FALLEN
SAIN†

FALLEN SAINT

A DARK ROMANCE

VOLUME
TWO

International Bestselling Author
MONICA JAMES

FALLEN SAINT
(All The Pretty Things Trilogy, Volume Two)

Cover Design: Perfect Pear Creative Covers
Editing: Editing 4 Indies
Formatting: E.M. Tippetts Book Designs

Follow me on:
monicajamesbooks.blogspot.com.au

OTHER BOOKS BY
MONICA JAMES

THE I SURRENDER SERIES
I Surrender
Surrender to Me
Surrendered
White

SOMETHING LIKE NORMAL SERIES
Something like Normal
Something like Redemption
Something like Love

A HARD LOVE ROMANCE
Dirty Dix
Wicked Dix
The Hunt

MEMORIES FROM YESTERDAY
Forgetting You, Forgetting Me
Forgetting You, Remembering Me

SINS OF THE HEART
Absinthe of the Heart
Defiance of the Heart

ALL THE PRETTY THINGS TRILOGY

Bad Saint

Fallen Saint

STANDALONE

Mr. Write

AUTHOR'S NOTE

CONTENT WARNING: *FALLEN SAINT* is Volume Two in a Trilogy. The final book in the series will release shortly after the second. This is a continuing story, therefore, not all questions will be answered in Volume Two. There is a cliffhanger. You've been warned.

FALLEN SAINT is a DARK ROMANCE containing mature themes that might make some readers uncomfortable. It includes kidnapping, captivity, strong violence, mild language, and some dark and disturbing scenes.

This twisted tale is not intended for the faint of heart…it will steal your soul.

CHAPTER ONE

All of this was for nothing...
No, that's not entirely true. I met
her. And now, I must protect her. But
first, I need to wake the fuck up.

Day 34

Even though I walk through the darkest valley, I fear no evil,
for you are with me...

-Psalm 23:4

This passage was my father's favorite. His go-to when times were tough. I remember sitting in my Sunday best with my small hands linked as I listened to his sermons. They always filled me with such hope, and whenever he spoke of this Psalm, I felt so connected to God.

How couldn't I?

The passage claimed that no matter what evils one faces, they will never be alone.

But sitting here bound, watching an unconscious Saint bleed out in front of me, I know that Psalm is a load of shit. Where is He now? I am walking…no, I am fucking staggering through the darkest valley, but I am alone. No one is with me.

There is no saving grace.

The only grace would be for a tidal wave to swallow this yacht and drag us all under to a watery grave. However, been there, done that, and here I am, still a fucking prisoner.

My feet and hands are bound tight. I've tried to wiggle free but gave up when it was clear I wasn't going anywhere. But where would I go? What would I do if I did escape? I'm trapped with a psychopath and his pet, who is far more dangerous than the man who kick-started this entire shitshow.

Zoey Hennessy hasn't taken her eyes off me, eyes so similar to her brother's, who lies bleeding at my feet. Rather than caring that her own flesh and blood is hurt, she's made it clear with her death stares that she only cares about making me pay.

In some ways, I'm thankful Saint doesn't have to see his sister, but he will soon rouse. You can't keep a good man down. And that's what he is. A good man.

The man who bought me in a game of poker, however, is not.

"Don't fret, ангел." The name I once held dear has been tainted forever. "You're safe now."

Safe? Is he fucking high?

The Russian mobster Aleksei Popov ruined my life, so

speaking to me as though we're friends seems ironic. As he turns over his shoulder and smiles, the hair at the back of my neck stands on end. I hate him. And I will do everything in my power to make him pay for what he's done.

"Wh"—I clear my raspy throat—"where are we going?"

Aleksei gestures with his head for one of his goons to take the wheel. It's that simple for him. He doesn't even need to speak for everyone to be at his beck and call.

But not me. And I never will be.

He saunters over but stops when Zoey commences to follow him—on her knees. "Stay," he orders, addressing her like a dog.

She does as he says.

Swallowing down my revulsion, I hide my disgust at having him near me when he sits down. It doesn't affect him in the slightest that I'm tied up. "We are going to your new home. Russia," he explains while every part of me riots. "You're going to love it there."

My mouth hinges open. "Love it?" The urge to hurt him mounts. "You're kidnapping me. I never agreed to this," I add in case he's lost in translation.

He's not, and what he says next confirms Saint was telling the truth this entire time.

"But your husband did."

And there it is. The harsh reality that's been staring me in the face this entire time.

Saint revealed my husband, Drew Gibbs, lost a game of poker, and to pay his dues, he agreed to give me to Aleksei. At the time, he didn't know me, so it could have been any girl.

But apparently, I fit the bill, and like an idiot, I fell for his lies.

I should have known something was amiss. But I thought, for once, maybe life would cut me some slack. I was wrong.

"You can't do this." I wriggle against my restraints. "I'm not some piece of property you can trade! I am a human being."

I'm hoping, by some miracle, my words appeal to him, and he'll see the error of his ways. And when he reaches into his pocket and produces a crisp white handkerchief to wipe away the blood from my face, thanks to the fact one of his men punched me in the nose, I think I've maybe done it.

But then he levels me with those steel blue eyes, and I know I've wasted my breath. "You are mine. And I will do with you what I please." He continues to clean my face, but his touch isn't gentle. It's possessive and filled with warning.

"The sooner you understand that, the easier this will become. There," he says, leaning back to get a better look at me. "Much better."

Is this what staring into the eyes of a monster feels like?

His eyes hold no compassion, no remorse for what he's done. He's ruined countless lives all because he can. And it seems mine is the next in line.

A guttural groan slices through the air, and although I wish it were any other sound, I'm thankful he's stirring. When those chartreuse-colored eyes flicker open, a trapped breath escapes me. For a split second, I forget I'm sitting beside a maniac because all that matters is that Saint is awake.

He takes his time, gauging where he is. When he gradually focuses on Aleksei sitting beside me, holding the bloodied handkerchief in his hand, Saint's jaw clenches, and he moves to spring up, intent on murder. But Aleksei knows Saint and ensures he stays down by placing his Italian loafer over Saint's throat.

Saint claws at Aleksei's foot, attempting to break free, but he doesn't stand a chance. Wounded and turning a bright crimson, Saint looks seconds away from passing out once again.

"No!" I scream, thrashing about to get free, but it's useless. My cries and Saint's struggles only fuel this narcissistic asshole.

"Calm down." Aleksei tsks Saint. In response, Saint flips him off, still attempting to pry Aleksei's foot off his throat.

Aleksei laughs, appearing to enjoy the banter as though they're two friends arguing over a football match. Eventually, he releases the pressure, allowing Saint to take in mouthfuls of air.

I watch with wide eyes because I can't believe this farfetched scene playing out before me is my life.

When he's finally able to breathe, Saint sluggishly props up into a half sitting position. He cups his shoulder, flinching. He doesn't speak, but his poignant eyes communicate. They're asking if I'm all right.

I give an imperceptible nod, wanting more than anything to console him. But I can't.

"Untie her," Saint demands, his breathing uneven, yet his gaze never wavering from mine. Aleksei raises an eyebrow, clearly surprised by Saint's orders, but Saint won't be intimidated. "I said untie her."

Aleksei leans back in the seat, casually crossing his ankles as he twirls the gold ring on his pinkie. "And why would I do that?" His English has just a slight accent, so you can barely ascertain where he's from. Like all chameleons, he's learned how to fit in to survive.

"Because you fucking shot me, you asshole, so someone has to help me take out the bullet. Unless you fancy getting your Italian silk dirty?"

I dare not breathe—surely, Aleksei will see through Saint's lies—but Saint must convince him. Aleksei shuffles close to me, inhaling deeply, and I remain perfectly still. A tic beneath Saint's eye reveals he's barely holding back, but when Aleksei produces a switchblade and reaches behind me to cut the rope, Saint nods subtly, hinting it'll be okay.

Aleksei cuts the rope at my wrists carefully, his shallow breaths coating my neck. When I'm free, he runs his fingers over the rope burn, humming in satisfaction. It seems torture is his thing. "You're worth a lot of money. Go get cleaned up. I want to see my prize," he whispers into my ear, loud enough for Saint to hear.

My stomach turns, and I shrug from his hold, instantly bringing my hands out in front me to rub my raw wrists. However, when he tosses the knife onto the floor in front of Saint, I freeze.

Saint peers down at the knife, then back up at me. We both know what this is. A test.

Saint could take that knife and end this bastard's miserable existence by slicing open his jugular. But he wouldn't get closer than two feet before one of Aleksei's men shot us both dead.

Aleksei is whipping out his dick to prove who's in control.

But we never forgot. How could we? I'm bound. Saint has a bleeding gunshot wound. And that's all thanks to him and his obsession for power.

Saint reaches for the knife, and with shaky fingers, he cuts the rope at my ankles. He takes deep breaths through his nose to work through his pain, but he continues to saw at it until I'm free. The moment I am, I exhale. It's one step closer to getting off this boat.

He extends the knife to Aleksei, just how I once did to him.

Aleksei keeps his cool as he reaches for the blade. This is all a power play. I wonder what'll happen when one of us breaks even though that time is not now.

Saint climbs to his feet unsteadily. "Come on." He grips my bicep and yanks me up roughly.

The harsh pressure causes me to flinch, but I allow him to manhandle me because I don't want to stay up here with Aleksei. When he sees Zoey, however, he pauses.

She's still on her knees, awaiting further instruction from Aleksei. I can't imagine what this does to Saint. She's the reason he's here—why we're both here—but she tricked him. She never wanted to be saved.

Expecting him to say something to her, I'm surprised when he drags me around her and down the stairs to the galley. A gasp leaves me when I see this place. It looks like a resort on water. The fully functional stainless-steel kitchen rivals any master chef's with a large fridge, stove top and oven, and white marble counters.

Off to the right, eight leather chairs surround a large

table. A fruit bowl in the center with red apples, bananas, and pears sets off a welcoming vibe. If someone didn't know any better, they'd think everyone aboard this yacht was here of their own accord.

When a group of men rise from their perches, replacing their playing cards for guns, I yelp, but Saint isn't intimidated in the slightest. "Where's the bathroom?" he barks, tightening his grip on my arm.

The one who struck Saint and me, a disgusting man with a bald head and long, thick beard, gestures to a door behind him. When two of them attempt to follow us, Saint shakes his head. "I don't need you to hold my hand."

But the man who struck us has other ideas as he raises his gun. "Adrian and Rahil will come with you."

The two men in question take a step toward the bathroom, but Saint stays rooted to the spot, not at all threatened. "Have you forgotten your place, Diak? You obey me. Not the other way around."

"The rules have changed since you've been gone," he replies smartly. The other men chuckle in agreement, but their hungry glances don't go unnoticed. I once again feel like a piece of meat.

"Oh, have they?" Saint quips, walking casually toward Diak, lugging me with him.

The closer we get to the guns and the ravenous grins of these wolves, the more anxious I become. But I trust Saint. And besides, I feel safer in his grasp because I know he won't let me go.

"Yes. Boss isn't too happy with you. He doesn't like

waiting, especially for pussy." Diak focuses his lifeless eyes my way, licking his fat rubbery lips.

Though I have the urge to shrink behind Saint, I stand my ground. I will not show them fear because I can't afford to show weakness; it will be the end of me if I do.

"But for pussy like this...it might be worth the wait." Diak attempts to reach out and touch me, but when I hear a snap and a crunch, it's evident that's the last thing he'll attempt for a while. Saint broke his wrist, disarming him with a snap, and then elbowed him in the nose.

It happened in the blink of an eye, but when Diak wheezes and tries to cup his nose with his floppy hand, it seems that's all Saint needs. The satisfaction I feel when I see blood pouring from his nose should leave me ashamed, but it doesn't because karma's a bitch.

The rest of the men stand motionless, ignoring Diak's cries for help as he drops to his knees. Saint acts as cool as cool can be when he jerks me forward to pick up the gun. I do as he proposes, the hard metal feeling like utter power beneath my fingers.

When the men's eyes widen, the whites to their eyes revealing their fear, it's an aphrodisiac. I should be afraid, but I'm not. Am I desensitized to such violence? I could pull the trigger and kill them all. But Saint clucks his tongue, hinting we choose our battles wisely.

I pass him the gun, which he slips in the small of his back.

"What happened to Kazimir?" Adrian asks, and when I take a closer look, I see the resemblance. A younger brother maybe?

Saint deadpans him. "That happened." He gestures with his head toward a howling Diak cradling his wrist as blood gushes from his nose. "But a lot bloodier. And a lot more dead."

Adrian's jaw clenches while the room falls silent.

"If anyone else has any other questions, now is the time to speak up." No one dares to utter a word. "I didn't think so." Saint drags me toward the bathroom, leaving the men to clean up his mess. I want to shrug from his hold because he's hurting me, but I know better.

He almost rips the door from its hinges as he opens it and shoves me inside. When the door slams shut, he finally releases me. If I wasn't being held against my will and fearing for my life, I would admire how spacious it is in here.

Besides a large glass shower and a bathtub, black marble covers as far as the eye can see. Everything gleams within an inch of its life. No expense was spared as everything down here allows me to shower in comfort. Nothing but the best for Alek it seems.

Saint's harsh breathing snaps me back to the now, and I turn around slowly. He's propped against the wall, clutching his shoulder, his snarled hair hanging around his face. Now that we're alone, the severity of where we are hits me, and it appears I'm not desensitized after all.

Tears well, but I bite my cheek to stop them from falling. Saint lifts his eyes to meet mine, but I can't read what he's thinking. The room turns explosive.

"You silly, stubborn girl," he chides, shaking his head slowly. "You should have done what I said." What he said was for me to run and hide—for me to be a coward—but I couldn't. I couldn't leave him to deal with this on his own. I don't know what that says for me and my sanity, but I wouldn't have been able to live with myself if I did.

"It doesn't matter now," I say, brushing the matted hair from my cheeks, trying to be brave.

"Of course, it matters!" Before I have a chance to reply, he storms over, gripping the back of my neck and pressing us brow to brow. "I'm sorry if I was rough with you, but I had to be. I can't show weakness when it comes to you because you'll pay the price if I do."

The feel of his hands on me is indescribable. "What are we going to do?" I whisper, rubbing my nose against his.

He inhales deeply, and this close to him, I can almost forget our troubles. When we're this way, nothing else matters. "I don't know yet. I have to talk to Popov and figure out his game plan. He knows something is going on between us."

His admission has me drawing back to look him dead in the eye. "And what's that?" I don't even know what this is between us. I never have. Maybe he can explain it to me.

But when he shakes his head, it seems he's just as confused as I am.

"Just trust me, ангел."

Closing my eyes briefly, I savor the way the nickname rolls from his tongue. I can almost forget the way it sounded when Popov spoke it.

"I may have to do some things you won't like."

"Like what?" My heart begins to race.

"I just need you to trust me," he repeats, squeezing my

nape softly.

With a hesitant touch, I place my hand over his, threading our fingers together. When he doesn't shy away, I sigh in relief. "Okay. I trust you."

We stay this way, both needing a moment to center and prepare ourselves for what's ahead. "Go shower. I'll take this bullet out."

The mention of his injury has me pulling away, attempting to tend to his wound. But Saint presses his hand over mine, right over the bullet hole, and simply stares at me. Who knew a look could convey a thousand words?

On instinct, my gaze drops to his lips. I want to kiss him. So badly. I want to stop feeling this constant fear and just lose myself in something that isn't swathed in darkness and gloom. But Saint releases me, putting an end to that train of thoughts.

"I wasn't lying when I said it's just a flesh wound. I can manage."

With a deep sigh, I know there is no point in pressing because he's made up his mind.

He goes on the hunt for a first-aid kit while I decide the thought of taking a real shower after all this time is too incredible to pass up. Without hesitation, I slip the green dress over my head and reach around my back to unhook my bra.

When it falls to the floor, I slip my thumbs into the waistband of my underwear but pause when I realize Saint is watching me. He's found a first-aid kit, but his bullet wound seems the least of his worries as he stands unmoving, focusing his animated eyes on my body.

My nipples instantly pearl, and my breasts tighten.

He places the kit on the counter, then walks over to me at a languid pace as his gaze peruses every inch of my skin. "I don't know when I'll be able to touch you again." He places his palm against the side of my neck, cupping it gently. "And it kills me inside."

I'm too afraid to move because if I do, I will smash my lips to his and beg he consume me while we have the chance.

"I want you, ангел." He slides his hand down my throat and it comes to rest on my chest over my heart.

My knees buckle, and my sex clenches. His overwhelming honesty leaves me at a loss for words.

"I haven't wanted anything more in my life. But no matter how much I want you." *There's always a but.* "I won't drag you into this mess. I will get you out of here. I promise."

He can feel the thrashing of my heart under his palm. "What about you?" I'm not stupid. The likelihood of us both getting out of this unscathed seems impossible.

He smirks something wicked, causing my chest to heave as I'm suddenly short of breath. "You let me worry about me."

"Saint…" But all conversation ends when he leans forward and suckles over my thundering pulse.

"I want to mark you. Like a fucking caveman, I want to rub my scent all over you."

My eyes roll to the back of my head because him rubbing me anywhere sounds like a brilliant idea. He's doing this to distract me, and it almost works.

"You have a gun. You're a good shot."

He hums against the column of my throat, sending an electrical current all the way to my toes. "Too much is at stake."

"What could possibly mean more to you than your life? Your freedom?" I question, refusing to surrender to the glide of his lips.

Saint kisses downward, licking a path from my neck to the top of my breasts. I arch into him, looping my fingers through his mussed hair and moaning softly. When he takes a nipple into his mouth, I see stars. But I persevere.

"Tell me."

He circles my areola, sucking my breast with a desperate hunger.

As far as distractions go, this is absolutely amazing, but I need to know what he has planned. Does he still intend to save Zoey? And if so, how, seeing as I was the bargaining chip?

But when my nipple pops free and Saint walks us backward until my ass hits the basin, I suddenly wish I'd kept my mouth shut because his reply changes everything.

"You."

My mouth hangs open as I'm at a loss for words. A simple word has just changed the course of it all.

I want to say so many things, but Saint presses a kiss to my cheek, then reaches for the kit, leaving me a wanton, needy mess.

When he opens the kit and yanks out a pair of scissors, I pale and make my way to the shower. Slipping out of my underwear, I turn on the faucets and stand under the warm spray. I've dreamed about this moment for weeks, but it suddenly falls short of my expectations because I'm distracted.

What happens next? But most importantly, what will I do to ensure Saint and I get off this boat together? As I remember his touches and get lost in his words, I know that I will do anything. Anything at all.

Even sell my soul...to the devil himself.

I've procrastinated long enough. It's time to face the inevitable.

Once Saint removed the bullet and bandaged himself up, he said he was going to talk to Aleksei. I wanted to go with him, but I know they have much to discuss. Alone.

I understand Saint and I will have to be careful, knowing Aleksei will use whatever this thing is between us as leverage. Just as he used Zoey as collateral to Saint.

When Saint protected me on the island by standing in front of me when Zoey pointed her gun, he no doubt clued Aleksei in. But knowing Saint, he will play it off as something else. We both have to watch our backs. Not only from Aleksei but also Zoey. She is a loaded gun, and I'm afraid of what she'll do next.

A banging on the door alerts me that my time is up.

I found a change of clothes on the marble counter when I exited the shower. The fiery red dress seems a little inappropriate, but I needed something to cover the barely there lace underwear set accompanying it.

Having everything in my size creeps me out, as it means Aleksei was preparing for my "homecoming." I wonder what else he has in store for me.

When the thumping sounds once again, I look in the mirror and take three calming breaths. I raided the drawers for a weapon, but all I found were toiletries and the makeup I used to keep from resembling the living dead.

However, I remember the scissors in the first-aid kit and quickly lunge for them. Without much choice on where to stash them, I lift the hem of my dress and tuck them into the waistband of my underwear. Even though it's not ideal, having them gives me a sense of security. No matter how false that may be.

Just as I'm straightening my dress, the door bursts open, and one of Aleksei's men appears. He seems disappointed when I brush past him. I think he expected a fight or for me to be lying in a pool of my own blood.

Putting my game face on, I walk out into the dining area, ignoring the glares from Aleksei's goons. When I don't see Saint anywhere in sight, I decide to go up onto the upper deck to find him. But Adrian has other ideas when he blocks my path.

"Boss said you stay down here."

Just as his brother did, he makes my skin crawl. However, while Kazimir wanted to defile me, I get the sense Adrian wants to defile my insides as he murders me.

Without bothering to argue, I walk over to a bench seat, away from my captors, and turn my back to them to look out the window. I still have no idea where we are, but I'm not worried about the journey. The final destination and what's in store for me when we arrive in Russia are what have me lifting the hair off my neck and twisting it into a high topknot. I'm burning up in panic.

When the room falls silent, though, I wonder if I'll even make it to Russia. If Zoey has her way, I'll be overboard come nightfall. The men mumble under their breath, clearly hoping to see a catfight when Zoey marches down the stairs. But I am not competition. She can have Aleksei.

The fridge opens, and the sound of a water bottle opening cuts through the static. I keep my eyes up front because even though I would give my right arm for a sip of cold water, I remain quiet. Zoey, however, doesn't share the sentiment.

When her bare feet pad across the floor, announcing her arrival, I brace myself for World War III.

"You may have my brother fooled, and Alek may be excited with the shiny new toy"—I curl my hands into tight fists to stop myself from slapping her—"but make no mistake, I am always going to be *their* number one."

I couldn't care less about Aleksei. But what she says about Saint turns my stomach.

"Know your place and we won't have a problem because my brother will always put me first. Don't you ever forget it."

Unable to hold my tongue any longer, I turn over my shoulder, pinning her with a glower of my own. "What's that supposed to mean?"

Zoey's bowed lips tip into a malicious grin. "It means if you even *think* about taking Alek away from me, I will give my brother what he's always wanted. The sweet, innocent sister he still thinks I am."

Wide-eyed, I gape at her.

"The fact he protected you means you've gotten under

his skin. But it'll only take some tears and hollow promises of going home for his protective big brother mode to kick in. I will wedge a wall between you by filling his head with insecurities, like he isn't the only man you want, and he'll believe me because he doesn't see himself as good enough for someone like you. Then he won't be so quick to protect you when I kill you with my fucking bare hands."

I thought I'd seen it all. I was wrong.

She steps forward, and with nowhere to go, I turn around to face her. "I will lie, cheat, and kill to get you out of my life. So if that means lying to my brother, then so be it. I know Saint. Even though he's loyal, his jealousy will make him weak."

"And what are you then?" I spit, refusing to back down. "Isn't this little pep talk because you're frightened Aleksei will throw your sorry ass to the curb?"

Furious, she advances forward but then abruptly stops and takes a calming breath. "I'm the person you don't want to fuck with," she threatens. "You may think you're safe with Saint here, but he has to sleep. And if I don't get to you first, the other men on this yacht will."

"I don't want Aleksei," I clarify in case she missed the memo. She simply chuckles, and it's not a pleasant sound.

"That's what they all say. But Aleksei is like heroin." Her face turns tranquil while I wonder where she's going with this analogy. "You become hooked with the very first taste, and you don't know you're addicted until it's too late. All you need is a little bump to get you through the day, but before long, you can't survive without it."

"Lucky for me," I say, coming to a slow stand, "I've always

said no to drugs."

Zoey looks surprised by my wit. "I wouldn't be so sure." She's a few inches shorter than I am, but like her brother, she oozes control. "Isn't Saint your heroin?"

My cheeks instantly blister because she's caught me off guard. But I squash down my embarrassment. "If you think that, then why are you so concerned I will come between you and Aleksei?"

She takes another step forward, almost pressing her nose to mine. "Because he will worm his way into your soul and make you forget a life before him existed. Believe me, I know." When she traces over the track marks on her arm, I *almost* feel sorry for her.

"I don't *want* to be here. I hate him," I spit, wanting to make that very clear.

But she reveals just whose show this is. "Didn't you hate my brother as well?" My silence says it all.

I don't know how she can tell, but she's right. And she knows it. And then she says the most frightening thing she could ever say.

"Who do you think taught him everything he knows? So just as you once hated Saint, you may hate Aleksei now, but sooner or later"—she rips the air from my lungs when she presses her lips to mine and whispers—"he will become your heroin too."

She seals my fate with a chaste kiss—the kiss of death.

She pulls away with a smug smile because she's won this battle. I'm too shell-shocked to move and watch with wide eyes as she saunters away from me. My knees threaten to buckle, so I slump onto the seat, needing a minute to catch my breath.

What the hell just happened?

Zoey has struck a nerve because she's right about Saint. I did hate him, and now...I don't. But Saint is *nothing* like Aleksei.

"Who do you think taught him everything he knows?"

Zoey's words haunt me.

A master manipulator, Aleksei clearly loves to play mind games with people. But so does Zoey. She made it clear she would put Saint against me if I didn't play by her rules. I want to think he'd see through her lies, but knowing she's the reason he's done all this, I'm not so sure.

But the fact she thinks I would ever feel anything other than utter hatred toward Aleksei reveals that I'm stronger than she is. He may try to fool me, but you can only fool me once, and Drew was a lesson learned. And I will never be like Zoey—hooked on the most potent drug of them all.

"He will be your tormenter, but he will also be the person who makes the pain go away."

Saint's words echo loudly in my head, seeming to confirm what Zoey just said. Suddenly, I'm more fearful for my soul than my virtue. And when I hear Aleksei's voice, my body breaks out into a cold sweat.

Saint walks down the stairs, instantly seeking me out. When he sees me stooped over, he raises a brow but quickly shrouds any emotion when Aleksei trails him. His men stop what they're doing, some even standing at attention, while Zoey leans against the wall watching me.

Taking a deep breath, I won't allow her words to affect me. I need to have a clear head because it's the only way I'll survive this.

"I almost didn't recognize you." I know he's talking to me, but I can't look at him. The scissors burn my flesh, screaming at me to use them against this vile man. When his shoes come into view, my breathing mounts, no matter how hard I try to keep calm.

"After everything you've been through, you must be exhausted. Saint told me that for most nights, you slept outdoors?" Hearing his name has me lifting my eyes to meet Aleksei's gaze.

I don't know what he expects of me, so I simply nod once.

"Now that doesn't sound very comfortable."

Neither is being held against your will, you asshole, I think to myself.

"Well, hearing all about your adventures has left *me* tired. I'm going to have a lie down."

I exhale in relief, but it's in vain.

When Zoey pushes off the wall, no doubt armed and ready to ease all the fatigue from his loins, Aleksei stuns us all. "You can stay here, Zoey. I don't require your presence. Willow?"

Even though I've just heard my name and see his extended hand, my brain can't comprehend that he requires *my* presence. Every part of my body protests, beseeching I don't follow the lion into his den.

But what choice do I have?

I'm thankful I haven't eaten because when I slip my hand

into his, the need to throw up almost winds me. His hand is warm, soft, but when I think of all the lives these hands have destroyed, Saint's included, it turns cold.

"You look absolutely beautiful, by the way. Red is your color." He accentuates his comment with a wink while a small piece of me dies.

Standing, I attempt to pry my hand from his, but he holds on tight. I'm a true prisoner.

When we turn around, I want more than anything to make eye contact with Saint, but he stares straight ahead, his jaw clenched and his eyes cold. Zoey, though, doesn't mask her emotions as well as her brother. She looks seconds away from ripping out my spleen.

Aleksei doesn't seem bothered by anyone as he leads me toward a door, a door which no doubt leads to his bedroom.

This is my last chance to make a run for it. But when I look at a rigid Saint, it's clear we're all prisoners and pawns in Aleksei's game. I follow him with my chin downturned in shame. Memories of being face first against that dirty carpet with Kenny's heavy weight pressing into me rob me of air, but I squash the memories down because I refuse to be a victim again.

Aleksei opens the door, leading me into an elegant bedroom draped in gold velvet and silk. Turning around quickly, I lock eyes with Saint, and his tormented expression tears a hole straight through me. Aleksei closes the door but not before Saint steps forward, primed on saving me as he always has.

Aleksei leans against the locked door, a reptilian smile

spreading from cheek to cheek. I back up, only for my legs to hit the king-sized bed. He watches me with hunger. "I think it's time we got to know one another without all the… distraction."

Distraction? He means Saint.

I gulp, the walls closing in on me.

Feeling behind me, I walk my way slowly around the bed, never taking my eyes off Aleksei as I cower in the furthest corner of the room. He watches on amused, a true cat and mouse game.

"And to do that, I need to see you."

My heart begins to pound against my rib cage. "You can see me just fine now."

Aleksei's animated laughter slashes the air. "Suit yourself."

When he pushes off the door, I frantically scan the room from left to right, searching for an escape route. But the man intent on trapping me forever has blocked my only way out.

Feelings of helplessness surround me, and the stench of Kenny's soaked breath crashes into me. But another smell overrides that weakness, and that's the combination of spicy, sweet, and floral—Saint's signature fragrance.

Thoughts of him and his belief in me that I'm the bravest woman he knows have me refusing to surrender. I will do him proud when *I* save us this time.

It's time I showed Aleksei my real worth.

CHAPTER TWO

I'm going to kill him. I don't know how or when, but it's inevitable. I should have done it years ago. After seeing the way he looks at her, it takes all my strength not to end him right now. But I have to bide my time. I have to be smart. Regardless of my feelings for her.

Day 34

My heart thrashes against my rib cage; so much so, the frantic rhythm deafens me. But I pull it together and don't lose sight of the predator stalking toward me.

Judging by the enormous bulge protruding from Aleksei's pants, he thoroughly enjoys this game. I have nowhere to go, seeing as I'm backed into a corner, so I scamper onto the bed, intent on running from this room.

But Aleksei is quicker and catapults onto the mattress, pinning me down.

Images of wild animal documentaries invade my thoughts as I suddenly feel like a gazelle being taken down by a lion. Aleksei holds me down with little effort, but I struggle against him all the same.

"Get off!" I bellow, thrashing wildly, but he's bound my wrists above my head.

"Shh," he coos, his heavy weight on top of me making it hard to breathe. "Don't fight it."

It? Does he actually think I feel an iota of attraction toward him? It's time I made my feelings very clear.

"Make no mistake. I will always fight you," I cry, attempting to buck him off. "I won't submit to you. Ever."

My response seems to amuse him as he laughs loudly. "We will see, ангел."

"*Don't* call me that," I grit out between clenched teeth, glaring at him.

"I thought you liked it," he replies, looping his leg around mine to stop me from kneeing him in the balls.

"You know nothing about me." Being this close allows me to take this monster in.

His dark brown hair has flicked forward, and the soft strands brush my forehead. His deep blue eyes would be a hypnotic color if not for the fact they belong to a murderer. His clean-shaven face exposes his sharp features and emphasizes the fullness of his pink lips. I turn my cheek to escape his suffocating sandalwood scent.

The rebellion just turns him on further because I can feel his hard-on pressing into me. It makes me want to vomit.

"You're right. I don't. But I want to change that."

"Why me?" I beseech for him to shed light on why I'm so special. He's rich, some would even say he's good looking, and he oozes power. He could have a million other women, women who would be more than willing to be at his disposal, but he's chosen to torment me.

"Because…" He lowers his lips to my cheek as I freeze in horror. "I haven't been challenged in a very long time."

He places a chaste kiss on my cheek before trailing to my lips. I thrash my head from side to side, but he grips my chin firmly, preventing me from moving an inch. I glower at him, my chest rising and falling rapidly. His attention drifts to where my breasts are exposed thanks to the low neckline of my dress. His tongue darts out to wet his bottom lip.

"And you challenge me. I like it because I can't wait to see you break."

"Fuck…you," I pant between pursed lips as he maintains his punishing grip on my face.

He chuckles hoarsely once again before licking the seam of my mouth.

Tears of anger sting because I can't do a damn thing, but the scissors in the waistband of my underwear reveal that isn't exactly true. Fighting seems to get Aleksei off, but what if I didn't? What if I was the docile submissive he wanted?

My body protests at the thought, as surrendering to this asshole is complete blasphemy, but it's the only way I can get him to lower his guard and catch him unaware. So I detach myself from my body and stop fighting, allowing him to slip his tongue past my slack lips.

The urge to gag or bite down overwhelms me, but I stare up at the ceiling, biding my time. Aleksei doesn't seem to notice or care and groans into my mouth, driving his hips into me. Everything about this feels so wrong, but when his grip on my wrist slackens, I quash down my uneasiness and focus on breaking free.

My flaccid lips allow Aleksei to molest my mouth any way he likes. Yet the way he bites, licks, and suckles me is in no way pleasurable for me. My stomach roils, but I remain still, thinking of anything other than being trapped under him.

A string of Russian leaves Aleksei as he rolls his hips and nudges me with his monster hard-on. I need to speed things up because I can't stay this way for much longer. So I arch into him, pressing my breasts into his chest.

Your looks are used for evil...

My mother's words spur me on because that evil has him releasing my wrists to grope me. Now that my arms are free, I slowly place them beside me, using my left hand to subtly lift my hem. Aleksei's grip on my chin never wavers because he knows it's hurting me. The pain gets him off. Just as being in control does.

But when he lowers his head to tongue the top of my breasts, the roles are reversed, and I'm the one in control. I lunge for the scissors and press them into his throat in lightning-quick speed. His head snaps up, but I only dig the scissors in deeper, daring him to move an inch.

I've caught him off guard, just as I did with Saint once

upon a time, but unlike then, I want to end this bastard's miserable life.

"I'm impressed," he says smoothly, eyeing me closely as he raises his hands in surrender. "But give me the scissors before you hurt yourself."

That arrogant asshole. "You're in no position to be making demands." To emphasize my point, I nudge the scissors in deeper. But the thought of following through suddenly makes me feel nauseous. "Get off me."

When he doesn't move, I threaten to draw blood.

"Okay, fine." He goes to move off me, which has me celebrating, but it's premature because the moment my grip on the scissors slackens, he slaps them from my hand. They skid across the floor, echoing the dire consequences headed my way.

I work on pure adrenaline and spring up, but Aleksei forces me back onto the mattress when he presses his forearm over my windpipe, holding me down. I claw at his arm and kick my legs, but he only pushes down harder. "You *are* a pleasant surprise. I must thank your husband."

The mere mention of Drew has me thrashing about like a wild cat, uncaring that Aleksei will probably choke me into submission. Without breaking a sweat, he reaches into the bedside table with his free arm and produces a pair of handcuffs.

He yanks my arms above me, snapping one cuff around my wrist before threading the restraints around the twisted steel of the Victorian style headboard and quickly removing his arm from my windpipe to fasten my other hand.

I lunge forward, but the movement only jars my shoulders from their sockets. "You fucking bastard!" The handcuffs rattle against the headboard as I yank at them, but I'm not going anywhere.

Aleksei smirks, shuffling down the bed and straddling me. I try to buck him off, but his strong thighs pin me to the bed. "I should force my cock down your throat as punishment for speaking to me that way."

His threat has me gritting my teeth together. "Try it and see what happens," I warn, as this time, I will ensure to not let go.

"But when that happens"—he leans down to whisper into my ear—"and it will happen. I won't be seconds away from exploding into that beautiful mouth like I am right now. You've got me so worked up, and I wouldn't want you to think I was lacking in stamina because with someone like you, I want to savor every last inch." He suckles my earlobe while I squeeze my eyes shut. "But right now, I just want to come. I suppose having Zoey here does have its benefits after all."

He is revolting because Zoey, it seems, is merely a warm body to jerk off into.

"Don't go anywhere," he quips as he crawls off me. I turn my cheek, refusing to look at him.

When the door closes behind him, I exhale in relief.

An electrical current pulses through me, but it's not the good kind. I tug at the handcuffs, but they're tight. My feet aren't bound, but in this position, I have nowhere to go. "Fuck!" I scream in frustration and flail madly, angry with myself for hesitating instead of growing a pair.

I had the opportunity to end this, but I faltered, and it's cost me dearly.

During the past few weeks, I've felt hopeless, but this, this is something else. With Saint, I never felt this terrified because deep down, I've always trusted him. Even when I shouldn't have. But Aleksei scares me because his promises aren't empty.

Sinking into the pillow, I rack my brain, attempting to piece together a plan to get the fuck off this boat. But the longer I think, the more desolate things look. I suddenly would give anything to be back on the island. There, things were complicated, but I was with Saint, and together, I never doubted we could accomplish anything.

Things were never black and white, but for a mere moment in time, that island was my own private oasis. I began to feel things that I have never felt before, and I was foolish not to embrace them because now…I've run out of time.

When the door bursts open, I curse my thoughts, but when I see who just entered, my heart fills with a sliver of hope. Saint quietly closes the door behind him, his eyes distressed when he sees me handcuffed to the bed.

"Ангел." He rushes over, brushing the hair from my cheeks. "Did he hurt you?"

"No." I lean into his touch, closing my eyes in relief. "Uncuff me. Please."

Saint nods and frantically searches the room.

"Try the bedside table." I gesture with my chin to the one Aleksei took the cuffs out of.

After hunting desperately, he runs a hand through his

hair, yanking at the snarled strands. "Fuck. He's probably got the key on him."

He should know. Didn't he do the same to me?

"Where is he?"

When Saint averts his gaze, I know where. He's no doubt gone to find Zoey. The thought turns my stomach.

"I don't have much time," he says, sitting near me and glaring at the cuffs. "I need to win back his trust. It's the only way I can get you off this fucking yacht! He's watching me closely. They all are."

"So how do you do that?"

His Adam's apple bobs as he swallows deeply. "I have to do what he says…regardless of my feelings."

He doesn't need to spell it out. We're both prisoners, and Aleksei is the puppet master, pulling both our strings.

"Then do it. You do whatever it takes," I reply, nodding slowly. "It'll be okay."

I know what he's proposing. For him to earn back Aleksei's trust, he's going to have to prove he's still Popov's number one hitman. He can't show kindness. Or compassion. He has to punish and kill without remorse. He has to treat me how he always should have but never did—like a hostage.

But Saint reveals he's no longer the man he once was.

"I-I don't know if I can," he confesses with regret.

My heart swells, but I soon squash down my emotion because there is no other way. "You have to. It's the only way we can escape."

When he lowers his chin, though, it seems there is only enough room for one.

"You're coming with me, right?" I know the answer, but I press anyway. "Right?"

"I can't leave Zoey," he replies. His hair shields his face, but his defeated tone tells me he's breaking inside as well. "He will slip up, and when he does"—he raises those hypnotic eyes—"I'll set you free. No matter what happens, you do what I tell you, okay?"

My stomach drops at his ominous command.

"Okay?" he presses when I don't reply.

"Yes," I finally answer.

With the slowest of movements, he leans forward. Resting one hand by my head, he hovers over me, combing over every inch of my face. "Don't look back. Don't *ever* look back," he whispers while unexpected tears break past my floodgates.

With his free hand, he brushes away my sadness with his thumb.

"I'm sorry I did this to you."

A sob escapes because it's the first time he's apologized for kidnapping me. But it's not his apology that I want. He's just as much a prisoner as I am.

"But I'll make it right. I promise."

I can't shake the feeling that this is goodbye. That whatever he has planned will end in us never seeing one another again.

I open my mouth, primed to argue that I don't want to go without him, but sealing his lips over mine robs all my words. It takes my brain a second to catch up, but when it does, I surrender and lose myself to the bliss.

With my hands bound, I'm helpless to Saint's lips and tongue, but who am I kidding? There isn't anything I enjoy more. I may not intend to submit to Aleksei, but with Saint…I beg for so much more. And more he gives.

Cupping my cheeks, he positions himself over me, wickedly devouring my mouth with a frantic kiss filled with urgency and uncertainty. Our tongues duel, our breaths melt into one. I arch into him, ignoring the pain in my shoulders because I want everything and more.

"Ангел," he pants into my mouth, his touch burning me alive.

The handcuffs rattle as I yank on them because each lash of his tongue drives me wild. His fragrance is a heady punch to my libido, and I scissor my legs to create friction, hoping to douse the flames. Saint kisses without apology because we both know this will be the last time.

I know what this is—the final kiss goodbye.

"Saint, no," I mumble against his lips, trying to keep him hostage, but without my arms, I'm helpless to stop him.

He kisses my lips a final time before severing our connection with a heavy sigh. We lock eyes, and I know he's lost to me because to become who he once was, he has to detach himself from feeling. It's the only way he can do this.

When the distinct sound of a door handle turning can be heard, Saint leaps from the bed, wiping his lips. All I can do is watch, fearful for what comes next. When Aleksei enters, he pauses, as he was clearly not expecting company.

"Saint?" he questions, looking from him to me. "What are you doing in here?"

Saint clenches his fists by his side, and his shoulders are raised. He looks moments away from springing into action and tearing off Aleksei's head. When he doesn't reply, I know this will not end pretty. So I think on my toes, hoping it works.

"Fuck you! You can't keep me tied up like some animal." I wriggle wildly, the cuffs straining against the headboard. The commotion has Aleksei and Saint turning their attention my way. "Let me go!"

Aleksei grins while Saint pales. But he soon pulls it together and clues on to my plans. "She was giving me a headache with all her shouting. I came in here to remind her what happens when she misbehaves. I didn't realize you had cuffed her."

I exhale in relief, thankful he's playing along.

Aleksei takes a moment to take everything in. When he sees everything is as he left it, he nods, closing the door behind him. "She's very disobedient."

I gnash my teeth together, livid he's talking about me so flippantly like I'm not here.

"*I know,*" Saint says, his comment filled with innuendo. If I wasn't handcuffed and fearing for my life, his annoyance would be entertaining.

"So how did you punish her? How did you manage to get her to call you master?" He leans against the door, crossing his arms as he waits for Saint to reply. "On the island, she called me мастер," he explains when Saint remains silent. "I presume that's because you taught her to address you that way. Am I correct?"

Saint clenches his jaw tight. I hold my breath and only exhale when he replies.

"Yes."

"Excellent," Aleksei says, his stance still relaxed. "Show me."

"Show you what?" Saint counters quickly, irritated.

"Show me how you were going to punish her. That's what you were going to do, right? You were coming in here to punish her?" Aleksei is a smart man. Even though he ends his sentences with a question, we don't have a choice. We never did.

"Yes," Saint manages to spit out between clenched teeth.

"Good. Show me," he repeats, gesturing with his hand that the floor is his.

Saint inhales, his chest expanding on his heavy breath. He trains his eyes on me, and all I see is utter torment. I understand why a second later. "Give me the key to her cuffs."

I know we agreed that to survive this, Saint has to win back Aleksei's trust. But to what lengths will he have to go to achieve this?

It's too late to turn back now, so I simply await Saint's next move.

Aleksei reaches into his back pocket, producing a small key. I suddenly wish I could remain cuffed. Saint doesn't hesitate and reaches for it. When it's in his possession, I exhale, but his stiff shoulders cause me to break out into a cold sweat.

He turns slowly, and resembling a robot, he walks over to the bed. I wonder what Aleksei expects to see. He believes Saint to be my мастер, my master, so I remain still. When he reaches over me and unlocks the handcuffs, he brushes over my wrist with the quickest and gentlest of touches. Aleksei cannot see the gesture, as Saint has deliberately turned his back in a way that shields me from prying eyes.

It gives me the strength to continue.

"Kneel."

Without question, I slowly rise from the bed and follow Saint to the middle of the room. When he positions himself so Aleksei can see, I know what I have to do.

I drop to my knees and bow my head.

"Oh my." A stunned gasp leaves Aleksei. "That is incredible. Just like a trained dog."

A strong metallic taste fills my mouth, alerting me that I've drawn blood by biting down on my tongue so hard.

"What is your name?" Saint asks numbly.

"Ангел."

"And who am I?"

"мастер," I reply softly, using my hair as a veil.

"What? I can't hear you."

Before I have a chance to reply, Saint reaches down and grips my chin, forcing me to look up at him. I arch my neck, locking eyes with him. The amber swirls mingle among the flecks of green and set me alight. He is barely holding on.

"мастер," I say, louder this time.

"Good girl." He releases me while I sag forward in humiliation. "You know what happens when you disobey me?"

"Yes, мастер." The truth is, I don't know what punishment he intends to deliver. He reveals what a moment later.

"Lift your dress."

And just like that, I'm transported back to the night when Saint first struck me with his belt.

I know for this to be believable, Saint has to make the punishments credible. But the thought of being hit again has me whimpering.

"I said lift your fucking dress." Saint's tone is venomous. With no other choice, I do as he demands.

When I hear his belt being unbuckled and threaded through the loops of his pants, I brace myself for what comes next.

My back faces Aleksei, so he has a clear view of my ass. My lace underwear leaves nothing to the imagination, but it appears he wants more. "Take them off."

I lock eyes with Saint, begging he doesn't force me to bow to this pervert's demands, but he maintains his apathetic façade. Yet underneath this disguise, I know he'll always protect me.

"With all due respect, Aleksei, you asked me to show you, so please allow me to do my job." Being called a *job* causes me to flinch as though he kicked me in the guts. I know it's part of the plan, but it's hard not to get lost in the past.

"You're right. Sorry. I got carried away. Continue." His politeness is beyond insulting, as he's apologizing for suggesting Saint strip me when he whips me into submission.

This is so fucked up.

Saint walks around me and kicks my legs apart. I suppress the need to scream. He doesn't give me any warning. I hear the vicious hiss slicing through the air just before the pain hits me. With a loud grunt, I propel forward but remain kneeling.

My ass throbs from where Saint brought down his belt, but I know he could have struck me a lot harder. When he hits me over the back of my thighs, I whimper but remain upright. This strike was softer than the first.

"Do you have anything you want to say to me?"

Whack.

Tears sting my eyes, but I refuse to cry. "I'm s-sorry, мастер. I won't disobey you a-again."

Whack.

"Are you sure?" Even though Saint barely breaks a sweat from hitting me, his breathlessness reveals it's taking every ounce of his willpower not to kill Aleksei.

When I hear the belt being swung into position, I cry out, "Yes! Yes. I'm sorry. I won't d-do it again."

I brace myself for another strike, but it doesn't come. "Put down your dress."

With shaky hands, I do as he says.

Since I'm facing away from Saint, I can't see what's going on, but I'm guessing from the silence it's not good.

"That's it?" Aleksei is far from impressed. It seems he will only be satisfied when I'm crying out in pain and begging for mercy.

"Yes. She submitted, did she not?"

Silence.

The air is thick with challenge. Saint's methods aren't satisfactory because Aleksei knows he could have been a lot crueler.

"She fought me like a wild cat. I think she likes you."

My cheeks heat, but I squash down my embarrassment because this exercise was supposed to convince Aleksei otherwise. I quickly rack my brain, hoping to prove Aleksei wrong, but Saint is two steps ahead.

"She fears me," he argues. "She doesn't know you yet, but I've broken her. Just allow me to spend more time with her, and I promise, she will fear you too. I'm the only one who can break her, so I need to stay close to her to ensure she stays in line. You can't have her behaving this way when we get back to Russia. What will The Circle say?"

The Circle? Who, or what the fuck are The Circle?

I soon forget my question because if I could throw my arms around Saint, I would. But I simply blend into the background, hoping Aleksei falls for Saint's lies.

Just when I think he's going to kill us both, a light shines from above. "You're right. Very well," Aleksei says. "I'm strapped for time as it is, so if you think you can tame her, then I'll allow it. I can't have her acting out when we get back home. But…"

There's always a but.

"But if your methods don't prove satisfactory, and I don't see a change very soon, I will take over. Are we clear?"

My blood turns cold.

"We're clear," Saint replies with bite.

"I won't have her behaving like a rabid dog because you know what happens to them?" Aleksei pauses while the room drops ten thousand degrees. "I shoot them."

Make no mistake, he's warning us both.

Saint grips the back of my neck, hinting I'm to stand. When I do, he leads me back over to the bed. He won't look at me, and the detachment has me getting onto the bed, desperate for them to leave so I can process this on my own.

Without him asking, I place my arms over my head after I lie down.

A tear leaks from my eye when he cuffs me, but I turn my cheek so he can't see.

"Let's go into my office. We have some things to discuss." Just as Saint moves to rise, Aleksei says something which has me questioning how good of an actress I really am. "Gag her. You said she was shouting earlier."

You're going to be a good little girl, aren't you, Willow?

I suddenly find it impossible to breathe.

I'm moments away from blowing our ruse when a tender caress floats across my flank. Though it's a subtle touch, it's enough. "That's not necessary. She won't scream." Saint recognizes my panic; he knows what memories claw to the surface when I'm gagged.

"I said gag her," Aleksei perseveres, needing to hold on to some semblance of control.

I know I told Saint to do whatever it takes, but that's my hard limit, so I don't know if I can stomach that. But I should know by now that Saint will always be the alpha. "Aleksei, you just said you're willing to allow me to do this my way. Are you going back on your word?"

I don't know why his word is so important. He's a fucking criminal, for god's sake. But I remember Saint saying that Aleksei does hold some honor among his men. I can only hope he's right.

"So be it. But if I hear a peep out of her, it'll be the last for quite some time."

I gulp as his threat is filled with promise.

"She'll be quiet," Saint assures, speaking for me as he knows I'm close to breaking. "Let's go."

When he rises from the bed, I turn my cheek to look at him. But when I lock eyes with Aleksei instead, I realize I have to be more careful. Although we have convinced him today, tomorrow may not be as easy.

Saint doesn't look back and is quick to leave. I soon find out why that is.

"Aren't you forgetting something?" Aleksei blocks the doorway while I watch on in horror. He's going to kill Saint and make me watch. We haven't fooled him at all.

When Saint reaches into his pocket and produces the key to my cuffs, I sense he has a plan after all. Aleksei seems disappointed he surrendered it so easily.

Saint opens the door, hinting for Aleksei to move. He eventually does but not before he grins my way. The gesture sends a shiver down my spine.

This is only the beginning of things to come.

CHAPTER THREE

Popov isn't fooled. But the thought of hurting her more than I already have...I don't know if I can.

Day 35

Once again, passing out from exhaustion allows me to forget where I am. But when I wake, it doesn't take me long to remember the nightmare that has been my life for the past thirty-five days.

I haven't seen Saint or Aleksei since they left this room. Others have brought me food and water, and uncuffed me so I could use the bathroom, but it's clear I'm to remain handcuffed to this bed until further instruction from Aleksei.

The clock on the bedside table reads just after 7 a.m. I wonder what the day holds and how close we are to Russia. The thought of reaching my final destination turns my stomach, but it's the lesser of two evils.

Being stuck on this yacht with Aleksei and his men is far more suffocating than being held prisoner in Russia. I may be naïve in thinking this, but being on land will present more plausible opportunities to escape than my current predicament of being trapped at sea.

If by some miracle I were to escape now, where exactly would I go? I'm surrounded by nothing but water. Truth be told, there is no need for me to be handcuffed because I'm truly a prisoner—a prisoner to the elements as well as to a maniacal psychopath.

When the door opens, I turn to see who it is. When Zoey floats in, wearing a grin from ear to ear, I instantly dread what's headed my way. "Time for breakfast." She's in a black bikini top and sarong with her hair piled high on her head. She looks like she's ready to laze about in the sun all day, circumstances be damned.

The mere mention of food turns my stomach. "I'm not hungry."

When she bursts into laughter, I know I've missed the memo. "That's a good thing for you then because until we've all been fed, you don't eat."

I raise my head off the pillow to get a better look at her. "Excuse me?"

She's clearly enjoying herself, and when she produces the key to my cuffs, I know why. She's in control for once, and I suddenly feel like an ant being roasted alive under a magnifying glass. "It's time you earned your keep."

"Unless you've had a lapse in memory, I'm here against

my will," I snap, tugging at the cuffs to prove my point.

But she doesn't seem to care either way.

She reaches over me and unlocks my cuffs but doesn't give me a moment to rub my raw wrists before she yanks me up by my arm. I try to shrug from her punishing grip, but she holds on tight. "Alek doesn't like to be kept waiting, and this will be the first breakfast we've had together that I didn't cook."

I'm soon brought up to speed.

It seems I'm to be a slave in every sense of the word. "Cook your own damn breakfast," I spit, prying her fingers off me.

My suggestion falls on deaf ears as she shoves me between my shoulder blades. "Move."

Not having much choice, I open the door and wonder if this is how someone feels when they walk into a room where everyone is talking about them. All heads turn my way and the conversations pause as the men gawk at Zoey and me.

I'm guessing most are placing bets on who would win in a fight because it'll come to blows if she doesn't stop pushing me. "Alek likes his eggs poached."

It takes all my willpower not to tell her to go fuck herself as I walk past the perverts to the kitchen. Saint isn't down here, which has me wondering where he is.

"The eggs are in there." When she points at the fridge, I realize she's serious. The men look at me and then at Zoey, and I know she's doing this in front of company to humiliate me. She wants them to see her as the top dog because even though I'm here to take her place, she wants to reiterate that she's still number one.

Without a choice, I hunt through the fridge and cupboards

to gather what I need. Both are well stocked. There is enough bacon to feed a small army, which I suppose I am. By the fresh produce on board, I dare say we are close to Russia because it'll run out in two, three days tops.

Or we could always dock somewhere.

The unknown adds to my nerves, so I decide to focus on feeding these assholes so I can go back to my prison. I find a monster glass bowl in the cupboard above the stove and go about cracking the eggs into it.

However, a pained *oof* leaves me when my head is yanked back—hard. "What do you think you're doing?" Zoey snarls, tugging my hair harder when I twist violently to break free.

"Making breakfast!" I cry, reaching behind me to force her fingers out of my hair. But the movement only infuriates her further.

"Are you fucking stupid? I just told you Alek likes his eggs poached."

I want to strangle her. But I can't move. Hair pulling is such a catty thing to do. I would respect her more if she knocked me out cold because then I wouldn't haven't to cook her fucking breakfast.

"I'm making scrambled eggs for the merry men," I explain sarcastically through gritted teeth. "Let go of me."

When she does, I spin quickly, intent on killing her, but she stops me in my tracks when she slaps my cheek so hard, I taste blood. I cup my face, eyes narrowed as I move my jaw from side to side.

Zoey isn't bothered in the slightest. "Alek and I eat first. Then they eat. Now do it again."

Anger spurs me forward, and I don't care if this action ends my life. It will be so worth it because if I go down, I'll make sure she comes with me. Sadly, all plans of killing her with my bare hands will have to be put on hold for now.

"What's going on?" Saint's voice booms across the room, reminding me that regardless of how badly I want to murder Zoey, she's still his sister. She may be a mega bitch, but that will never change who she is to Saint.

And judging by the winner's grin she's sporting, she knows it.

"This bitch is useless," she says with a condescending chuckle. "She can't even do a simple thing like make breakfast."

When I turn slowly to lock eyes with Saint, he discovers my reddening cheek. He inhales deeply through his nose, like someone would when asking God to give them strength.

I don't know how he'll respond since we're all on show. I want nothing more than to go to him, but I can't, so I stand here like a trained poodle and not say a word. But Saint, it seems, has enough words for us both, and that has me nodding in gratitude even though his sentence is a double-edged sword.

"She isn't your slave."

"No, but she's Alek's," Zoey counters, folding her arms in challenge. But she doesn't stand a chance against her brother.

"Therefore, only Alek has the right to command her."

Technically, *no one* has the right, but I understand what he's doing.

Zoey's eyes narrow, and her lips twist into a bitter scowl, but she doesn't argue. It seems she's submissive to Alek *and* her brother.

"Go wait for him," Saint commands, which I can only imagine eats him up inside. He's giving her orders like a dog to save her punishment. She's chosen this life, and this is the only way Saint can guarantee she stays safe.

She doesn't argue but pushes past me forcibly, ensuring I lose my balance. I grip onto the counter to stop myself from face planting. She floats through the room and does what Saint said—she waits on her knees by the golden chair at the head of the table, which looks like a throne, for her master.

I turn my back, sickened.

Although the last thing I want to do is make her breakfast, I commence poaching the eggs and frying the bacon because I need something to do with my shaky hands. As I'm brewing the coffee, I can feel someone watching me closely.

No guessing who.

"Something smells good."

A shiver passes over me; an automatic response, it seems, to whenever Aleksei enters a room. However, I continue preparing breakfast because it allows me to keep my back turned.

"Good girl," Aleksei says to who I presume is a kneeling Zoey. She hums in response. I can imagine him patting her head. "Come sit."

This is so fucked up, and I can't do a damn thing about it. I desperately need to speak with Saint in private, but these walls have ears, and I have to be careful.

Once I've prepared Aleksei's breakfast, I hunt for crockery. When I open a drawer and find it filled with plastic forks and knives, I don't know whether to laugh or cry. It appears Aleksei has thought of everything.

Gathering everything I need and serving up two plates of food, I take a deep breath and turn around. Saint stands off to the left of Aleksei with his eyes forward in what I assume is his usual post. He is Aleksei's hitman, after all.

Shaking such thoughts from my mind, I make my way over to the table and place Aleksei's breakfast in front of him, ensuring I don't stand too close. I do the same with Zoey sitting to his right. The rest of the men remain standing. It appears their boss eats first without them encroaching on his space.

It's amazing that he commands this much power, and I wonder if any of them are here against their will too. What has he promised for them to exhibit such loyalty? Or are they just fearful for their lives?

I go back into the kitchen to pour the coffee.

When I make my way back over to the table and place the mug in front of Aleksei, he reaches out and gently grasps my wrist. I flinch, as I'm still sore from being handcuffed, but I don't struggle. What would be the point?

He strokes his thumb over my skin, peering up at me. "Thank you for breakfast. It smells wonderful."

I blink once, taken aback by his manners. But I quickly recover as it's clear he's waiting for my reply.

"It's my pleasure. I hope you enjoy it." I swallow down my lie because it feels like acid against my tongue.

I chance a quick glance at Saint and find his jaw clenched tight. He may appear docile, but I know better. In order to convince Aleksei that Saint is the key to curbing my behavior, I need to behave.

Aleksei nods once. He's brushed back his damp hair after taking a shower, and the slight graying at his temples only adds to the refined look. He doesn't look like a monster, but I suppose those are the most dangerous types.

He lets me go, examining me closely as he can't seem to read me as well as he does Zoey. I will use this to my advantage because it's the only way to survive whatever I will face. I quickly make my way back into the kitchen.

I'm guessing the men have to wait to eat until after Aleksei finishes, so I'll make their breakfast when he's done. This is so incredibly sexist, but the more time spent out here, scoping out my surroundings and what's at my disposal, the better it is for me.

There is some chitchat, mostly in Russian, but Saint stays as quiet as a ghost. I wonder what's going through his mind? Is he searching for an escape route just like I am?

A loud clutter causes me to jolt.

Pausing from where I'm washing up, I turn and look over my shoulder, taking in the sight of Zoey's breakfast spilled on the floor. The upturned plate leaves a trail of yellow yolk marring the polished surface. "This is disgusting," she spits, glaring at me.

Aleksei stops midchew, appearing just as confused as I am. "What's wrong, любимая?"

I remember Saint told me Aleksei used this nickname for Zoey, which means favorite. Irony at its finest, considering he treats her like dirt.

She leans back in her seat with her arms folded and her lips pressed into a scowl. She looks like a spoiled little girl. "The eggs are overdone. The bacon is soggy. Do it again."

My hands are buried in hot, soapy water, so no one can see me clench them into fists. This is just a power play. Aleksei places his plastic fork and knife on the rim of his plate, watching this unfold. Technically, I am to obey him, not Zoey, so how am I supposed to respond?

The men watch on eagerly, ready for a catfight. But I won't lower myself to her level.

Channeling my inner yoga goddess, I take three calming breaths as I dry my hands on a dishcloth. I grab a roll of paper towels and some all-purpose spray to wipe down the floor. Without a word, I walk over to the mess Zoey made and drop to my knees.

A heavy exhale leaves Saint, but he doesn't say a word.

As I'm wiping up the gooey eggs, which are cooked just fine, I'm coated with a spray of coffee. Yelping, I shrink back, but it doesn't make a difference. I'm covered in the coffee Zoey just poured onto the floor. It seems her breakfast wasn't enough of an insult, and she had to add her coffee as well.

Clenching the paper towel in my hand, I keep my eyes peeled to the floor as I'm afraid of what I'll do if I look at her. I see Saint's boots kick into action, but I subtly shake my head, demanding he stay put.

"This coffee tastes like dishwater. You really are good for nothing, you stupid whore."

I know what she's doing—she's baiting me—and it's working. Just as I lift my chin, poised on telling her to go fuck herself, a fist slamming onto the table has me pausing.

Aleksei's cool composure has been replaced by a dark cloud of anger. Zoey still sits smugly, but that soon changes when she turns a ghastly shade of white. "I will not tolerate this behavior at my breakfast table."

"Alek—"

"Silence! Since when do you speak when I'm talking?"

Zoey doesn't think twice as she springs from her seat and drops to her knees beside Aleksei. I'm also on my knees, cleaning up her mess, but she doesn't even acknowledge me. She knows she's in trouble.

"You want to throw your food on the floor and behave like an animal? Then you can eat like one."

I gulp, eyes wide. Although she deserves this, I can't find any satisfaction in seeing her being treated this way.

"This breakfast is wonderful, Willow," he says, looking at me with a smile. All I can do is nod numbly. "Don't listen to Zoey. She seems to have misplaced her manners this morning."

"I'm sorry, Alek," she cries, her lower lip quivering.

But it's too late.

"I'm not the one you should be apologizing to."

This must kill her, but she raises her chin slowly. "I'm sorry. That was very rude of me. The breakfast is delicious." She doesn't mean a word, but I accept her apology nonetheless.

Aleksei, however, doesn't seem convinced. "Prove it."

We are facing each other, both on our knees, both puppets to a man who thrives on pain. Without a flicker on emotion, Zoey lowers herself onto her hands and begins to eat what's left of her spilled breakfast off the floor.

I shuffle back, horrified. Is he doing this to show me he cares?

"Good?" Aleksei asks, peering down at her with a wicked grin.

She hums her approval while I'm about to be sick.

"You can make the men their breakfast now," he instructs me while I stare at Zoey, tears filling my eyes.

This is the most degrading thing I have ever seen, and I can't do a damn thing about it. "Move." Saint's sharp voice has me snapping to attention.

Looking up at him, I beg for him to stop this. But what can he do? He acts out, and his entire life will crumble around him. We have to be smart and devise a plan, I know that. But seeing this...I don't know how long I can last.

Coming to a slow stand, I walk around Zoey and into the kitchen. When my back is turned, I allow one tear to trickle down my cheek, but I wipe it away just as quickly with the back of my hand. I work on autopilot, preparing a mountain of food. Subconsciously, I'm hoping to fill the void in my chest, but nothing will.

The moment Aleksei finishes his meal, the men dig into their breakfast. Zoey has finished hers but remains on her knees by Aleksei's side. Saint stands rigid like a trained solider. If not for the heavy rise and fall of his chest, I wouldn't even know he's breathing.

"You may eat," Aleksei says to Saint, as if doing him a favor by giving him permission to eat, but he shakes his head.

"I'm not hungry." Waves of anger roll off him.

Aleksei reaches for a toothpick from the table and goes about picking the food from his teeth. "Very well then. Take ангел into the en suite to shower. I have a few calls to make, but I'll meet you in the bedroom soon."

A foreboding panic overcomes me because what exactly will happen when he meets us in the bedroom?

Saint doesn't need to be told twice and practically rips my arm off as he drags me in the direction of the bedroom. When he opens the door and shoves me inside the en suite, I grab onto the towel rack to stop myself from falling.

He slams and locks the bathroom door, placing his splayed hands against it. Lowering his head between his spread arms, he inhales deeply through his nose. He is visibly shaking.

"Saint?" I whisper, afraid.

When he hears his name, his hands curl into fists. "We have to leave. Tonight."

"Tonight?" I question, a hitch to my breath. "How?"

As he spins around, his anger hits me, and I instantly back away. I know he won't hurt me, but he looks intent on murder. "We are three days away from reaching Russia," he reveals, unsnapping a black band from around his wrist and tying his hair back. "By eleven seventeen tonight, we will be fifty kilometres away from a port in Romania. It's the only opportunity we'll have to escape."

My mouth opens and closes, but I can't speak. He's clearly been studying our route.

"We have five minutes."

I gulp, wringing my hands in front of me. "Five minutes to do what?"

I know what, but I need him to say it. I need for him to make it real.

"Kill that son of a bitch and get the fuck off this yacht," he says without pause.

My legs feel heavy so I slump onto the toilet seat, needing a moment to process what I always knew to be true.

Saint storms over, dropping to his knees before me. He looks up at me, gripping my thighs, pleading for me to speak. And when I do, I barely recognize my own voice. "How do we do that?"

He exhales in what seems to be relief. "We throw a party."

I scrunch up my nose. Has he lost his mind? "A party?" Clearly, I've misunderstood.

I haven't.

"Yes. Zoey has enough sleeping tablets to take down a dozen horses, and there is an abundance of vodka on board. It'll be easy. We just have to convince Aleksei."

"How do we do that?"

Saint's grip on my thighs tightens, which means I'm not going to like his proposal. "We have to give him cause to celebrate. We have to make him think it's his idea to throw the party."

His tone has a knot forming in the pit of my stomach.

"He's going to come in here, and most likely"—he swallows deeply—"he's going to want to see what he bought. He won't take no for an answer this time. But if you tell him… if you tell him you're a virgin and that you're afraid, it'll buy us some time."

My cheeks rival a tomato. "How is that going to work

in our favor? You once said that being a virgin is a crime." I think back to that conversation and what seems like years ago. I didn't understand what he meant.

"All he wants is for you to submit. This isn't about lust. It's about power. He wants to control you. So if you act like the perfect victim and beg he protect your virtue until you get to Russia, he will."

"This isn't going to work," I cry, shaking my head.

Saint refuses to allow me to think otherwise. "It will," he presses. "You're a virgin. And it *is* a crime because to someone like Aleksei, you are the ultimate conquest. He will want to break you slowly and not force you. Because when you do break, he'll see it as a victory. Aleksei may be many things, but he's not a rapist."

"How can you vouch for him? For his honor?" I beseech he help me see something I simply cannot.

When a frown tugs at his bowed lips, I wish I never asked. "Because every woman he's been with has done so on their own free will."

Because he will worm his way into your soul and make you forget a life before him existed.

Zoey's words of warning sound loudly because she and Saint seem to share the same opinion on Aleksei's charm. But those women are not me.

"Is that why you didn't"—I pause, chewing my bottom lip—"want to sleep with me? You knew we could use my virginity as a bargaining chip?"

Saint jerks his head back, clearly stunned by my question.

"On the island, when I asked—" But he doesn't allow me

to finish.

"I remember," he interrupts, looking at me with those hypnotic eyes. "And no, that's not the reason."

"Oh."

He lowers his chin and takes a deep breath as if weighing what to say. "I haven't"—he clears his throat—"I haven't been with someone I...care about in a very long time."

"Oh," I repeat, my stomach full of butterflies.

I want to press, but it's enough. For now. I know how hard that was for him to admit.

"So how do we convince him to throw a party? What are we celebrating? My virginity?" I quip, but when he doesn't see the humor in my comment, I know he's proposing exactly that.

"This is fucking crazy." I sigh, running a hand down my face.

Saint squeezes my legs before standing. "It's the only thing I can think of. We need to disarm his men, and we can't rely on them falling asleep at the same time. This is the only way we have a fighting shot."

He's right, but this plan isn't foolproof, and honestly, I'm doubtful it'll work. But we have to try.

"So when he comes into the bedroom, I have to play the docile little lamb he wanted?"

Saint nods slowly.

"And somehow convince him to throw a party to honor my virginity?" It's as ridiculous as it sounds.

"It'll be okay. I'll be with you. Just follow my lead, all right?"

Forever my guardian, Saint looks out for me when I want to give up. "Okay. So if this plan works and we manage to drug the men, then we...kill Aleksei and escape on the inflatable raft?"

I need to say this aloud to ensure I've got it right.

"Yes," he replies. "Everything will come down to timing. Those sleeping pills take up to twenty minutes to kick in, and we need to make sure all the men are out for the count before we kill that motherfucker. We can't risk any of them waking up to raise the alarm or to run to his aid."

I gulp.

"Why do we have such a small window? You said we have five minutes?"

"Because when we reach a certain point, the waterways will split. I've studied the nautical charts countless times. The current will take us in a direct route to Russia, bypassing any ports to stop. Aleksei has done it this way so we avoid passing any people along the way. This is our only opportunity."

I was nervous before I knew what he had planned. But now, I am petrified because there is no room for error.

"We don't want this plan to kick off too early or too late. Timing is everything. It's the difference between life and death."

Saint isn't being melodramatic.

And neither am I when I ask, "What about Zoey?"

"She'll be out cold. She won't have a choice this time when I throw her ass into that raft."

"And what happens then?"

The question is inevitable. Zoey and I have no love lost

between us, and honestly, I can't see us ever getting along. But Saint has never promised me anything other than my freedom. He's never painted a picture where I live happily ever after with him.

This was always about saving Zoey. But things have changed. Well, they have for me.

"Let's just focus on getting out of here alive."

He's right.

"So please"—he lowers his lips to my forehead—"for once, do what you're told, ангел."

His touch calms my racing heart. "Okay. I promise."

He kisses my brow before straightening. "Go shower. I'll bring in a change of clothes. Is there anything in particular you wanted to wear?"

"A suit of armor? A chastity belt?" I offer, only half joking.

Saint smirks, but it's laced with exhaustion. Once he's out the door, I strip out of my clothes and step into the shower. I wash on autopilot, going over the plan in my head. This is insane. *If*, and that's a big if, we pull this off, what happens when we get to Romania?

Do we go our separate ways? I have no identification. No money. What would I do?

I don't know for certain, but I assume killing Aleksei will upset a lot of people who will then be out for revenge. We'll be fugitives so going back and living a normal life doesn't seem probable. What a mess.

One thing is for certain. I intend on getting my own vengeance against my beloved husband. He is the reason this entire nightmare began, so it seems fitting to end it with him.

Such dire thoughts have me quickly switching off the water.

When I've dried off, I see that Saint has left me a change of clothes on the edge of the sink. It's a pretty white sundress with a red bow at the waist. It seems Aleksei has an obsession with red. Probably because it reminds him of blood.

After applying deodorant and body lotion, I slip into the underwear and bra set and am thankful when the dress Saint chose covers a lot more skin. I know it's a false sense of security, however, because god knows what I'll be walking into when I exit this bathroom.

I leave my hair down and apply a little makeup. I'm not here to impress anyone.

Once I look presentable, I stare at my reflection in the mirror and assure myself that this will all be over by tonight. I hope.

Knowing I can't hide in here forever, I open the door, only to pause in my tracks when I see Aleksei in the bedroom. I thought I had a little time to prepare myself, but here he stands, smiling at me like we're friends.

"You're a vision."

Saint stands behind him, eyes heavy with venom. But he remains quiet.

"Thank you," I whisper, walking into the room and standing in front of Aleksei awkwardly.

When he inhales, then takes a step forward, it takes all my willpower not to recoil. He reaches out and brushes my hair behind my shoulder, taking in my appearance closely. I feel like a bug under a microscope, but I keep my gaze trained on Saint.

Aleksei circles me slowly as it seems he needs to observe me from every angle. He comes to a stop when he's at my back. His warm breath bathes my neck as he twirls a strand of my hair around his finger. "Pictures don't do you justice."

I know he's talking about the photograph Saint sent to him.

"May I see you?"

He's asking me as though I have a choice.

Saint's poker face hasn't slipped, reminding me of our plans. This is my opportunity to play Aleksei. I just hope it works.

When I nod shyly, a hiss leaves Aleksei as my submission pleases him. I'm not sure if he wants to do it himself, but I'd rather remain in control of at least one aspect of my life, so I lift the dress over my head, then drop it to pool by my feet.

Saint and I face one another, and when the green of his eyes are consumed by black, I know the sight of me standing in nothing but my underwear affects him. The moment shatters, however, when Aleksei walks around me.

He stands in front of me but takes a step back as he devours me whole. I want to cover myself, but I don't. I allow him to view his property because that's what I am to him. The thought has me locking eyes with Saint, which is a mistake on my behalf.

"Why do you keep looking at him? Can he provide you something that I cannot?"

I avert my gaze quickly, but it's too late.

"She obeys me, Alek," Saint says stiffly. "Nothing more.

Don't you, ангел?"

I nod, too afraid to speak because Aleksei has clearly seen what I thought were discreet exchanges with Saint.

Aleksei seems convinced. "I've seen you do this to other women, break them, I mean, but she's different."

Time stands still as I take a moment to process what Aleksei just revealed about Saint.

Other women? How many *other* women? Saint never told me there were others. I thought I was the first one to take Zoey's place. But I suppose his comment earlier now makes sense. He knows Aleksei's track record with women because it seems he's trained them all.

I suddenly feel sickened by the fact. I knew he wasn't, well, a saint but other women? I don't know how to feel. Betrayed comes to mind. But I rein in my emotion and remain passive.

"Something about her intrigues you, and well, that intrigues me."

The more Aleksei speaks, the angrier I become. I am not a science project. I am also in the room and to hear him speak about me like I'm not pisses me off.

"She *is* different," Saint says, staring me straight in the eyes.

Only he can read my annoyance because he knows me. But it seems I don't know him.

"How so?" Aleksei asks, looking at me like an anomaly.

Every part of my body challenges him to explain because I, too, am curious to know the answer.

"She is good. Pure," he says, which has my mouth parting in surprise. "She fights so hard because she is virtuous."

Aleksei's brow lifts. "Virtuous?"

Saint nods and kicks our plan into motion. "Yes. She is still a virgin."

I stand tall even though my heart threatens to burst from my chest.

Aleksei's mask slips as he zeroes in on the cross around my neck. "Is this true?" he asks me, visibly stunned by Saint's revelation.

I am not ashamed. "Yes."

A string of Russian words leaves him as he grins and shakes his head in awe. "That useless American really came through," he mumbles under his breath.

I remain unaffected because just the thought of Drew will ruin this innocent act.

But when Aleksei cocks his head to the side, appearing to have just had a thought, I hold my breath. "How can you be certain? Maybe she's said that to protect herself?"

I knew this wouldn't be easy. There really isn't a way to prove that I'm a virgin unless Aleksei probes for himself, which, according to Saint, he won't do until I want him to... which will be never.

"I'll prove it to you. Come here, ангел."

Stunned, I blink once, wondering exactly how he's proposing to *prove* my virginity. But remembering my promise to do what I'm told, I walk toward Saint, ensuring not to touch Aleksei as I move past him. Aleksei turns to watch the show, appearing truly entranced.

My back is to Aleksei, so he can't see me glare at Saint. I desperately want to ask just how many women there have been. But when he reaches out and spins me around to face Aleksei, I know the questions will have to wait.

He draws me back against his chest. He's warm and the feel of him is so familiar, but I don't allow Aleksei to see my comfort of being in his arms. "I can whip you until you bleed…or I can fuck you. Which would you prefer?"

Both sound horrific, and I prefer neither option, but I see what he's doing. Most would opt for the fucking, as it would be far less painful, especially if one didn't have their virtue to protect. "Whip me, мастер."

Aleksei's eyes sparkle. It's just another day at the office for this asshole.

"Are you sure? The fucking would be a lot less painful." My body, the traitorous whore, wants that, but considering where we are, and the fact I just found out I'm not the only woman Saint has probably fucked into submission, I nod firmly.

"No. I'd rather the punishment."

Saint hums low; the scorching warmth of his body pressed to mine has me breaking out into a sweat. "Why is that? I promise I'll make it feel good."

To my horror, he presses his lips over my pulse and licks my slickened skin. I refuse to buckle.

"Thank you, мастер. I'm sure that you would. But I'm saving myself for marriage. Or at least, for someone I love." The falter to Saint's lips betrays his feelings as that comment had a double meaning. I'm not acting now, and he knows it.

I wanted to have sex with him, so that must mean I…I don't love him, well, I don't think that I do, but I meant it when I said I wanted him. I am so fucking confused, and the way my body responds to his touch doesn't help.

"You *are* married," he says, dousing my flames as he toys with his pinkie ring.

"I never got a chance to consummate my marriage," I reply truthfully.

Aleksei smiles broadly, watching the shitstorm unfold.

"Your values are rather old fashioned, don't you think?"

"My father was a Baptist minister, and it's one principle he believed firmly in. I want to honor his memory by respecting something he had faith in."

Christmas has come early in his eyes as he claps once. "You are so much more than I expected." I'm the ultimate conquest, it seems.

"I think I can change your mind," Saint says, interrupting the celebrations.

I don't have time to ask Saint what he means because I'm robbed of air when he wraps his hand around my waist. Aleksei's attention drops to Saint's fingers as they walk their way over my hip and drift to the front of my underwear.

"Wh-what are you doing?" I ask, suddenly forgetting Aleksei is here.

"Shh," he orders, rubbing slowly over my sex.

He can feel my arousal, but this is so twisted. I don't want to perform in front of Aleksei like some trained circus animal.

"Please, no, мастер." And I mean it.

"Why not?" He suckles my earlobe all the while continuing to caress me.

My body craves his touch, just as it always does, but when I look at Aleksei and see his dilated pupils and labored breathing, I feel disgusting. I don't want to share this with anyone. This is private.

Any other time, I would feel Saint being turned on, but the fact nothing prods me in the back confirms he's doing this to prove a point.

"Because…" When he rubs over my ripened clit, I gasp and sag forward, my entire body flushing in utter embarrassment. I've just gotten used to Saint touching me, especially after my childhood, so this PDA leaves me mortified.

Which is exactly what Saint wants.

"A virgin's blush," Aleksei says in awe. "She's telling the truth. I know a liar when I see one, and you, sweet Willow, are not a liar. You really are a virgin…and you are mine."

Saint instantly recoils, ending our little peep show.

Humiliated, I wrap my arms around my body, needing to veil my nakedness. I feel so dirty, which is ironic seeing as something pure has led to these feelings of shame.

"As you can see," Saint very matter-of-factly states, "she is modest. Over the years, we have been forced to weed out the liars, but she is not one. What she says is true."

Aleksei nods in agreement. He looks at me as though he's just witnessed the second coming of Christ.

"Shall we drink to your good fortune?" Saint suggests, planting the seed and hoping it'll grow. And it does. Just as he said it would.

"Yes, we shall. I think there is much to celebrate, don't you?" Aleksei runs the back of his fingers down my cheek. I flinch, which only seems to excite him all the more. "Get dressed, дорогая."

I don't even want to know what that means.

Making a beeline for my dress, I slip it over my head in haste, keeping my back turned to Aleksei and Saint. I'm unable to face either of them.

"You're a rarity. Thank you, Saint, for protecting my investment."

I close my eyes, sickened.

"You truly are a diamond in the rough. But we will work on that to unearth your true shine."

A tear slides down my cheek.

I expect him to touch me, but he doesn't. He leaves the room to no doubt gloat to his disciples about his virgin hostage. I don't know how I feel right now. Numb is probably the best word.

But I eventually find my voice. "So other women?" I whisper, shaking my head in defeat. "You left that part out. Did you, did you sleep with them?"

Saint exhales heavily. "Of course not! It's not like that. Alek picked the girls he wanted. I was to make sure they... behaved. What do you want me to say?"

"Nothing," I reply honestly.

"Don't do this. He did what we wanted."

But at what cost?

"How many?" I press. I don't know why it matters. It just does.

"I don't know!" he exclaims, his boots pounding along the floor as he storms over and turns me around to face him. "Hundreds. Thousands. I've lost count! But I never had...*this* with them."

With a scoff, I jerk out of his hold, scowling because I don't want his hands on me even though he professed what we have is different. "Thousands?" I ask, unable to hide my disgust.

Something ugly passes between Saint and me, and I don't like it. I knew he wasn't a knight in shining armor, but I can't stop thinking about all the lives he's destroyed—like mine.

Saint can read my thoughts before I have a chance to mask them, and a wall, the one which took me so long to break down, resurrects quickly. "You know what I am. I never said I was the hero."

And there it is, the truth. Saint is right. He never offered me anything but himself, but now...I don't know if it's enough. How can I even think about having a future with him knowing what I do?

Looking into those eyes which held me captive long before I was bound, I'm heavy with regret when I confess, "I know. So what does that say about me?"

I'm waiting for Saint to make it better, just as he's always done, but when he doesn't reply, it's apparent the silence says it all.

Having my head elsewhere is a dangerous thing, considering what I'm supposed to be doing very soon. I just can't stop thinking about Saint and his harem of "other" women.

His actions will never be excused, and the fact he's done this to other women—even though he said he never slept with them—has me wondering just who he really is. It shouldn't matter because I know it was done against his will, but it does. I thought I knew who he was, but I'm realizing I don't know anything at all.

However, I can question myself later because right now, I need to get my head back in the game.

The sexism has come in handy because when Aleksei declared we were going to have a celebration, I was expected to cater for all. Saint, of course, knew this would be the case, and although it pains me to serve these murderous assholes, it has allowed me to set our plan into motion.

Saint stole enough sleeping pills to drug a small nation. He said Zoey wouldn't notice because, judging from her comatose state as she lays sprawled out on the sofa, it seems Aleksei has already ensured she stays in her own private drugged bubble for the night.

I believe this is punishment for today's outburst. If he's doing this to buy his way into my good books, he will be sorely disappointed when I stand back and watch Saint end his miserable life.

I keep my hands steady as I pour drinks for everyone. It seems simple enough, so I can only hope this plan doesn't backfire. Ensuring I keep the blue cups pumped full of crushed sleeping tablets and other drugs Saint ensured me would knock them out cold from the non-lethal red cups, I pour the top shelf vodka, hoping my nerves don't betray me.

When I was ordered to go into the kitchen, Saint made

some excuse to be in there too. Aleksei was too euphoric over my virginity and his guard was lowered which allowed Saint to slip the drugs into the cups and also the bottle of vodka with the blue label.

I was convinced we'd get caught, but Saint's sneakiness came in handy, and he laced the cups and vodka before my eyes. The tension was toxic between us, making this plan even harder because it seems we both need to put some space between us.

But we don't have that luxury because when Saint looks at his watch and meets my eyes, I know it's time.

The men have been drinking all night, and the stereotype that Russians love vodka seems to be accurate. Some are already a little tipsy, but Saint is clearly not leaving anything to chance as he scoops up the blue cups and bottle, indicating I'm to follow.

Aleksei sits at the table playing cards, and judging by the wad of cash piled high beside him, I dare say he's whipping everyone's asses. The thought turns my stomach because this shitstorm all started when I was sold in a game of poker. The thought of ending this bastard's life is becoming easier and easier to accept.

"дорогая," he says when I walk behind Saint, drinks in hand. I still don't know what that means, but by the way he smiles at me, I dare say it's his term of endearment for me. "You are a wonderful cook."

The vast amount of food on board allowed me to whip up quite an assortment of party food. As I prepared the beef sliders, I couldn't stop thinking of this as the last meal because that's what it will be for Aleksei if Saint and I are able to pull off our plan.

"Thank you," I reply, pushing sentiment aside and placing a blue cup in front of him.

Just as I attempt to move, he launches forward and takes a hold of my wrist. I dare not breathe, and from the corner of my eye, I can see Saint watching the exchange closely. "If I didn't know any better," he purrs while I brace for him to tell me our jig is up, "I'd say you were trying to take advantage of me by giving me all this alcohol."

Relief swarms over me, but I try my best to remain unmoved.

"But I know that's not true because why?" He looks up at me, a shit-eating grin glowing from ear to ear.

Every part of me rebels, primed on telling him to go to hell, but this is what we're celebrating, after all. All the men look at me with a new hunger reflected in their glassy eyes. I am the guest of honor, or rather, my hymen is.

I'm sickened beyond belief.

With that as my mindset, I ensure to play my part and not rouse suspicion. "Because I am holding on to my virtue."

Aleksei sighs in victory, finally letting me go. "Yes, you are."

When one of the men says something in Russian, causing the table to erupt in laughter, Saint turns to glare over his shoulder. Getting off this yacht can't come soon enough.

Aleksei joins the commotion, which is just fine because when he reaches for his cup, I will have the last laugh. As I attempt to move away, he gestures for me to stay. "I want to make a toast."

I stand by his side, taking steady breaths so I don't give away my nerves.

"To you, дорогая. I know we're going to be very happy together." This man is fucking delirious, but when he raises the cup in salute, I know our plan has just begun. "To my little девственница."

The men follow suit, raising their drinks to salute my virginity, I'm guessing by the clenching of Saint's jaw.

But they can salute all they want because when they, one by one, gulp down their laced drinks, it'll be the last thing they do for a while. I'm on eggshells as I wait for Aleksei to take the fatal sip, but he doesn't.

My heart begins to race.

He brings the cup to his lips but then stops, eyeing the drink closely. Can he see the small white particles? Or does his sense of smell hint that something is off?

Whatever it is, he has to drink it now because as the men top off their cups with the laced vodka, I know they'll be out for the count before too long.

Aleksei peers over at Saint, who stands rigid, and then at me. He surely suspects something. And when he addresses Saint, I know that I'm right. "Where is your drink, my friend?"

"I'm not thirsty," Saint replies as beads of sweat collect along his brow.

"Come, drink with me. It's because of you that this is possible. If you hadn't been the loyal friend you are"—his tone drips with innuendo as he offers Saint his cup—"then my beautiful девственница wouldn't have come into my life."

Aleksei isn't offering; he's challenging Saint. He still doesn't trust him. And this, just like everything else, is a test.

This is really it this time. Aleksei will kill us both. Saint steps forward, knowing he doesn't have a choice. If he doesn't drink the vodka, then we're as good as dead.

But I can't allow all this to have been for nothing. I refuse to accept this is how my story ends. So without thought, I drop to my knees by Aleksei's side. My eyes are cast downward, but I know I have his attention.

"Is there something you want?" he asks sweetly while I nod slowly, playing his game. "What is it then?"

"May I have a drink?" I try my hardest to sound submissive and innocent because if this doesn't work, we're screwed.

"Ангел!" Saint scolds, his horror clear. But he soon recovers. "I've taught you better than to ask for anything. Do *not* forget your place."

This exchange to onlookers would appear he's reprimanding me for talking out of line, but I know what he's doing. He's demanding I don't do this. But this isn't his decision. It's time I saved myself.

"It's all right, Saint," Aleksei states. When I feel him pat my head, a piece of my soul is lost forever. "She can have a drink. Here. I offer you my cup."

Again, he seems like a good Samaritan, offering his very own drink to his slave, but we both know what this is. If I drink from his cup, then his suspicions are wrong. If I don't, well...There really isn't any other option.

"Thank you, мастер." Aleksei hums his approval as I slowly peer up at him from under my lashes and timidly accept the cup from his hands.

I know what this means, but what other choice do I have?

Without reservation, I draw the cup to my lips, and I…drink. The urge to throw it all up overwhelms me, but I swallow it down, as I do with my tears. Aleksei places his fingers under the rim, forcing me to down it all.

I do.

When the cup is empty, I wipe my lips with the back of my hand and wonder how long I have before the drugs hit. Before that happens, however, I whisper, "I don't like drinking alone," and pass the cup back to Aleksei. Please, let this work.

It does.

He accepts, and all suspicion vanishes as he reaches for the bottle of vodka off the table. My stomach gurgles as it feels like I've just downed acid. Aleksei pours himself a glass and raises the cup in my honor. "You will never drink alone again."

His words are filled with promise, and when he throws back the vodka, savoring every last drop, I see that he means it. Aleksei has a way of making it seem like I'm here because I want to be. He hasn't been cruel, as such, but I know this is his way of manipulating people into becoming his pawns.

I risk a glance around the table and notice a few of the men's eyes slipping to half-mast. Their chins droop to their chests because they can no longer hold up their heads.

Thy drugs are quick.

Thankfully, Aleksei is too preoccupied with patting his new pet to notice.

"Fuck it," Saint says, cutting through the silence. "Let's drink. Your success is mine." I risk a glance at him and see he holds the bottle of vodka with the red label—the non-drugged one.

Aleksei nods, and when his head wobbles slightly, I know the drugs, mixed with the copious amount of alcohol he's consumed, are kicking in. He raises his bottle to salute Saint, and they both gulp down the vodka. Saint guzzles his, baiting Aleksei to beat him, and he does.

Aleksei consumes the entire bottle, then attempts to slam it onto the table. However, it seems his hand-eye coordination is failing him because he misses the table and the bottle shatters into tiny slivers when it hits the floor. He tries to pinpoint the noise but blinks quickly as though he can't focus.

"Wh-what d-did you doooo?" he asks in a slur, sagging low into his seat as he tries to grab me. But all he clings on to is air.

The effects of the drugs hit me too as I grip the edge of the table to maintain my balance. I blink once as the world flickers into blurred lines. The world moves in slow motion around me as I peer around the room, noticing the comatose men.

Some are slumped onto the table while most are sound asleep in their chairs or mumbling incoherently as the drugs seep into their system.

I know the drugs have hit them quicker because of all the vodka they've had, but I am half their body weight and don't drink nearly as much as they do, so I know I only have minutes until my fate matches theirs.

"Y-you wi-will pay." And those are the last words I hope to ever hear from my kidnapper because his head hits the table with a harsh thud. He's out cold.

I can finally breathe again.

"Ангел, come! We have to be quick." I feel someone slip their forearms under my armpits and yank me up. I'm as floppy as a rag doll.

I have no control over my body and sag forward, but Saint won't allow me to fall. Regardless of how I feel about him right now, he will keep his word and give me back my freedom. Just as he promised he would.

"I'm sorrreee." My swollen tongue makes it hard for me to speak, but I need to apologize to Saint. I judged him when I shouldn't have, and my anger was misdirected. I'm angry with myself for...for falling for the bad guy. Because when I inhale his scent and bask in his touch, I know that's exactly what I've done.

I blamed him for me feeling this way, but there is no one to blame but me.

"Shh, it's okay. Just lean on me, okay?" Like I have a choice. My legs are like overcooked spaghetti.

We commence a slow stagger, but to where, I don't know because my eyes are sealed shut. I've read that before one dies, the last sense they lose is their hearing. I wonder if maybe I've poisoned myself because that's the only thing I'm relying on right now because my body feels like it's shutting down.

"I-I can't feel m-my...body," I wheeze, my heart beating frantically.

"I've got you, and I promise, I'll never let you go." Those words throw a warm blanket over me, and I allow Saint to lead the way. But one thought pounds against my temples, and I fight the urge to surrender to the darkness.

"Kill...him," I push out between winded breaths.

I can't leave this yacht knowing he's still alive. After everything he's done, this stops now. No more women are to take my place because I want this to end with me.

"We don't have time."

With the last bit of strength I have left, I use my weight to try to hold him back. It's a lame attempt, but it has the desired effect. "Please."

I want to say so much more, but I can't, and I know we're running out of time.

Just when I think Saint is about to pick me up and haul ass, he exhales loudly and then groans. We take a few steps forward, then I feel the soft plush sofa under my body as Saint lays me down gently. "Cover your ears," he instructs before placing a frantic kiss to my forehead.

If I could move my arms, I would.

It feels like minutes, not seconds, but when I hear a gun being cocked, I know it's really over. I'm safe.

Or so I thought.

"Drop your gun."

There must be some mistake. I'm surely hallucinating. But when I feel myself being hauled to my feet and the cold barrel of a gun being shoved against my temple, I know this is really happening.

"Zoey," Saint wheezes, his anguish clear as we are once again at gunpoint because of her. "Don't do this. Come with us. We can finally go home."

I don't know how she's awake, but she is, and with

everyone out cold, it's only us. Considering how this entire thing started, it seems fitting.

"What did you do to Alek?" she screams. The sound shreds my brain, and I moan in pain. The need to sleep overpowers me, but I force myself to stay awake. "Saint!"

I hiss when the metal stings my slick skin. Her patience is wearing thin, but so is Saint's as our window of time to escape closes. "Give her to me and…and you can live."

Both Zoey and I gasp because what he just said has drawn a distinct line in the sand.

"You'd chose this *bitch* over me?" Zoey cries, her betrayal and surprise apparent. "Over your own flesh and blood?"

Time stands still.

"I will always, *always* choose her. You're dead to me, Zoey."

The ultimate "fuck you" one could ever say to a sibling or to anyone, for that matter. My heart swells, knowing he chooses me. *No one* has ever done that for me. I was never important enough to be someone's number one.

All the warm and fuzzy feelings soon disappear, however, because when Zoey roars and cocks her gun, it's now or never. "Fine then. Her blood will be on your hands!"

I try to fight, but it's useless, so I brace for death.

It never comes.

"Drop it, Saint, or I kill your ангел."

That voice belongs to the man whose brother we killed. It seems not even being drugged can stop him from seeking revenge for his brother's death. I don't need my sight to know what's unfolding. Two guns versus one.

All this because of me. But I am done. Tired. The fight in me withers, so I surrender.

"Let," I pant, trying to stand upright on my own. "Let him go. I won't fight."

"That's not an option," Zoey says, her grip on me weakening. It seems that even though she woke from her drug coma, she's still drowsy. I wish I could use that to my advantage, but I can't.

I can taste defeat.

"Yes. She must pay for what she did to my brother, Kazimir. You both must." He's always been privy to what went down. He was just biding his time.

When Saint bursts into laughter, I wonder if he's finally lost his mind. I know I have. "Your brother cried like a little girl. Begging for his life."

"Shut up!" roars Adrian, but Saint does nothing of the sort.

"He pissed his pants right before I put a bullet between his eyes."

I recognize what he's doing. He's baiting Adrian to train his gun on him and not on me. I know Saint, and my life is always more important to him than his. I don't need my vision to recognize that.

The room explodes into pandemonium as Russian words boom around me. Zoey shrieks when gunshots sound around us. The deafening noise splits me into two. I expect her to let me go, to duck for cover, or at the very least, to cover her ears, but to my horror, my hearing doesn't fail me as I hear the trigger squeak. She's going to shoot me.

"No!" A guttural scream leaves me, and I try to break free, but it's hopeless. And I do something I haven't done in a very long time.

I pray.

Please God, give me the strength and welcome me home.

I await my death, but it seems God isn't done with me yet.

"Forgive me, ангел."

I don't know what he's seeking absolution for…until I hear an echoing boom that rattles me to the core. I propel backward, the force so fierce that it knocks the sandals from my feet. I don't feel the pain in my body until I hit the floor.

Everything grows numb, and all I can focus on is the pain.

"Forgive me, ангел," he said.

Why?

Because Saint has caused this searing pain eating me whole—he just…fucking shot me.

I carry that certainty with me as I finally succumb to the darkness, unsure if I'll ever see the light again.

CHAPTER FOUR

I shot her to save her because if I didn't, Zoey or Adrian would have, and their shot would have been fatal. But it doesn't seem to make a difference because now, I'm just as much of a prisoner as she is.

Day 40

I have no idea of the time. Or day. Or where I am, for that matter. I feel neither here nor there. One thing is certain; I'm wrapped in silk sheets that smell of lavender. A strange thing to notice, but my senses are on high alert because I'm smelling something different from the past few weeks.

No longer the open sea.

The fact I can't feel the subtle sway to the waters has me guessing I have finally arrived where I was always destined to end up.

I'm on land. I'm in Russia.

Through my fuzzy brain, I try to think back to the last thing I can remember, but all I feel is pain—literally. My left shoulder feels as though red-hot pokers have pierced it, and my whole body aches.

With the slowest of movements, I gradually open my eyes, blinking rapidly to clear my blurred vision. It takes a few seconds, but when I eventually focus, I can't deny my surroundings are quite a sight.

I'm clearly in a bedroom, but this room looks like it once belonged to royalty.

A gold wallpaper ingrained with blue and gold flowers covers the walls. The high ceiling is domed, I think, and covered with the same wallpaper. The wooden furniture has red velvet cushioning. Thick silk drapes the king-size bed I'm lying in, and the color scheme matches the wallpaper.

Regardless of all the gleam in this lavish and comfortable place, it's still a prison—just with shinier bars.

I try to sit up, but my head spins, and I groan, falling back down onto the pillow and rubbing my brow. When the door opens, and a young woman enters with a jug of water, I can't help but shrink back. "W-who are you?" It takes me two attempts to speak, but she understands me perfectly fine.

"Oh, you're awake?" She has a definite French accent.

"Where am I?" My voice sounds like I gargled glass, and that pitcher she holds suddenly has me wetting my very dry lips.

She closes the door gently and walks over to the bed.

"You're in Russia. At Aleksei's home," she explains, reaching for a glass on the bedside table and pouring me some water.

Even though she confirmed what I already knew to be true, my stomach still turns at the thought.

"My name is Sara." She passes me the water, and I am far too thirsty to care if it's drugged or not. I reach for it and tip back my head to drink it all down. It gurgles in my empty belly.

"How many days have I been here?"

"Two."

My exhausted brain attempts to do the math. Remembering Saint said we were roughly three days away from Russia, that means I've been unconscious for five days.

What the hell happened?

"Where is the man I arrived with? Saint," I ask, hoping she knows who I'm talking about. But more importantly, hoping I did, in fact, arrive with him in tow.

When she averts her gaze, I sit up, ignoring the pain shooting straight through me. The blankets pool around my waist, allowing me to see I'm in a white nightgown. I can also see a bandage poking out of the collar where my shoulder is strapped.

Memories crash into me, followed by a deafening BOOM! Instinctively, I reach for my shoulder...the one Saint shot me in. My mouth pops open because the image of me being manhandled by Zoey before she was seconds away from blowing out my brains comes to life.

I would be dead by now if not for Saint's bullet, which is ironic in every sense of the word. He shot to wound, not to kill. But I don't understand why I've been out for five days. Unless Saint is playing down his gunshot wound to the shoulder, then something else caused me to be comatose for the past five days.

"I don't know where he is," Sara explains, placing the pitcher on the table.

"Has he come to see me?" I ask, but it's in vain. I know the answer.

"No."

"Why have I been unconscious? I don't remember coming here."

Sara frowns. "Aleksei, he made me do it."

"Do what?" I ask slowly, sitting against the headboard.

"He told me that I was to keep you…comfortable." Her pause has me guessing that means he did to me what I did to him.

He drugged me.

"I need to leave." I'm about to throw the blankets off, ready to flee this prison once and for all, but Sara's eyes widen, and she latches onto my forearm.

"Please, don't! He will kill me," she pleads, and I see the truth in her eyes.

I owe this woman nothing, but I can't help but feel sorry for her. She's being held captive by Aleksei as well.

"Why are you here?" I ask, needing to know what role she plays, and if she can be trusted.

Sara looks similar in age to me with long dark hair. Once upon a time, I would have guessed her dull and lifeless light brown eyes sparkled. "I'm a prisoner too," she says. Even though she doesn't know my situation, it's evident I'm here against my will.

"Alek has me working off my father's debt. He borrowed money from him but couldn't pay it back."

She doesn't need to continue. I can fill in the blanks.

The inevitable looms. "Is he...?" I gulp, unsure how to even phrase this. "Is he your master too?"

She nods slowly, her large eyes filling with tears.

I don't understand any of this. If Alek has ample women at his disposal, then why does he want me?

However, when I think of my purpose, that I'm to take over for Zoey, his number one, I assume that Alek parades one "special" girl around to all his friends like a prized pig while the others, like Sara, are there to scratch an itch when he gets bored.

Judging by her clothes, which look like something Cinderella would wear when scrubbing the floors, she serves as his slave in every sense of the word. We all have a purpose to Alek, chess pieces to move to win the game.

"Zoey has been in here." My blood turns cold when she shares this with me. "Be careful of her. She will do anything to make sure no one takes her place. You aren't the first girl."

Her confession leaves a bad taste in my mouth as those other girls were "trained" by Saint.

"At first, Alek makes you think he cares, but his true colors will eventually shine through." She tugs at a loose thread on the duvet, betraying her guilt. "We're all just his property to do with as he pleases."

Saint was right. It sounds like Sara fell victim to Alek's

charm too.

"I want to see him. Alek," I add, and she turns a ghastly shade of white.

"He's attending to some business. He won't be back for an hour or so."

"Well, in that case"—I kick the blankets off and turn my body, placing my feet on the soft carpet—"I want to see what my cage looks like." Because that's what this place is.

Sara must read my determination because she quickly offers her hand to help me. I feel like a ninety-year-old woman as I come to a slow stand. My legs wobble, but once I gather my bearings, I commence a slow shuffle toward the door.

However, when I see an en suite, I make a beeline for it as I'm desperate to use the toilet and brush my teeth. Sara gives me privacy to do my thing. When I look at my reflection in the oval mirror, I almost fall backward as I don't recognize the person staring back at me.

The dark circles under my eyes look almost bruised. My skin is a sickly white, and my hair is a knotted mess. But appearance aside, the sparkle has gone. When I look at myself, I see a stranger. I have lived her life, but I no longer see the Willow Shaw I once was.

This person is angry and intent on revenge. She will do anything to make sure those who hurt her pay.

A red toothbrush in a wrapper sits on the marble counter as well as toothpaste. I make use of both. As I'm brushing my teeth, I open the drawers and am disgusted when I see all the things you'd expect to see in any bathroom.

But I don't want any of the expensive makeup or perfumes.

The drawers are filled with lotions, as well as brushes and other beauty implements. I slam the drawer shut and spit out my toothpaste.

I wash my face with water, which will have to do for now. I'll take a shower after I take a look around.

Sara waits for me by the door. "We have to be quick. Alek didn't give me permission to let you out of your room."

I can't stop my eye roll. "Permission? Screw him. I don't need nor do I want a minder."

Sara looks saddened by my claim. "Willow, you will soon learn that here at красная долина, we don't have any choices."

What the hell is красная долина?

"How long have you been here, Sara?" I ask, her sorrow palpable.

She straightens out her white apron, eyes downcast. "Thirteen months."

I gasp in horror. "How long until your father's debt is paid off?"

"I am enslaved to Alek for the rest of my life."

I don't know what to say because I want to say so much. "That must be some debt your father owes."

She doesn't reply.

I don't press because Sara may be my only ally in this place. We walk, or I hobble, toward the door as I know she will be my shadow from here on out.

When we step out into the long hallway, I stop in my tracks to take it all in. Countless doors branch off the corridor. The carpet has a Persian design, and the same wallpaper as in my room covers the walls.

This doesn't appear to be a simple house but, rather, a mansion or a palace. As we continue our journey, I gape at my surroundings. When we walk out into the foyer, I extend my neck as far as I can to study the domed ceilings. They are painted with artwork like something you'd see in the Sistine Chapel.

Sara gently coaxes me along as she clearly worries Alek will return soon.

We venture into the living rooms, dining rooms, ballrooms, and kitchens, and each one is more elaborate than the one before it. Artwork complements the gold décor, and it seems no expense is spared. But Alek can afford it. He enslaves people and profits from their exploitation.

"Who is Alek?" I ask, more to myself. Saint said he's the most powerful man in Russia, but what does he do to obtain his wealth?

"He's a drug lord," Sara explains, filling in the blanks. "But to the unsuspecting, he's just a businessman with connections all over the world. Not much happens in this country without Alek's consent. The government are corrupt, and together, they have unrivaled power. He's untouchable."

A shiver passes over me because this is a lot worse than I thought.

"Who are The Circle?" I ask, remembering Saint mention this ambiguous group.

Sara slams her hand over my mouth, eyes wide as she shakes her head. "*Never* say that name."

But I don't listen. "Why not?" I shrug from her hold, refusing to be silenced.

Sara backs up, appearing as though she's seen a ghost. "Because *they* don't exist."

It's futile to ask who *they* are because it would go against her entire claim. "Where's the front door?"

Sara looks at me as if I've just asked her to give me her right arm. "You can't just walk out."

"Watch me," I challenge, deciding to find it myself. I don't care that I'm barefoot and traipsing around in a nightgown. I want to draw attention. Hopefully, my disheveled appearance will alert law enforcement so I can tell them all about the vile monster named Aleksei Popov.

"Willow, please." Sara runs after me, yanking on my arm. I understand her fear because if I leave, she will suffer because of my actions. However, if I...

Without a second thought, I turn around and slap her cheek—hard. She staggers back, cupping her cheek in horror.

I flinch but don't regret my actions. "Now you can tell him I knocked you out and escaped while you were unconscious."

She blinks once—whether admiring my courage or mourning my death, I'm not sure—but I don't plan on sticking around to find out. I run through the house, intent on finding a way out. Door. Window. I don't care. I just need an exit, and I need one now.

Remembering the main kitchen was down to the left, I decide to try there first. Surely, there is a back door or even a servant's entry because I have no doubt Alek has many of them. No one was in there before, so the coast should be clear.

And it is.

My feet skid along the polished tiles as I desperately

search for an exit. But there isn't a door. "Goddammit!" I curse angrily, about to flee, but something from the corner of the room catches my eye. An old red rug looks out of place, so going with my gut, I dive for it and kick the edge away, and what I see has my heart almost bursting from my chest. It's a trapdoor.

I don't know where it leads, but it's better than being stuck in here. Besides, someone like Alek has to have a secret passage, and I bet this is it. Just as I drop to my knees and hurriedly roll the carpet away, I hear a voice that makes my skin crawl.

It's Alek, and I have mere seconds until he busts me.

The old brass handle has a lock on it. "No!" I cry in a mere whisper when I yank at it, only to find it's locked. I was hoping by some miracle it would be unlocked.

Wishing I had more time to look for a key, I know if he finds me here, my only escape route will be foiled. I *will* find that key. Just not now.

I look over my shoulder quickly to make sure the coast is still clear. Then I cover the trapdoor and leave it as I found it, springing up and making a mad dash to the stainless steel fridge. Yanking open the door, I bury my nose inside and exhale when I hear Alek enter.

"дорогая?" His surprise is clear.

I take a few moments to catch my breath and calm down. "Hello." I feel so strange addressing him this civilly. All I want to do is kick him in the balls and make a break for it, but I can't. I have to be smart, especially since I've found my way out.

"You're awake?"

"Yes." I refrain from adding he probably should have amped up the dose of whatever drug he gave me.

Unable to hide in this fridge forever, I close the door slowly and come face to face with the man I hate with every fiber of my being. He looks casual in a white linen shirt and fawn-colored pants, but I don't let his looks deceive me.

"I wasn't expecting you to be up. I wanted to show you around your new home personally. I see Sara failed to do what was asked of her," he says, his nostrils flaring slightly.

"She tried to stop me, but I get cranky when I'm hungry. Her red cheek proves just how cranky I can get," I innocently say while Alek's lips slowly lift into a sly grin.

"We are one and the same."

We are *nothing* alike, but I smile nonetheless.

"I'm sorry about the commotion."

I raise an eyebrow. "Commotion?" He needs to be a little more specific because this entire shitshow has been a commotion.

"Yes, on the yacht. With Saint shooting you and all." He points at my wounded shoulder.

The moment I hear his name, my façade almost slips, but I pull it together. "I don't remember much." I need to know what exactly Saint told him before I go divulging what I remember.

Alek leans against the counter, folding his arms casually. "Of course you don't. You drank the drugged vodka. Saint explained how Zoey was trying to hurt you. How she drugged us all because she was green with jealousy over you."

My legs tremble, but I keep calm. Saint said that? He threw his own sister under the bus to save me? "That would explain the lapse in memory," I say, nodding as if I've just solved an ambiguous puzzle.

"Zoey is spoiled. I blame myself," he explains offhandedly while I wonder how the hell he's come to that conclusion. "I should be harsher with her, but she loves me. I can't punish her for that."

It takes all my willpower to remain cool.

"Saint revealed how jealous Zoey has been over my need to"—he wets his bottom lip—"broaden my horizons. She thought if she killed you, then that would prove her love for me. Thankfully, Saint didn't drink the drugged liquor, so he was the only one awake to tell the tale. Zoey, of course, had a far different version of events."

I gulp because her version is the truth.

"But I know that she's lying."

"How do you know that?" I ask, feigning innocence.

Alek never takes his eyes off me when he coolly replies, "Because Saint doesn't miss. If you had, in fact, done all the things Zoey claimed you did, then you wouldn't be standing here today."

No further explanation needed.

"He told me she used you as a shield as she held a gun to your head. He had no other choice but to shoot you so he could disarm Zoey. Adrian, on the other hand, was intent on revenge because of what happened to Kazimir. He was stupid to think he could ever compete with someone like Saint." His tone holds an almost pride at the killing machine Saint is thanks to him.

Saint has tied a big red bow on this entire story, and Alek has fallen for it. The only other witness is now dead, which only leaves Zoey. But I remember Alek's words before he was out cold.

You will pay.

At the time, I thought our ruse was up, but it appears I was wrong. I don't know the full story, but from the pieces I've gathered, it seems Saint has blamed everything on Zoey, and it's stuck because she hasn't hid her hatred for me.

Alek believes Saint because why would he lie to save me? Zoey is his sister. She's the reason he's here in the first place. He owes me nothing, but that's exactly what he did. Alek may have clued on to some kind of connection between Saint and me, but he would never suspect Saint to do what he's done. And neither did I.

I want to ask where he is, but I don't.

"Tonight, I have some very important guests coming to visit. I will have Sara help you get ready."

I don't appear to have a choice in the matter. But thinking of my escape behind me, I nod. The sooner I figure out the layout of this place, the better, and I can't do that locked in my room.

"By the way, I'm sorry I had to drug you. I didn't want you to feel any pain. A gunshot wound can be excruciating," he says as though he did me a favor.

"Who took out the bullet?" I ask, wishing I could remember.

Alek pushes off the counter. "Saint. He's a godsend," he

replies, his response filled with complete innuendo. "I couldn't have chosen a better man."

I gnaw the inside of my cheek to stop myself from hurling abuse. He is the only one who has a choice while we are forced to bend to his will.

"Will Zoey be there tonight?" I need to know where my enemies are at all times because that's the only way I will be able to escape.

Alek runs the tips of his fingers over the styled side of his groomed hair. Not one lock is out of place, which has me guessing this might be a mannerism of his indicating something has pissed him off. "No, she won't. She must learn her place. She is no longer my number one girl."

When he floats toward me, I hold my breath. He sweeps a piece of hair behind my ear. "Because who is?"

He's not a tall man, but I still feel dwarfed in his presence, especially when he looks at me with that hunger in his eyes. He waits for my reply, but we both know there is only one answer.

"I am." Bile rises as I confess something which makes me physically ill.

He inhales happily, but it seems my skills as an actress suck.

Leaning forward, he places his lips against the shell of my ear. My chest rises and falls rapidly as I try to steady my breathing. "One day, you'll really mean that."

I brace myself for a punishment, but I don't get it. Instead, Alek leaves me standing in the kitchen with my heart in my throat as he exits.

"I'm sorry for hitting you."

Sara pauses from applying shadow to my upper eyelid. "It's okay."

I figure I owe her an apology seeing as she's doted on me all day. Of course, this isn't either of our choices because Alek ordered her to help me get ready. As she pulled out lavish dress after lavish dress while she stood in some ratty maid's outfit, I couldn't help but feel like one of the wicked stepsisters from *Cinderella*.

I picked a green A-line dress with long sleeves and an even longer hemline. The top is fitted, but the skirt flares out slightly past my waist. I wanted to cover as much of my body as possible. When Sara walked me into a closet that technically could be a room of its own, I gaped around at all the shoes, clothes, and accessories on the shelves.

Sara said Alek liked heels, so she picked out a pair of pointy black pumps. When she asked what jewelery I wanted to wear, I clasped the cross at my neck. She didn't question it but decided my outfit wasn't complete without pearl drop earrings.

I showered, dressed, and now, I am getting primped within an inch of my life. Sara decided my hair down would complement the dress, so she curled and styled it to fall around my shoulders. Once she was happy with her handiwork, she began to paint my face to hide the real me.

The layers of foundation she applied indicated I needed the excess to make me look human. We remained quiet, both of us lost to this foreign world.

"I'm almost done," she says, snapping me from my thoughts.

"Take your time. I'm in no hurry." I have no idea what awaits me out there, but I'm guessing it can't be good.

Where is Saint? And why hasn't he come to see me? I need to speak with him to discuss what happens now, but getting two seconds alone in this place seems impossible.

"I know you're nervous about tonight," Sara says, uncapping a tube of mascara and coating my lashes. "Just do what you're told. It will be less painful that way."

I know she's trying to be nice, but I'm not nervous. I'm angry. "One thing you'll come to learn about me, Sara, is that I don't do what I'm told very often."

Her lips twitch. "I can see that."

It's nice to share a lighthearted moment because we don't experience them often.

When she caps the mascara and leans back to admire her creation, I wonder what she sees. "You look beautiful."

When she shifts and allows me to look in the mirror, I see she's done a great job. My skin looks flawless and sculpted, thanks to her contouring skills. My blue eyes pop because of the gold shimmer eyeshadow, the brown liner, and mascara she's applied.

An almost nude lipstick coats my full lips, but the subtle rose undertones seem to draw out the pink.

My makeup isn't overdone. As it appears, I'm hardly

wearing much at all. But that's the look Sara has gone for. "What do you think?" she asks nervously.

Leaning forward to take a closer look in the dresser mirror, I gently bring my curls over my shoulders to frame my face. Her skills rival any makeup artist in Hollywood. "You've done a great job."

"Then why do you look like you're seconds away from bursting into tears? You look beautiful."

Peering at her reflection, I frown sadly. "Isn't that the problem? The reason I'm here." It's because of my beauty that I was chosen, and at this moment, I would give anything not to stand out in a crowd. I want to blend in. I don't want to be special. I just want to be left alone.

Sara doesn't know what to say, but truthfully, there isn't a thing she can say.

"Let's get this over with." I stand, straightening out the soft material of my dress. The heels add a few extra inches to my frame.

Sara nods and retrieves a cell from her apron pocket. My eyes widen, but she soon puts an end to my excitement. "I can only make calls to Alek and some of his men. He's blocked any other numbers. Besides, he monitors all our phones." Regardless, I have to try.

"Can you reach Saint?" I ask, almost lunging for the cell.

"Yes, but like I said, Alek would know."

"Sara, please," I beg, but she shakes her head firmly.

"I'm sorry, Willow. I can't. He would kill me." Her lower lip trembles. She is clearly terrified, so I let it go.

"I understand."

"I'm sorry, I just can't risk it. The last girl who disobeyed Alek…" She doesn't continue, but there is no need for her to. I can fill in the blanks on my own.

She nods, her remorse clear that she can't do more. She texts someone, and within five minutes, there is a knock on the door. "My chariot awaits," I sarcastically quip, taking three deep breaths as Sara opens the door.

A young man stands outside my bedroom, but when he locks eyes with Sara, I see it. Something is going on between them. The blushing of her cheeks confirms it. From the way they politely greet one another, I'm guessing any relationship under Alek's roof is strictly forbidden.

"Hi, I'm Hans. I'm to take you to where Alek and his guests are." His has a strong German accent. I don't fear him because his gentle brown eyes reflect the same sorrow as mine and Sara's.

"Hi, Hans."

He nods, but there is no time for small talk. He gestures I'm to follow him. Bidding farewell to Sara, I find her wringing her hands together, and the sight only adds to my nerves.

Hans wears black pants, a black T-shirt, and boots, similar attire to when I first met Saint. The gun at his hip isn't concealed. I wonder what he did to end up here because it seems everyone within these walls is here against their will.

We walk the corridor, my heels clicking on the polished flooring as we make our way to the foyer. It's still hard to believe how lavish this place is. Sara called it красная долина, and I wonder what it means.

"They are in the den," Hans says, but every corner we

turn looks the same. This is a different way from where I went today.

I follow quietly, trying my best to establish a path, a pattern because I need to learn the blueprint of this place. That trapdoor in the kitchen leads somewhere, and I'd rather I know where, instead of jumping down the rabbit's hole without any idea of what's headed my way.

A sketch of a naked woman on the wall will act as my marker because down the small corridor, I can see a group of men sitting around a poker table, smoking cigars and sipping from their crystal glasses.

My stomach turns when Alek comes into view. He's seated at the head of the table with a deck of cards in his hands. When he hears us approaching, he turns to look over his shoulder, and his eyes come alight when he sees me.

I'm caught off guard when he stands. It's such a chivalrous thing to do when a lady enters the room, but we all know Alek is no such thing. He makes no secret of examining me from head to toe. Three other men are with him, and instantly, the hair at the back of my neck stands on end. Not because they are malevolent in appearance, but because they are completely normal.

A wolf in sheep's clothing.

They look like upstanding citizens, and judging by their expensive attire, they are extremely wealthy. But the fact they're here socializing with Alek proves they are monsters just like him.

"I'm at a loss for words," Alek says as I enter. Hans stands off to the side with his hands linked behind his back. "You are even more beautiful than I imagined."

He extends his hand, indicating for me to approach, but I am suddenly frozen to the spot with what I see. On a large leather sofa in the corner of the room, Zoey lays with two other women. All are naked. Their limbs are entwined as they are sprawled out languidly in what appears a drug-induced state.

My cheeks blister. Even though they are merely lying there, it sets the mood for what's about to come.

"Alek, you were right. She is exceptional," a man says, sipping his drink as he devours me with his eyes. At a guess, I would say he's in his 40's and in great shape. His full head of groomed blond hair and baby blues would leave many admiring his good looks. But not me. He makes my skin crawl.

I'm too afraid to move when he stands. "I'm Oscar." His accent is definitely Russian.

The other men watch on, and I do the same to them as I examine my enemies.

All are around the same age and look like doctors or businessmen—people you wouldn't look twice at if you passed them on the street. However, Oscar stands out from the bunch, and that's not a good thing. He reeks of authority, and by the way he looks at me, I think it's safe to say he wants to assert that power over me.

"She's shy," Alek explains, making excuses for my suddenly clamming up.

Oscar nods, a ghost of a smile tugging at his lips. "There is no need to be shy. We are all friends here." He spreads his arms out wide, indicating Zoey's lewdness is just a normal occurrence among acquaintances.

We are anything but friends, but I stay perfectly still when he walks toward me.

Alek watches carefully, but he doesn't move. He allows Oscar to inch closer and closer. When we're feet apart, he slowly reaches for my hand. My instinct is to recoil, but I refuse to cower in fear. He draws my hand to his lips and kisses the back of it, observing me attentively. His breath is warm, too warm.

"Is she housebroken?" he asks Alek, his mouth lingering on my skin.

Offended, I take back my hand and narrow my eyes.

In response, he laughs hoarsely. "Oh, Alek, I envy you. She is a treat."

It's on the tip of my tongue to tell him I'm not a fucking delicacy, but the world stops spinning when heavy footsteps announce someone's arrival. Every fiber in my body prickles in awareness because he's here—he's really here.

Unable to stop myself, I turn over my shoulder quickly, and everything quiets for just a fraction in time. Saint appears stunned to see me but soon recovers. He wears his hair tied back, but it's still not long enough for all of it to be held back, so some lose strands fall free, framing his chiseled cheeks. His beard has also grown.

He looks all the more rugged and wayward, standing here in all black, but that could just be the pissed-off look he sports when he sees Oscar standing near me. I want to go to him, but I don't.

Oscar soon forgets about me as he zeroes in on Saint. "Well, hello. Where have you been hiding?"

Something shifts, and the room drops about a hundred degrees.

I watch with interest as something comes over Oscar. He seems…spellbound by Saint. I don't understand what I'm seeing because if I didn't know any better, I'd say he was more excited by Saint's arrival than by the three naked ladies who lay feet away.

Saint ignores Oscar's quip and walks over to Alek. "Everything taken care of?" Alek asks. Saint nods in response while I gulp.

What has he done?

Alek claps once, clearly excited by the news. "Oscar was just asking about ангел."

Saint trains his gaze on me slowly. How is it possible he can set me alight with a look alone?

"He asked if she was housebroken," he continues with a wave of his hand while Saint's jaw clenches. "I didn't have a chance to explain your situation."

"What situation?" Oscar asks, his interest piqued.

Too afraid to make a noise, I keep my breathing shallow.

The other men at the table are clearly not interested in the conversation and have decided to join the three women on the couch. When one of them bends low to suckle the brunette's nipple, I instantly look away.

"Saint was the one who brought her to me, and because of this, he seems to be the only one who can…control her. Well, for now anyway."

Oscar turns to look at me, grinning sinisterly. "I am utterly intrigued." His ravenous look makes me feel sick, and I shrink away, afraid of what he'll do.

"Would you like to see?" Alek's tone is smug as though he's showing off a new car to friends.

"You never disappoint," Oscar replies, walking over to the poker table and taking a seat, clearly ready for a demonstration.

"Saint?" Alek says, hinting they're waiting, but he doesn't move. Saint continues to stare at me, undressing me with those hypnotic green eyes. The explosive moment between us causes everything inside me to combust into a million tiny pieces.

He clears his throat and walks toward me slowly. I don't move a muscle because the closer he gets, the faster my heart beats. My memory has done a poor job remembering him because when he stops in front of me, it's like I'm seeing him for the first time.

And when he speaks, everything collides into me, and I inhale, needing the oxygen to feed my deprived lungs. "Kneel, ангел. By my side."

Without question, I do what he asks.

It's sensory overload as my body needs this—I need to be close to him, to obey him. I know how sick that sounds, but I can't help it.

Oscar squeals and claps excitedly, but he can go to hell because when Saint reaches down and runs his fingers through my hair, everything else fades into the background. I've craved his touch. I've craved him. I can't help the mewl that escapes me as I lean into his caresses.

We are facing both Alek and Oscar, and I know how this looks—like the good submissive, kneeling by her master's feet—but truth be told, being here is the safest I've felt in days. Saint continues stroking my hair, and even though the parallels can be seen between this and how Alek strokes Zoey when she kneels at his feet, this is different.

Alek owns Zoey, and his touch is one of control, ownership. But the way Saint touches me—his caresses are filled with nothing but…love. And that fact has tears filling my eyes.

"I want her to meet my Dominic and Ingrid," Oscar says, ruining the moment. I don't know why, but something shifts between Alek and Oscar.

It feels as if Oscar is challenging Alek in some sense. Why?

Alek is soon to settle the mood. "Yes, that sounds like a wonderful idea. I was going to host a party in her honor. A masquerade ball maybe? When the time is right, I will unveil my девственница. The suspense is the best kind of foreplay."

Oscar almost falls off his seat. "What? It can't be."

Alek's victorious grin is all the answer Oscar needs. My virginity is clearly something to celebrate.

"You lucky bastard. She is ripe for the picking." Oscar runs his tongue over his thick bottom lip, watching Saint and me.

I huddle closer to Saint who places his hand at the back of my neck. His thumb circles over my racing pulse. His touch calms me until Oscar speaks.

"I would give anything to see you break her in." The protruding at the front of Oscar's pants reveals just how much so. "Actually, I think a few of us would. How much?"

Alek blinks once as it seems Oscar has caught him off guard.

"What's the matter? Friends share, do they not?" This is personal for Oscar. What did Alek do?

There doesn't seem to be an option for Alek, which has me thinking he owes Oscar for something. "I think we can come to an agreement where everyone wins."

Saint's body hums with violence while I attempt to decipher what the hell is going on.

"Excellent. I will await your conditions then. This will be quite the show. I haven't seen а девственная жертва in so very long."

I have no idea what he just said, but I know it can't be good.

Pleasured moans cut through the room, alerting us to the tangled bodies on the sofa. I can only imagine what this does to Saint to see Zoey spread open as a stranger feasts on her. She is barely conscious, but he doesn't mind.

Oscar unbuckles his belt as his insatiable eyes watch this orgy unfold. I clutch my cross, needing an anchor to some form of purity. Alek walks over to the sofa, unbuttoning his shirt as it seems he's not interested in being a voyeur tonight.

Is this what my future holds?

My immediate future, however, is saved. "Alek, I'm taking ангел to her room." Alek barely hears Saint and dismisses him with a quick flick of his hand.

When his broad back comes into view, Saint yanks me up. I exhale, but it's in vain. "I can't wait to see if you blush all over."

When I see Oscar working his thick cock in his hand, I reveal that I do because my cheeks burst into flames. However, my embarrassment shifts because what I see next leaves me confused, but most of all, it has me wanting to rip out Oscar's eyes.

Instead of gaping at the lewd scene just feet away, Oscar has directed his attention on Saint and is using him as jerk-off material. Focusing on him, Oscar pumps his dick and groans when he eats Saint up from head to toe.

I am speechless. This is too much.

Saint hurriedly escorts me from the room, never looking back. I can barely keep up as he drags me down the hallway, his breathing getting heavier and heavier the farther away we go. He is shaking in rage and all I want to do is console him, but when we pass my bedroom door, I realize it'll have to wait.

I have no idea where we're going. I can only hope out the front door.

When we get to a door at the end of the hall, and Saint bursts through it, I exhale because everything in here reeks of him. I don't have a chance to speak however because the moment the door closes, Saint wraps his arms around me, and with violent delight, he presses me into his chest. I go willingly, losing myself to him, crying happy tears.

I clutch him tightly, but it's still not close enough. I want our bodies to become one. "I'm sorry," he whispers, his lips pressed to the top of my head. "I didn't want to shoot you."

"Shh." I hush him because I understand. I don't want to talk. I just want to cherish this moment of being lost in his arms. Everything falls silent, and I surrender.

We both need the connection as Saint holds me tightly, inhaling my scent and humming contentedly. "I wanted to come see you," he explains.

"It doesn't matter. Alek had me drugged anyway. I wouldn't have known if you were there."

A growl escapes him. "I told Sara to watch over you. I am so fucking sorry, Willow."

Each time he uses my name, he alleviates some weight inside, and I feel like I can breathe. "It's okay. It's not your fault."

"All of this is," he corrects with nothing but regret as he wraps his body around mine.

We stay this way for minutes. Truth be told, I could stay like this forever, but nothing lasts forever.

"We're in here, in my room because it's one of the only places that doesn't have a camera. That's why I couldn't come see you. Alek would have seen."

"What?" With great sadness, I slowly break our embrace. I instantly miss his warmth.

He peers down at me with nothing but defeat overshadowing him. "This entire place is bugged and has hidden surveillance cameras. We have to be careful."

"So even when Alek isn't in my room, he or someone else is watching?"

Saint nods with a sigh. "Twenty-four seven. You are being watched."

This just goes from bad to fucking diabolical.

Needing to sit, I stagger over to the foot of the king-sized bed and slump onto it. "If only Zoey hadn't woken up, we wouldn't be here," I mumble to myself, staring at a spot on the floor.

Thoughts of her and the night on the yacht have me remembering Saint's story.

"You sacrificed her to save me. Thank you." I slowly meet his eyes, wishing I could say and do more.

"I promised you your freedom, and I don't intend on breaking that promise," he replies, but regardless of the fact that Saint is a man who sticks by his word, I know he did this because he cares.

"What is девственная жертва?" I ask, trying my best to pronounce what Oscar said to Alek.

Saint's nostrils flare. "It means...virgin sacrifice."

"Oh my god," I gasp, covering my mouth in horror. "He intends to"—I pause, needing to gather my words—"to what? Have sex with me in front of people? At this masquerade ball?"

Saint looks about ready to punch the wall as he squeezes his clenched fists. "Yes."

Not only is that barbaric, but it's also horrific. But these people are a different breed. "Who are The Circle?"

My question has caught him by surprise. He shakes his head firmly, suggesting I drop it.

But I won't. "Tell me."

When he reads my determination, he levels me with nothing but sincerity, and reveals, "They are the most powerful, most wealthy people in all of Europe. They are your lawyers. Doctors. They are untouchable because no one would ever believe upstanding citizens would engage in the heinous things they do. They are bored with too much money to burn. They stick together, ensuring they never get caught because if one goes down, they all do. They are all sick, twisted individuals with an appetite for pain."

"So I'm fucked?" I don't see the point in being coy.

"No." Saint rushes over and sits beside me. "This masquerade ball is your out."

"How?" I laugh hysterically, skating close to the edge.

"Because a masquerade ball means anyone can be you."

My maniacal laughter soon dies.

"There is a trapdoor—"

"In the kitchen. I know," I interrupt, watching as Saint's eyes widen.

"It shouldn't surprise me that you know this," he says with a hint of a grin. "Anyway, that door leads to the gardens. I will have someone waiting for you on the other side. I will disrupt the live feed to the cameras to give you a window to escape. It'll be small, but it'll be enough."

The inevitable lingers. "Wh-what about you?" I can't keep the fear from my tone.

He reaches for my hand and squeezes softly. "I will be here watching you on the cameras. Alek's men won't allow me in the control room unsupervised for too long. But I will do everything, everything in my power to keep you safe."

"Saint—" But I can't speak because tears replace my words.

"Don't cry." He wipes away my tears with his thumb. "This is the only way."

"I-I..." I choke on my words, my heart shattering into

two. "I can't go without you."

"You have to," he presses, and his stern tone divulges this isn't negotiable.

"I won't," I sob, shaking my head.

"Please, ангел, let me do this. Let me make this right. I owe you this."

"You owe me nothing! If you want to owe me anything, come with me." Unable to control my emotions, I smash my lips to his, desperate to bridge this gap between us. I have survived this because of him, so the thought of doing it without him…I don't know if I can.

"You don't need me," he says against my mouth, moaning when I bite his bottom lip.

But I do.

Threading my fingers through his hair, I tug hard, needing to anchor myself before I fade away. When our tongues duel desperately, I'm struck with an idea. "My virginity is the reason for all this," I whisper between kisses. "But there is a solution."

"And what's that?" He melts in my mouth, affirming my thoughts.

Pushing my bashfulness aside, I slowly walk my fingers over to the front of Saint's pants, rubbing over his bulge.

His eyes pop open as he pulls away. "No," he firmly presses, gripping my wrist to stop me from touching him.

"It's the only way," I reason, attempting to set myself free. But Saint holds on tightly, exposing his thoughts on the matter. "Alek only wants me because I'm a virgin. He sees me as an even bigger conquest now. But if I'm not…"

"If you're not, then you're as good as dead," he counters with bite. "That's the only thing keeping you alive."

"You call this being alive?" My voice quivers as my desperation surfaces. "I won't give myself to him willingly. But I will"— I nervously lick my trembling lips while Saint follows the action with longing —"to you."

He hisses, recoiling as if my words have burned him. "Ангел, no."

I can't help but feel rejected because this isn't the first time he's said no. However, I'm not deterred and forget my coyness. "Why not? I-I want you."

He groans, tipping his head back to look at the ceiling. "I can't. Please understand."

But no, I won't.

Gripping his bicep, I force him to look at me, and when he does, my heart sinks with his. "I have already ruined your life. I won't ruin this for you too."

His response should remind me of all the horrors we've faced, but all it does is prompt me to remember how Saint has saved me in this fucked-up, cruel world. "You couldn't," I whisper, hoping my bravado stays strong. "I want my first time to be with someone like you."

"Someone like me?" he scoffs angrily. "What's that supposed to mean? A liar? A felon? A…killer?"

But he's misunderstood.

"No." With trembling fingers, I place my hand on his cheek. "Someone who steals my breath every time he enters the room. Someone who has sacrificed everything to ensure my safety. Someone who has invaded every inch of my soul."

Saint gasps, clearly stunned by my revelation. "How can you forget everything I've done?"

"I can't, and I won't," I reply, slowly crawling onto his lap and straddling him. "But it's because of those things that I want you…all the more. You focus on the negative"—I lean down and gently kiss over his throat while he arches his head back with a groan—"while I refuse to dwell on the past. Which is why…we make a perfect pair."

Saint hums low as I continue kissing and suckling the column of his neck. I'm in control, which is a rare thing, and I've never felt more powerful than I do right now. He falls back onto the mattress, taking me with him. He lifts the hem of my dress, caressing my thighs as I devour him.

His scent punches me low, and I can't help but rub myself over his hard-on. We both moan as this feeling is just too much. "I know you want me too."

"Oh, fuck," he growls, detouring to my ass and squeezing hard. "For once, I'm trying to do the right thing."

"I don't want you to," I counter, biting over his racing pulse.

Each flick of my tongue shatters Saint's resolve, and before long, he surrenders. He doesn't fight me as I smash my lips to his and kiss him fiercely. Nor does he move a muscle when I unbuckle his belt and unfasten his zipper.

The moment I thrust my hand down his pants and grip his luscious cock, his hips rocket off the bed with a guttural growl. He is hot and heavy in my hand. I don't know where to start, so I gently push my underwear aside. I want to feel him pressed up against me. I position my hips and rock forward, gasping when I feel his blunt head nudge at my entrance that is slick with my arousal.

Our lips are still locked—our breaths heavy and mingling as one—so feeling this connection down low just adds to the heightened sensation, and I whimper, needing more. I have no idea what I'm doing, but I continue rubbing him over my heated flesh because it feels so good.

All it would take would be a slight shift of my hips, and my bargaining chip would be gone for good. To feel him buried deep within me, claiming every part of me—mind, body, and soul.

I know it would hurt because of Saint's size, but I want the pain. I welcome it. Pain makes me human. So with a deep breath, I brace myself for the intrusion…but it never comes.

The room spins before me as Saint flips us so I'm now the one lying on my back. He hovers over me, his eyes wild. "I said no," he breathlessly pants, biting over my jaw.

I groan in desire and frustration. "Saint—"

But he doesn't let me finish because what he says next leaves me a whimpering mess. "What I should have said was no, not now." He trails kisses down my throat and over my breasts as he slithers down my body. "However, once you're safe, and if you still want me…then the answer will be yes."

I arch my back when he nestles between my legs, lifting my hem. His lips form an absolutely wicked smile when he focuses on my sex, and with a quick tug, he rips my underwear clean off. It pleases me for two reasons. One—it gives me great pleasure seeing something Alek bought for me destroyed. And two—it's fucking hot.

But I can also play that game. "I will always want you, Saint."

My words are like a trigger because a primitive growl bursts from him before he lowers his lips to my core and suckles. I cry out, threading my fingers through his long hair, needing something to hold on to before I float away.

The ferocity with which he consumes me leaves me in twisted, desperate knots. He isn't gentle, but I don't want him to be. He spreads my legs open and goes in deeper. I am lost to his tongue, his mouth as he samples me without apology.

I ride his face, uncaring that I demand he put me out of my misery because I just want to come. He sinks two fingers into me, spreading me impossibly wide. I cry out, but soon realize these walls have ears, so I use my fist to mute my pleasured screams.

My body reaches the pinnacle impossibly fast, and I'm too weak to fight it. But before I am lost to the quiet, I whimper, "Teach me to be like you. Teach me how to fight."

Saint's hot breath ignites my skin, and I writhe madly. "Okay, ангел, I will."

When he drives his tongue deeper into me, I bow my back on the cusp of exploding. "Thank...you," I pant, squeezing my eyes shut. "The next time I meet those men, I will be prepared."

He doesn't need me to elaborate who.

"I will always protect you," he promises between fucking me with his mouth.

The sentiment along with his actions has me embracing my orgasm, but not before I confess, "And I...you. Oscar wants you…but he can't have you because…you belong…to me."

Saint pauses, surprised that I'm privy to Oscar's attraction to him, before he slaps his tongue over my clit, making me see stars. "And you belong to me…Willow." I'm swathed in everything Saint, and without a choice, I come…and I come hard. And loud.

Crawling up my body, he smashes our mouths together to mute my scream. I can taste myself on his lips, which just heightens my orgasm. His kisses destroy me, and I grow lax, my body trembling with the aftermath. My heart pounds fiercely, and I can't wipe the smile from my cheeks.

We lie entangled, both our guards lowered as we rest nose to nose. We don't have to say a single word because our lust-ridden gasps are all the speech we need. However, when a soft knock sounds on the door, my ecstasy shatters, reminding me this is all Saint and I will have—stolen moments in time.

"Willow, please come back to your room. Alek will be looking for you." It's Sara.

Saint brushes the hair from my cheeks, nothing but regret pooling in his eyes. But we both know she's right. "You look beautiful. I'm sorry I didn't tell you sooner."

And just like that, I fall even harder.

Once I've said a sorrowful goodbye, I creep back to my room, ensuring to stay hidden in the shadows because just like Saint—I now belong in the darkness.

CHAPTER FIVE

She is safe...for now as Alek is blinded by her perfection. But aren't we all?

Day 47

"**H**arder!"

I'm coated in perspiration, and my muscles ache, especially my wounded shoulder, but I embrace the burn because each bead of sweat takes me one step closer to regaining my life. Or, at least, a small sliver.

Saint stands before me shirtless, his ripped body shimmering under the bright lights, but I don't allow the sight to distract me because we're here for a reason. He's teaching me how to fight.

So far, I've ended up on my ass more times than I care to admit, but I don't see that as a failure. It spurs me on to get back up and try harder because each punch and kick on the focus pads and boxing bag has me feeling stronger.

"You're not even trying!" Saint mocks loudly to be heard over the pop music blaring through the speakers. He waves the focus pads at me while I gnash my teeth together, attempting to prove him wrong.

But he is fast on his feet, and it's easy to see why he's good at being a…hitman. It's still hard for me to stomach that fact, but I have come to accept it because that's who he's become to survive. Just as I have become Alek's perfect submissive.

I have behaved as expected, and because of this, Alek has loosened up a bit, allowing Saint to train me. Saint invented the genius ploy that for me to stay in shape, I was to undergo brutal physical training. He called it bootcamp. He said it was an American thing.

Alek didn't question it because I did what I was told. He thought the physical exercise was a part of my coaching for Saint to mold me into the perfect docile little lamb. And besides, there were cameras in every corner of the room, so it's not like we could plot his death.

Saint was right. My virginity seems to be far more important to Alek than a quick roll in the hay. He has respected my wish to have my own bedroom, which has surprised me. I wouldn't think a man like him would behave remotely like a gentleman.

But that's exactly what he's been.

I'm not fooled, though, as I know he's just looking after his "investment." That's all I am to him. Come the night of the masquerade ball, which the date is yet to be announced, it'll be a completely different story as he will have no qualms taking my virginity in front of a room full of perverted strangers. And I'm sure once I'm no longer a virgin, his chivalry will be long forgotten.

But that won't happen. I'd rather die than allow myself to be used that way ever again.

"Oh, I'm sorry." Saint's sarcasm whips me into the now. "If you've got someplace better to be, like kneeling at Alek's feet, then don't let me stop you."

Everything fades into the background as I narrow my eyes, intent on knocking that smug grin off his handsome face. "Fuck you."

With a rumble, I charge forward, punching the focus pads he holds with all my might. He's taught me a few boxing combinations, so when he attempts to knock me on my ass, I duck and deliver an uppercut. He staggers back, smirking.

"Again."

This continues until I can no longer feel my arms, but giving up isn't an option. Whenever I lower my guard, Saint knocks me to the floor, scolding me for not trying harder. I know what he's doing, and it's working because over the past few days, I have felt myself grow stronger and I've learned how to defend myself.

It's still early days, but with Saint as my teacher, failure isn't an option. He isn't gentle. When I lower my guard or am too exhausted to jump to his command, he makes me pay. Bruises cover my body, but each blemish only has me more determined to succeed.

"Jab!" he exclaims, flashing me the mitt, which I punch.

"Jab to the body!" He holds the mitt low, which I strike. "Jab to the head! Then body!" I do as he demands, following the sequence and watching his hands...a rookie move.

He kicks out his leg and trips me. I tumble onto my back, cursing my slipup.

"What did I tell you?" he asks. Shaking his head, he removes a mitt and offers to help me up.

"Never take my eyes off my opponent," I reply between clenched teeth as I reach for his hand. He yanks me up, and thanks to my equilibrium being off, I topple forward.

He's the only thing to break my fall, so I clutch onto his biceps, which are slick with perspiration. His scent is amplified, and unable to help myself, I inhale, relishing his unique fragrance. My body hums in awareness because he is hot and hard, and I desperately want to lick the beads of sweat collecting in the light hair on his chest.

The barbell in his nipple just adds to the appeal, and I wonder what it would feel like under my tongue. I focus on the cursive font across his chest which reads *Only God Can Judge Me.* The more time I spend with him, the more I come to understand its meaning.

When the word *Sinner* tattooed along his flank catches my eye, I gently squeeze his biceps as the tattooed feathers beneath my fingers contradict that claim. Yet his angel wings inked across his back and shoulders complement his name. But who he is and what he does would warrant his wings to be clipped.

Maybe they already have been. Hence the tattoo.

Suddenly, I'm hit with a heartbreaking epiphany. The black

armband he has inked under his elbow. I always wondered what it meant, but now, being faced with so much loss, I now know what it means. Tracing it with my finger, I watch as his golden skin breaks out into goose bumps.

"You got this for every person you've…?" But I can't say it. I may accept it, but saying it aloud…baby steps.

"Yes." He has no problem with what he is. How can he? He is in eternal mourning for his victims, and that armband will forever remind him of what he's done. I run my fingers over it, knowing it signifies so much. His own personal scarlet A.

His breath is hot and heavy, and I know I'm not the only one affected whenever we touch. I peer up at him from under my lashes. God, I want to kiss him. I want to scale up his hulking body and lose myself forevermore.

His sweatpants sit low on his tapered waist, emphasizing his glorious V muscle. The scars all over his body are like a roadmap, and I want to follow each one with my tongue. He is ripped, rugged, and oozes decadent sinfulness. Each second spent with him has me slipping further into hell.

"Ангел," he quietly cautions. His eyes dart to the corner of the room, reminding me to never make the mistake in thinking we're alone.

With regret, I let him go.

He casually walks over to the water fountain while I reach for my towel. To onlookers, it appears innocent enough, and with the loud music playing over the speakers, if one of Alek's men were to listen in, all he would hear is Britney Spears.

We have been training in this well-equipped gym each day, ensuring not to rouse any suspicion. So far, we've slipped under the radar, but when the doors open and in strolls Alek, I panic, thinking our hoax is up.

Saint slowly wipes the water from his lips, his demeanor as cool as cool can be. I mute the volume on the stereo before coming to a stand by Saint with my arms behind my back and my eyes downcast. The position he told me to take whenever Alek enters a room.

"Sorry to interrupt." Alek's smooth, unruffled voice makes me think we're safe—for now. "We have some business to attend to this evening."

"Let me get cleaned up. I'll show ангел to her room." Saint grips my elbow, ready to escort me, but it appears Alek has other plans.

"No, she's coming too."

I measure my breathing, not wanting my nerves to show.

"Okay. If that's what you want," Saint replies calmly, tugging on my arm. "Come on."

However, it seems Alek wants to speak with Saint alone. "Sara is waiting outside. She can help you get ready."

Just as Saint taught me, I slowly lift my eyes to meet Alek's. When he addresses me, I'm to look at him. When he doesn't, I'm not. Alek looks casual in khaki chinos and a blue button-down shirt. But I don't let his relaxed vibe fool me.

I don't look at Saint for permission because Alek is my supposed master now, and when he gives a direct order, I'm to jump to command. Nodding, I make a beeline for the door, but I'm not quick enough because Alek reaches out and snares my arm.

Every part of my body wants to rip from his hold, but I

stand passive, awaiting Alek's next move. He runs a fingertip down my forearm, causing me to break out into goose bumps—the kind when something scary is about to happen.

"Tomorrow when you train, I want you to wear something a little less revealing." He pinches my chin between his thumb and forefinger, forcing me to look at him, and I find myself staring into the steel blue eyes of the devil. "I don't want my men ogling you. Understood?"

With a jerky motion, I bob my head once.

I can't help but wonder if his comment is directed at Saint. Has he been watching us? I'm hardly parading around in my underwear. I'm in NIKE training leggings, sneakers, and a crop top. The standard gym wear. But tomorrow, I guess I'll be forced to wear a burlap sack.

"Good girl. Now go get ready."

I don't wait for further instruction because when he releases me, I can't get out of the room quick enough, though I'm worried for Saint. What does he want to talk to him about? But he can look after himself and obeying my "master" is the reason I'm not cuffed to my bed.

Sara is a ball of nerves when I walk out into the hallway. She quickly drags me away, mumbling in French. "Sara?" I question, wondering why she's edgier than usual. "What's wrong?"

"Alek has asked me to come with you tonight. That's never happened before," she reveals, chewing her bottom lip. I can now understand her concern.

"Where are we going?" I ask, suddenly sharing her apprehension.

She lifts her shoulders, revealing we're both going in this blind. If that's the case, I do the only thing I can to show her she's not alone. I reach for her hand and squeeze it tight.

Seeing as we had no idea where we were going, Sara and I decided to wear something causal. She's in a yellow pinafore dress while I opted for a dark blue chiffon mini dress with brown belt. Although it's sleeveless, the neckline is high, so I don't feel too exposed. I would give anything to wear my cowboy boots, but as there are none here in my closet, I've decided to wear brown ankle boots instead.

Sara waits nervously by the door, and when there is a knock, she yelps, betraying her nerves. She opens it to find Hans standing before her and reveals just how terrified she is by leaping into his arms. Even though this PDA is definitely forbidden, neither seems to care.

They hug one another tightly as Hans assures her it'll be all right. These walls lack love and warmth, so seeing this foreign sight has tears threatening to break past the floodgates. Something I took for granted once upon a time now has the ability to leave me a blubbering mess.

"It's okay. We are going to meet a new supplier. That's all," Hans says, rubbing Sara's back as she cries into his chest. "Alek just wants to show off his prettiest girls." He nervously meets my gaze, which I quickly avert as to not encroach on a private moment.

"Are you sure?" Sara sniffs, slowly pulling away. The moment may have only lasted a few seconds, but it's enough for now.

"Yes. I overheard him talking to Saint. Don't worry. I will be there."

"That's what I'm afraid of," Sara whispers, placing her palm to his cheek.

My heart breaks for these two secret lovers who have been brought together by heinous circumstances yet still managed to find beauty in the storm. I admire that. I wish they could watch their love grow freely, but we're all caged birds with our wings clipped.

"Let's go." Saint's sharp voice has Hans and Sara breaking apart quickly. Her cheeks redden while Hans stands tall, pretending Saint didn't just catch him in a compromising position.

I know he's mostly bark, but I wonder if they do. He does do Alek's bidding. What do they see when they look at him?

When he comes into view, I know what *I* see, and that's a man who isn't interested in small talk. Something bad is about to go down. Hans may not know the full story or he may have played it down to calm Sara, but whatever we're about to walk into can't be good.

Saint takes a moment to take me in, and when he doesn't mask his appraisal, I realize Hans and Sara can be trusted. The holster on his hip ruins the moment, and I swallow nervously.

Hans leads Sara out into the hallway while Saint waits for me by the doorway. I want to say so many things, but instead, I close my bedroom door and silently follow him through the rat maze. I'm slowly familiarizing myself with the layout, but this place resembles a labyrinth, which, of course, is done with intent.

When we get to the garage and a large Hummer SUV waits for us, I brace myself for what's ahead. Saint walks to the driver's side while Hans opens the door for us, indicating we're to get in the back. I breathe a sigh of relief, hopeful Alek has decided to ride in another car, but when I climb in and see him in the passenger seat, my optimism takes a nosedive.

Hans closes the door, hinting he won't be riding with us. Saint adjusts the mirror, positioning it so he can see me. The small gesture is enough to calm my racing heart. Until Alek turns over his shoulder and smiles at me.

"Buckle up," he says lightly as though we're simply going out for a casual outing. I do as he says, my fingers trembling as I fasten my seat belt. Saint takes off with speed, his patience already wearing thin.

The radio provides background noise, and when Alek speaks to Saint in Russian, it's clear he doesn't want us to know what he's saying. Although curious, I decide to lose myself in the landscape because this is the first time I've been outside.

Although it's night, the sky radiates a royal blue. The color could be from the abundance of lights illuminating the heavens. Though some of the architecture is quite contemporary, the feel is old world mixed with modern.

Although summer has come and gone and it's early September, tourists still walk the streets, taking selfies and marveling at the beauty. Something so mundane seems so foreign to me now. I can't take two steps without looking over my shoulder. I wonder if my life will ever return to normal if I escape? When I meet Saint's eyes in the rearview mirror, I know the answer is no.

Nothing will ever be the same again.

We drive for about forty-five minutes, and when the neighborhoods become run-down, I guess we're close to our final destination. The abandoned buildings have graffiti scribbled on them and faded advertisement posters rustle in the wind. The vibe points to these structures being vacant for years.

A flashing bright neon pink sign up ahead seems to be the only functioning establishment in the neighborhood. Saint pulls up in front of the building where two beefy security guards stand watch over the front door.

Craning my neck, I see the sign reads The Pink Pussycat. I dare say this is a strip club. My suspicions are confirmed when two women in jeweled thongs and silver stilettoes walk out the door and make a beeline for our car.

Saint looks at me in the mirror and nods subtly. His reassurance makes me feel remotely better. But when one of the women opens his door and leans in, batting her false lashes seductively, that assurance turns into the green-eyed monster. It seems he and The Pink Pussycat are well acquainted.

She says something to him in Russian, pursing her shiny red lips as she zeroes in on his. His gaze flicks to the mirror, watching me narrow my eyes as I challenge him on his next move. When he stops her advance by placing his hand on her shoulder, she peers down at it, confused.

Alek's door then opens, and woman number two appears.

The corner of her mouth lifts into a slanted grin. She goes in for a kiss, but he too stops her, mimicking Saint's pose. "Nadia, I want you to meet Willow."

The moment I hear my name, I stop glaring at Saint and remember where I am. Both women scowl at me, considering I'm the reason they're not locking lips with their beaus. But Nadia knows better than to upset a man like Aleksei.

"Hello," she says in a thick accent, nodding.

I nod back.

The thick tension can be cut with a knife, so I'm thankful when Alek gently pushes Nadia aside so he can exit the car. Saint does the same with his admirer, who unhappily walks back into the club with Nadia hot on her heels. When he opens my door and offers me his hand, I peer up at him, wondering if the surprises will ever cease.

Not wanting to rouse suspicion, I place my hand in his, ignoring the sparks crackling between us, threatening to electrocute me where I stand. We instantly drop hands when Alek walks over.

"There is no need to be frightened. You will be by my side." If that's supposed to make me feel better, he's sorely mistaken.

Another car pulls up, and when Hans and two other men exit the black truck, Sara sighs. That soon turns into a strangled wheeze.

"Hans, you will wait outside. I need someone to watch the door."

Hans nods, but something doesn't feel right.

"Shall we?" Alek offers me his arm as though he's some gentleman. With no other choice, I hook my arm through his, hating how close I am to him.

Saint leads the way, our own personal shield as he scopes out our surroundings. The guards at the door move aside, allowing us entry. When Hans takes his post outside, Sara whimpers softly, but she follows us, not wanting to make a scene in front of Alek.

The moment we step inside, I wish it didn't look like your sleazy stereotypical strip club, but it does. It's so dark, I can barely see three feet in front of me. The disco ball reflects the hue from the stage lights, showcasing a naked woman clumsily gyrating against a silver pole. Money litters the small glitter stage she dances on. She barely seems to notice, though, because it's clear she's high.

Men in suits, their ties loosely knotted, sit around ogling the women with drinks and cigars in hand. The bar is well stocked, and when the bartender sees Alek, he stops polishing the glass he's holding and instantly reaches for the top shelf vodka.

Saint leads us to a red booth in the back. Alek gestures for me to enter first. I feel trapped, but I slide along the vinyl. Alek sits close to me, placing his hand on my thigh. Even though it's on the material of my dress and not my bare skin, my stomach still roils.

Sara sits on a wooden stool as it seems she's not good enough to sit with us. Saint stands with his back facing us and his arms crossed. By his stance, it's clear he's watching the door, and when a group of men walk through it, I can see why.

There are four of them, but the older man in the middle, the one with the piercing eyes, is definitely the leader. The others flanking him have their hands on their guns as they scan the room for any threats. Once they see Saint up ahead, they huddle closer to their boss.

When they reach the booth, Saint doesn't move an inch. His rigid position reveals he isn't playing. One wrong move, and they'll all pay dearly…with their life.

"Are we allowed in?" teases the man in the middle. The well-dressed man smiles, flashing a gold front tooth. Nothing about him screams mobster, but that's exactly what he is.

"Saint, it's okay." Alek taps his back, indicating he's to move to allow our guests to join us. After a few seconds, he does as Alek says. The man enters the booth but doesn't hide his surprise when he sees me.

"Adam, this is Willow." It seems I don't need further introduction because Adam instantly nods graciously at me.

"Lovely to meet you," he says in an accent I can't place.

I wish I could share the sentiment.

Adam's men loiter near the booth, but Saint makes it clear there is an invisible line they are not to cross. If they do, they will lose a limb.

"Shall we get down to business?" It's Alek who doesn't want to dabble in small talk and just go straight in for the kill.

The bartender doesn't say a word. He places three glasses and the bottle of vodka on the table, then makes himself scarce. He knows the drill, but I don't. I don't know why I'm here. Or what I'm about to witness.

"Alek, I am so pleased we can do business. I guarantee the best product out there." One of the men passes Saint a black briefcase.

He slams it onto a table and pops open the lock while I hold my breath. A single brick of white powder appears. No guessing what it is. He reaches for the switchblade in his pocket and cuts through the plastic. Scooping out a tiny portion, he balances it on the tip of his knife.

He offers it to Alek, who shakes his head. When he gestures to Sara, I shift in my seat nervously. Saint has avoided making eye contact with me, and I know why. I've seen the real him, and this cold, callous bastard is not that.

"No," Sara gasps, gripping the edge of the stool.

Alek simply looks at her, and it's enough for her to nervously brush her hair back and lean forward so Saint can place the knife under her nose. She presses down on one nostril and inhales sharply, the white powder disappearing up her nose.

She rubs her nostril and closes her eyes tight as she sniffs repeatedly and clears her throat loudly. My attention flicks back and forth between Sara and Saint. Both look in pain. When she stops sniffing, she opens her eyes, and I can't help but notice they're wet. Alek may think it's just the burn of the drugs, but I know better. They're her tears.

Alek looks at his gold Rolex, and when a few minutes pass and Sara isn't convulsing on the floor or foaming at the mouth, he nods at Saint. Sara is the lab rat. He used her to test the drugs to ensure they weren't poisoned. That's how little her life means to him.

Saint does the same thing, but with a bigger portion this time and passes Alek the knife. Alek smiles, before offering the drugs to Adam. Adam isn't offended because, in this business, you can't trust anyone. He accepts the knife and snorts the drugs like it's candy.

Satisfied, Alek licks the tip of his pinkie. He inserts it into the brick, then slips his finger into his mouth and rubs it vigorously along his bottom gum. I watch all this in utter shock. In my line of work, I've seen drug use, but this is something you'd expect to see on the set of *The Godfather*. Alek squeezes my leg and hollers in delight.

"That's some good cocaine!" he exclaims, reaching for the bottle of vodka. Adam claps happily as the mood lightens.

"I'll have my men deliver the first shipment tomorrow at the drop-off point."

Alek pours three glasses of vodka, nodding happily. "Excellent. I will want to triple that amount every month, and I'll organize payment the first of each month. As long as we're clear that you sell to me and *only* me."

The whites of Adam's eyes reveal his excitement. "That can be arranged."

The vibe may be tranquil, but this is just the calm before the storm because when Adam asks, "And Chow?" it kickstarts the real reason we're here.

Alek slides a glass of vodka across the table, which Adam accepts. "You let me worry about Chow."

Sara's foot bounces uncontrollably, a sure sign the drugs are kicking in, and when Alek slides his hand up the hem of my dress, I know he's following her in hot pursuit.

I desperately want to flee, but where do I go? I'm trapped in yet another cage with my captor.

"You like this one?" Adam says, watching me closely.

If Saint had hackles, they'd be standing on end.

Alek caresses his fingertips along my flesh. Back and forth. Back and forth. His touch is like fire and ice, and I don't mean that in a good way. "Yes, I do."

He walks his fingers higher, inching way too close to my underwear. As much as I want to recoil, I don't. I won't show this bastard weakness, so I stare straight ahead, focusing on the barely legal stripper straddling the silver pole. It seems we're all prisoners in our own personal hell.

A winded gasp has my attention shifting because I wonder what has captured Sara's attention. What I see, though, has me realizing her gasp is in pure fear, not interest.

"You double-crossing asshole," says a man, edging through the door. The reason Sara looks seconds away from passing out is because the gunned man has Hans as a hostage.

Saint instantly springs into attack, drawing his gun. But the man uses Hans as his shield. He has the barrel of his gun pressed to Hans's temple, who has his hands raised in surrender. Saint snarls angrily, coming to a standstill with his gun trained on the assailant.

"Hello, Chow," Alek says calmly. Regardless of what is happening, his hand caressing my leg doesn't falter. Adam's eyes are wide as he watches the scene unfold.

"Don't hello Chow me!" he shouts, peering over Hans's shoulder as he seems to know that Saint doesn't miss. "What are you doing with this slimy bastard?"

Adam's men also have their guns drawn, but they don't have a clear shot. They gather closer to our table, flanking us to protect us.

"Put down the gun, Chow, before you get hurt," Alek mocks, coming to a slow stand. I exhale, thankful he's removed his hand, but when I see Sara, I know there is nothing to be grateful for.

"Fuck you!" he screams, pressing the gun into Hans's temple shakily. "Why did you tell me to come here?"

Alek tipped him off? Why?

Everything soon unravels although I wish it didn't.

"Because our dealings have come to an end," Alek explains, reaching for his glass of vodka. "You're indiscreet and can't be trusted."

The music over the speakers soon mutes, and the patrons are quick to leave. They too sense the tension hanging thick in the air and don't want to hang around. The ladies on the stage grab their money and quickly exit through the red curtain behind them.

Even though this is foreign to me, I can imagine it happens in here far too often.

"What are you talking about?" Chow says, but he knows.

Alek leisurely takes a sip of his drink, savoring the burn. "You sold to my rival"—he inhales sharply, hinting this is personal—"when I'm supposed to be the only person you sell to. That doesn't look good for business, especially when that person undercuts me and sells the product for half of what I do. You know what happens to people I don't trust? To people who betray me?" He is calm, like psychopath calm, while Chow desperately looks for an out.

My breathing is measured as I'm too afraid to make a sound.

So that's why we're here. Chow is Alek's supplier, and he double-crossed him by selling product to Alek's rival. How can you be the number one drug lord when someone else sells the same product and for half the price to greedy consumers?

"I will kill him!" Chow screams, creeping closer and closer to us. The entire time, Hans's eyes are locked with Sara, who is muting her sobs behind her hand. But their ruse is up. It's clear to anyone watching that what they share is a lot deeper than simply the mutual respect of two colleagues.

Saint tries to get a clear shot, but Chow isn't stupid. He knows this will end in bloodshed. And what Alek says next kickstarts the shitstorm.

"He means nothing to me."

"I'm not playing!" Chow is a desperate man, but his seconds are numbered. He never should have come here.

"Good. Neither am I."

"You're going to regret this." But it's too late for Chow.

It happens in the blink of an eye.

Sara's blood-curdling scream echoes the exact moment a single gunshot rings out around the club. The remaining patrons flee or duck for cover while I simply stare wide-eyed and unbelieving at the sight before me.

Hans drops to the floor with a sickening thud, and a small part of me hopes he's okay. But as Sara continues howling, covered in her lover's splattered brains, I know that the blood and gore hint that none of us will be okay ever again.

Gunshots echo loudly around us. Neither Alek nor I move yet for entirely different reasons. Alek gets off on the violence, but I am frozen in utter shock as I watch Saint shoot

Chow dead without breaking a sweat.

Adam and his men dive behind the booth, not interested in being involved in a war that isn't theirs. My feet are rooted to the floor, and no matter how badly I wish I could black out the horrors unfolding, I can't. I watch as Saint charges forward and shoots Chow in the head again, ensuring he's dead. He has taken this man's life and has done so without remorse.

I've allowed this coldblooded killer into my world, knowing full well what he is. But actually seeing it, seeing him covered in blood and brains…is something else. Those hands have touched me in ways no other man has. They've given me pleasure. But now, they only deliver pain.

Alek finishes his drink, wiping his lips with the back of his hand. He peers over the edge of the booth where Adam is hiding. The red stage lights catch the disco ball, showering Alek in a sheen of crimson and making him look monstrous. "Let this be a lesson to you, Adam…don't fuck with me."

Adam's head bobbles nervously because this was a lesson learned for us all.

Sara slumps to her knees, sobbing into her palms. The sight breaks my heart because she has just lost a small comfort in this bleak, cruel world. However, when Alek looks at her, unmoved and unsurprised by her emotion, I know why she's here. Why he insisted Hans was to man the door.

This is what happens when you try to go behind Alek's back. People die.

This was *her* lesson. Alek knew she and Hans were a thing, and to punish her for her betrayal, he killed her lover in front of her. Is this a warning to us all?

"Clean this up," Alek orders Saint coldly, gripping my bicep and lifting me to my feet.

My legs are like Jell-O, causing me to stagger, but Alek isn't playing. He drags me along, leaving Sara on her knees as she grieves for Hans. Saint spins around quickly, his eyes a cesspool of rage. When they focus on me, they soon realize what he's done, what I've witnessed him do, and they fill with sheer shame.

A look alone can express so much, and right now, Saint wants me gone. And truthfully, I want to go. I can't unsee what I've just witnessed as it has changed the way I look at him forever. He told me he has a darkness within, and right now, covered in blood and other matter, I can see that he does.

He may have been forced into this world, but to kill so efficiently, I wonder was that darkness there all along? Did meeting Alek only feed the beast? If, and that's a big if, we get out of this alive, how can Saint return to being "normal" after everything he's seen and done?

How can I because, at this moment, no matter what he's done…I don't care, and for that, I'm ashamed of myself. The line between right and wrong blurs because whenever Saint is involved, I always manage to find an excuse.

But what plausible excuse is there for taking another man's life?

I clutch the cross at my neck, an action which doesn't go unnoticed as Saint averts his gaze. Alek sighs in victory, revealing why I'm here, revealing what *my* lesson was. He wanted me to see Saint for what he really is. But more importantly, he wanted me to see what *I* am.

A woman…in love with a killer.

My heart shatters in two because I was denying it all along, but I am. I'm in love with Saint. It may not be the conventional hearts and flowers kind of love, but what I feel for him is my own kind of love, a love that's unique like a fingerprint.

The connection between us has always been present, but instead of it fading when I see him for who he really is, it's only grown…grown into this.

Alek doesn't allow me to speak to him, not that I'd know what to say. And it seems he feels the same way. We've both stripped back the layers, and now, it's time to see what comes next.

I step over Hans's and Chow's lifeless bodies, their blood staining the soles of my boots red. I say a prayer for them both, hoping wherever they go, it'll be better than here. We walk out the door and see the security guards slumped by the doorway. Chow made sure he took down as many as he could with him.

Alek opens the passenger door for me, and I enter the car, numb. He jumps into the driver's side and starts the engine, navigating away from the mess he made but doesn't have to clean up. The silence as he drives us back to his home speaks volumes.

I press my forehead to the glass and squeeze my eyes shut, hoping to erase what I've witnessed…but deep down, I know this is just the start of things to come.

CHAPTER SIX

She's seen me kill. Seen the true monster that I am. So, now that she's seen me, the question is what will she do?

Day 48

I thought taking a shower and scrubbing away the remnants of last night would make me feel slightly better, but it hasn't. All I can think about is how Hans and Chow will never have that privilege again.

When I could no longer distinguish between my tears and the running water, I decided to switch off the faucets because I couldn't hide forever. I hunted through the closet, wanting nothing more than to wear a pair of sweats and a baggy T-shirt, but I settled on skinny jeans and a blouse instead. It's forbidden, it seems, to dress in anything casual.

I'm in the bathroom brushing my teeth when I hear the bedroom door open.

I wanted to go to Saint, but after my revelation, I needed some time to clear my head. I always knew that the feelings I had for him resembled love, but after last night, it seems all the smokescreens had faded and I was left faced with the stark truth.

Ironic, isn't it? Seeing him take someone's life was the key to unearthing what lingered under the surface all along. I know how incredibly fucked up that is.

Rinsing out my mouth, I know it's now or never. I can run and hide, but I'm not going to be a coward now. Taking a deep breath, I open the door and brace myself for anything and everything. However, when I see a disheveled Zoey standing in my room with her hands behind her back, it appears I'm not prepared at all.

Before I have a chance to speak, she reveals why she's here. "He took you. And Sara," she spits, her eyes on fire.

After everything I've seen, her jealousy is so trivial. "Believe me, it was against both our wills."

"That's what I don't understand! He never kidnapped me. He chose me. He wanted me. And I wanted him!" Just how Saint once said, Zoey, just like all the others, have stayed with Alek by choice. "You don't want anything to do with him, but he is smitten by you. Why?" she questions, shaking her head in bewilderment. "What do you have that I don't?"

It's on the tip of my tongue to express the obvious—like morals and that I'm a good person—but when I think about my feelings for her brother, I remain quiet.

She's angry, but more so, she's hurt. She loves Alek with all her heart, and in return, he trades her in for another. I understand why she resents me, but she seems to be missing the vital point that I don't want to be here.

When she saunters forward, I stand my ground, wondering what she plans on doing. She reveals what a moment later.

"It's 'cause you're a new shiny toy. That's all," she reasons with herself. The last time I saw her, she was naked and being exploited by Alek's "friends." It seems she's forgotten all about that because why would he do that to her if he loved her in return?

"But if you weren't so…shiny"—her pause has me swallowing, suddenly nervous—"then things would go back to the way they were."

"Zoey…" However, my words die in a garbled mess when she uncovers what she's holding behind her back.

"He loves me. Not you." The sunlight streaming in from the windows reflects off the pair of silver scissors she holds. She opens and closes them, the clear-cut noise displaying just how sharp they are.

Instantly, I retreat with my hands raised in surrender. But Zoey isn't interested in waving a white flag.

"You think you're better than me," she exclaims, cutting the air with the scissors.

"No, I don't. I'm nothing," I state, unable to keep the panic from my voice as I continue backing away from her.

"That's right. You *are* nothing. You may have Alek and my brother fooled, but I see you. And now, it's time they do too."

She lunges for me, but I make a mad dash for the en suite

door. Sadly, it seems anger has turned Zoey into a superhero because she grips the back of my blouse, preventing me from escaping. I twist and turn, attempting to flee, but she only holds on tighter. Saint's training is now obsolete because there is no fighting Zoey. I've made a rookie move and lowered my defenses.

My heart sits in my throat because I don't know what she intends to do with those scissors. The thought has me thrusting my elbow backward, connecting with something soft. When she howls in pain, I think I've struck her in the stomach.

When she lets me go, I don't waste a second and dive for the safety of the en suite. But Zoey reads my intentions, and I curse my decision to leave my hair down. She grabs a fistful and yanks hard. On instinct, I claw at her hand, hoping to pry myself free, but she only pulls harder.

"Let's see who Alek prefers now!" she cries, dragging me by my hair back into the room.

"Zoey!" I scream, violently trying to escape, but it's futile. She comes up behind me, cups my head, and slams my face into the wall. A lump instantly forms on my forehead, and I see painful stars. To ensure I don't fight back, she presses on my tender shoulder where I'm still recovering from the gunshot wound.

She doesn't give me time to recover before smashes my face into the wall again. And again.

By the third blow, the world tips, and everything grows blurry. I attempt to reach out for something to hold on to, but the blood dripping into my eyes from the gash to my brow prevents me from focusing on anything other than passing out.

"Everything was perfect until you came along and ruined it!"

Bang.

"This is your fault, you bitch!"

Bang.

Each knock against the wall has my grip on reality fading, and it won't be long until the darkness pervades me. And I welcome it.

"He thinks you're the most beautiful woman he's ever seen. Well, we will see."

I brace for another blow, but instead, all that comes is the sharp slicing of scissors cutting. At first, I have no idea what she's cut because I don't feel any pain. But when I sag forward because the pressure in my head is no longer, I realize that's because my *hair* is no longer.

I slump into the wall, splaying my hands against it to support myself from falling, but Zoey is on me like a rabid dog, hacking into my hair and cutting it away while I detach myself from my body, helpless to stop her.

She came here to take my beauty, and she isn't leaving until she's satisfied she's won. Her maniacal laughter has me closing my eyes, wondering what happens when merely cutting off my hair isn't enough. The blood pouring from the wound on my forehead trickles into my mouth as I gasp for breath. I'm growing accustomed to the metallic burn.

At some stage, I collapse to my knees, head bowed as I cradle my waist, but that doesn't deter Zoey. She continues mumbling to herself while slashing away at my hair. When she cries in victory minutes later, I know that she's done.

"Much better," she sings with one final slice.

I'm too far gone to care what comes next. My soul and body are finally defeated by this cruel world. If she were to take those scissors and pierce my heart, she'd be doing me a favor because at least in death, there will no longer be pain.

But she doesn't show me the mercy because killing me would be easy. Instead, she exits the room, leaving me to deal with the aftermath alone.

With trembling fingers, I attempt to gauge the damage, and when I'm met with uneven, frayed clumps of hair, I realize it's worse than I thought. The coagulated blood has sealed my eyes shut, but I don't need to see it. The remaining strands of hair barely cover the back of my neck. She missed a few locks which fall around my face, but the only way to fix this mess is to start afresh. To shave it all off.

"Ангел!"

His voice shouldn't soothe me after everything I've seen, but it does. In this dark, cruel world, he is the only light I have.

"What happened?" The panic is clear as Saint runs into the room and drop to his knees in front of me.

He attempts to raise my chin so he can see the damage, but I curl myself into a ball, shielding my face into my palms.

"Let me see!" he demands, but I shake my head, ashamed of what he'll see.

The fact clumps of my hair litter the room doesn't leave him guessing to what happened. But my bloodied hands point at something a lot more sinister than me deciding to cut my hair because I needed a change.

"Who did this to you?" His voice is murderous, and I suddenly want to save him the pain of knowing his sister is the antichrist reincarnate. So I remain silent.

He places his hands over mine, his touch filled with desperation and fear. "Please, let me see."

"Go away," I whisper, but he inhales sharply, hinting that isn't an option.

"I'm not going anywhere," he presses, drawing me into his chest, and God strike me down, I go willingly.

He rocks me gently, allowing me to weep, not for my hair—because that will grow back—but for my soul. What has happened to me? How can I allow those hands to touch me after everything I've seen them do? I may have been able to admit my feelings for Saint, but that doesn't make me feel any less ashamed for them.

"I'm sorry you saw me do...that last night. I wish you didn't have to see any of this," he says with his lips pressed to my head.

More tears follow, flowing a deep crimson to reflect the heartache buried deep within. "They'll be here s-soon," I manage to get out between stilted breaths as I bury myself deeper into his chest.

Saint said my room is under surveillance. No doubt, Zoey convinced Alek's men to turn a blind eye for five minutes while she wreaked havoc. Her time is up, though, because when we hear footsteps pound down the hallway, it's time to slip into character.

"Боже мой!" Panicked, Alek bursts into the room. I can

only imagine what he sees.

To my surprise, Saint doesn't let me go. But no matter how good it feels, I slowly untangle myself from his arms and gradually pry open my eyes. Dried blood cakes my eyelashes, causing my vision to blur. Alek and Saint both gasp when they see me.

"Zoey did this to you, didn't she?" It's Alek who speaks. I'm surprised he knows it's her, but who else would do this?

I meet Saint's wide eyes as he shakes his head slowly. It's evident everyone can see Zoey for what she is, bar him. I wish I could save him this heartache, but I can't. With vengeance running through my veins, I nod, my heart breaking with his.

Alek roars, startling me because if I didn't know any better, I'd say he cares about me. "She must be punished," he snarls, staring down at me and Saint. "Look what she's done to you."

When he curls his lip in disgust, I wonder if maybe I've been looking at this the wrong way. Has Zoey just done me a favor? If Alek no longer finds me desirable, will he let me go?

"Saint, find your sister and leave her downstairs. I will tell Igor to expect her."

When Saint closes his eyes for the briefest of moments, appearing to say a prayer for Zoey, I wonder who Igor is. But more importantly, what's downstairs.

Alek also notices Saint's reaction. "If this is too personal for you, I will get someone else to find her."

Saint lifts his chin slowly, deadpanning Alek. The room turns violent. "This *is* personal. Just not for the reasons you think."

I gulp because the tension is thick as Saint has openly expressed to Alek that reason is…me. There is no doubt about it. What is he doing? But when he comes to a slow stand, it seems he doesn't care anymore. "I'll find her," he promises, unflinching, as Alek stares him down.

There is no question who the alpha is when Alek eventually averts his gaze. "Good."

"Come." Saint offers me his hand, which I look at confused. "I will help clean you up."

Is he trying to get us killed? When I hesitate, he nods, promising me it's okay. The gun at his hip assures it.

"That's not necessary." Alek finds his balls as he slaps Saint's hand away. "I will take her to see Nikita. She will fix her hair. I'll have you looking like yourself again." His demeanor changes as he peers down at me.

I don't understand any of this. Why is he being so nice to me?

"I will accompany you," Saint says when he reads my confusion.

"No, that's not needed. I will take Willow myself. After you deliver Zoey to Igor, I imagine you'll need some time to yourself. Take the day off. Go get laid," he adds with spite, digging into his pocket and producing a few crisp bills.

I'm assuming that's to pay for whatever woman Alek has lined up for Saint.

But Saint shakes his head. "I don't need the day off. Nor do I need to get laid," he adds heatedly.

"Suit yourself." Alek has regained control, and I know this will end ugly if I don't get Saint away from him. Which is why

I come to a slow stand.

"Thank you, Alek. I would like to see Nikita." I presume she's a hairdresser.

Alek's smug grin, although sickening, is rewarding because he doesn't seem to see through my lies, which will work in my favor down the line.

"Excellent." He claps his hands together, practically beating on his chest like a gorilla in the wild. "You might want to wash your face first, and in the closet are some scarves you can use to cover your hair."

My hair—or lack thereof—is the least of my concerns, but Zoey achieved what she wanted as my ravaged hair is a clear eyesore for Alek. He can't have his property looking less than perfect. But when I look at Saint, I feel more than perfect—I feel complete.

I hope he can read why I agreed to go. And it has nothing to do with wanting to fix the mess his sister made.

And he does.

"Very well. If you don't need me, I'll go find Zoey." He gives me one last look before he turns on his heel and leaves me alone with the devil.

Alek sighs, liberating his lungs with victory, but if he thinks he's won this battle, then he doesn't realize that sooner or later, Saint and I will win the war.

Each day takes me further and further away from who

I once was. And now, staring at my reflection in the mirror with my hair cut short, I can almost believe this stranger to be someone other than me.

Nikita didn't bat an eyelash when she saw me. She's probably seen this before when Alek is involved. There wasn't much she could do to save my hair, so she styled it into a short pixie cut with long bangs. She also added some blonde highlights.

Alek was pleased with what he saw. He thanked Nikita, and when we got into the car, he complimented me on my new look. To celebrate, he told me he has a surprise for me. He was going to wait, but thought I needed cheering up, seeing as I was attacked by a maniac he created.

I nodded blankly, too numb to even care.

The entire drive back, I thought about Saint and Zoey. What was happening to her downstairs? I have a feeling that "downstairs" is a torture chamber, clad with sharp objects and contraptions that would put the medieval period to shame. It may seem farfetched, but a room such as this is probably a normal necessity in the world of mobsters and drug lords.

Alek has asked—and I use that word lightly—me to join him for dinner. I would rather starve to death, but here I am, fastening the straps on my heels. I assume this dinner isn't a casual affair, so I'm wearing a burgundy A-line dress with short sleeves and scooped neckline. The hem stops just above the knee.

I don't know what this surprise entails, and I've given up on guessing because anything is possible in this place. When the clock strikes seven, and a knock sounds on the door, it's now or never. Being escorted everywhere seems to be the norm, so I don't make a fuss when I see a man standing out in the hallway, ready to show me to the dining room in case I've forgotten where it is.

I hide my disappointment that it's not Saint and follow him down the corridor.

My appetite is completely shot, but the aromatic smells hint that the menu contains something delicious. I wonder what the occasion is. When we enter the dining room, I see that it indeed appears like we are celebrating something because the table is set for royalty.

Alek stands at the head of the long table filled with every food imaginable to mankind. There is too much to list, but the bright colors bring the room to life. "I didn't know what you liked to eat," Alek explains when he notices me appraising all the food. "So I had the chefs prepare a bit of everything. I hope you like it."

"It looks lovely. Thank you." I keep my reply to a minimum because it's on the tip of my tongue to tell him the best dish he could ever serve would be his head on a silver platter.

Alek pulls out the seat beside him, hinting I'm to sit near him. With no other choice, I walk toward him and nod in gratitude. Before I have a chance to sit, he grips my bicep, stirring a panic within. I wait for him to speak, but he simply eats me up from head to toe.

"You look stunning. I usually don't like women with short hair, but if possible, you look even more beautiful. The blue to your eyes will be the death of me." He takes my hand and kisses the back of it. His lips linger for a little too long, but thankfully, he lets me go when a maid enters with more food.

I take this opportunity to sit and subtly shift the seat away from him an inch.

On instinct, I scan the room, looking for an out. Apart from the doorway I entered through and a side door which seems to connect to the kitchen, I'm trapped. Alek pours me a glass of red wine from a crystal decanter.

"Let's make a toast." He raises his own glass, gesturing I'm to do the same. "To new beginnings."

My grip on the glass tightens because I have no idea what that means. Nonetheless, I clink my glass against his and sip the sweet wine. Alek downs his in one gulp while I nurse mine because the liquor turns my already queasy stomach.

He appears awfully animated tonight, like he's bursting at the seams to tell me something. An excited boy, bouncing in his seat has replaced his usual calm state. I have no idea why that is.

A convoy of servants brings in more food before they begin to serve us. Alek points at what he wants while I merely allow them to choose for me from the selection of cooked fish, sausage, some sort of crumbed frittata, salad, and what looks to be homemade bread.

I don't mean to be unappreciative because it all looks delicious, but I don't want to share a meal with his man. But looking down at my mountain of food, I know this isn't optional.

"Try the fish," Alek says around a mouthful of food. "It's simply delicious."

Picking up my knife and fork, I envision stabbing both

utensils into his eyeballs. The vision pleases me more than I care to admit. But it will have to remain a daydream for now. I cut off a piece of the tender fish and try my best to swallow it down. Even though it does taste wonderful, I can't do this without wanting to be sick.

"So how do you like it here? Is your room comfortable?"

I pause from chewing, wondering if I heard him right. When he tears his bread roll in half and mops up some juice off his plate, I know that I did. He expects us to converse over dinner like we're friends.

Once I've swallowed my mouthful of food, I reach for the wine. "Yes, it's very comfortable. I would love to see the gardens one day." I need to familiarize myself with every corner of this place.

Alek chews his food, nodding. "Of course. But baby steps," he says with a condescending smile. "I can imagine you're an outdoorsy kind of girl. Growing up in Texas and all."

I keep my cool as I place my glass onto the table. How did he know where I grew up? I don't recall ever mentioning it to him. "Yes. I love the outdoors."

He nods, continuing to eat his meal. "Don't look so surprised. I've done my research on you. You told me your father was a religious man. Are you still religious?"

The cross at my neck burns under his scrutiny. "Not really. How can I be?" I instantly seal my lips shut because I've spoken out of line. But Alek has mistaken my response for something else.

"Is that because of your father's passing?"

The blood drains from my face. How does he know so

much about me?

I mentioned my father was a Baptist minister, but I never shared with Alek that he had died. For all he knows, he could have left the church and joined the circus. He knows an awful lot about me, and I don't like it.

He places his silverware against the rim of his plate, waiting for me to reply.

Swallowing, I nod slowly. "Yes. My father was a wonderful man. He didn't deserve to die so young."

I have no idea why I'm sharing anything sentimental with this monster. He wouldn't understand.

"Dying is a part of living," he says, cementing my thoughts. But what he says next surprises me. "My father also died young."

If I didn't know any better, I'd say he was genuinely upset over the fact.

"So, you see, I can relate to your loss. My father was a wonderful man too. I was young when he died. Ten."

We are *nothing* alike.

I have no idea why he's sharing this with me, but I can't help but feel there is a reason.

"My mother was a weakling. A pathetic excuse of a woman," he spits, not hiding his disgust. "She was too busy spending my father's money to look after her children."

As much as I hate to admit it, I'm utterly fascinated by his story because there is a moral, and I need to find out what that is.

"And when she welcomed every lowlife into our home, hoping to find her Prince Charming, I knew things would change forever. About a year after my father died, she remarried. One year was all she needed to forget about the so-called love of her life."

There is clearly no love lost between Alek and his mother. I wonder what happened to her.

"What was your stepfather like?" As I delve deeper, I'm hoping to unearth just who Alek is. Because to defeat your enemy, you have to think like them.

Alek pushes his plate away as he seems to have lost his appetite. "Boris Ivanov was a vile man. He would never fill the shoes of my father. And when he tried...I showed him that he never could."

"Showed him?" I question, gulping.

Alek nods casually.

"How?" I dare ask.

A hint of a smirk plays at his lips. "I killed him."

I blink once, unsure if he's joking or not. But someone like Alek doesn't joke, especially when it comes to taking someone's life.

"Y-you killed him?" I need clarification in case we're lost in translation.

We're not.

"Yes."

"How old were you?" I can't keep the horror from my tone.

Alek shrugs, spinning the gold ring on his pinkie absentmindedly. I've noticed him doing this before. I suddenly realize there is a reason. "Thirteen."

This is far more horrible than I ever imagined. I never

gave much thought to the adolescent Alek, but it seems this one event in time triggered the psychopath in him. Killing someone at that age changes a person. But maybe in Alek's case, it only confirmed to him what he always knew to be true.

"I cut this ring from his finger"— he holds up his pinkie so I can see—"as it's a reminder of who I am, and what I've done to get here." He confesses this so flippantly as though he's justifying his actions. But nothing can excuse taking another person's life.

Even with what Kenny did to me, I don't think I could ever do what Alek did. I guess that's what distinguishes us from human and monster.

"Anyway"—he claps, breaking the somber mood—"I think it's time for dessert."

Eating is the furthest thing from my mind, but the servants come running from every corner of the room to clear the table.

My mind reels from everything Alek has just shared. I doubt he wanted to have a D and M talk, so I wonder why he told me this. A man like him doesn't do anything without deliberate thought. He chose to tell me that story and had a reason for asking me to dinner…and I find out what that is the moment a woman in a maid's outfit comes into the room holding a silver platter.

At first, I arch a brow in confusion because her serving tray doesn't appear to hold anything. But when she places it in front of me, I recoil backward, my seat scraping along the polished flooring when I see what she holds.

"It's okay," Alek coos, gripping my upper thigh to stop me from fleeing.

But it's not okay. How can it be when before me sits a large knife?

The long blade has a handle made out of what looks like ivory. It's a decorative piece, like one would use in a ritual. My mouth grows dry, and my palms begin to sweat.

"Wh-what's going on?" I stumble over my words, terrified.

Alek seems to be in his element as he smiles. "I told you. It's time for dessert." Unless we're about to carve a cake made of rock, then I'm clueless to how this knife relates to dessert.

"Lev, we're ready," Alek calls out, grinning broadly.

I have no idea what's going on. So I wait, my eyes peeled to the doorway. Seconds feel like hours but when the grand reveal occurs, I don't understand a damn thing.

The man who escorted me here enters, but he's not alone. Beside him is a man with a sack draped over his head. His arms are tied behind his back, and by the spilled blood on the front of his white T-shirt, I dare say a bloodied mess exists under that blindfold.

Lev drags the struggling man toward us, who seems to be gagged because his cries for help are muffled... just how mine were because the closer he gets to me...I smell it.

Whiskey.

"No," I whisper, the walls closing in on me. I can't move a muscle because I am frozen in fear.

It can't be, I repeat over and over. There is no way the boogieman has returned. But as Alek hollers in delight, I know that he has.

Lev stops a few feet away, restraining the man who's struggling to break free. He waits for further instruction from

Alek.

"My gift to you," he says, leaning in close while I'm dying on the inside. "Take off the blindfold."

Lev nods, screaming at the man thrashing about wildly in Russian. To ensure he knows they're not messing around, he punches him in the stomach, winding him. The man buckles forward, gasping for air. Alek hums his satisfaction.

Lev rips the sack from his head, and when he does... time stands still. My past crashes into me, and I'm suddenly fifteen years old again. I now understand why Alek shared his story with me about his stepfather because before me...stands mine.

"No," I repeat, shrinking back in my chair. I'm desperate to flee, but Alek holds me in place.

The moment I speak, Kenny's eyes fly open. It takes him a moment to focus on where he is, but when he does, they widen in utter disbelief. He may be covered in dry blood and his face beaten and bruised, but without a doubt, it's him.

"Willow?" Although muffled, thanks to the gag, I understand him perfectly.

A fear so fierce scratches at the surface, threatening to leave me scarred for good. "Alek, p-please. I...ca-can't." I try to escape, but he doesn't let me go.

"Shh. You can. You can do anything. It's time for vengeance, just like I got mine."

But he's wrong.

Kenny is my kryptonite, my weakness because everything I've worked so hard to achieve shatters around me, leaving me the scared little girl I once was.

"I've done my research on you. I know what this vile man did. You and I, we are cut from the same cloth. Take back your life, my darling."

Kenny glares at me, spittle foaming from his mouth around the gag. I shrink in my seat, shaking my head violently as I tremble in fear. Those eyes are still cruel, and although he's aged, he still looks like the revolting predator he always was.

"H-how is he h-here?" I ask, not understanding any of this. How did Alek know about him?

Alek levels me with those eyes, and for once, I don't see cruelness. I see my salivation. "Leave a trail for a scavenger, and he will follow," he replies, brushing the back of his fingers along my cheek.

I'm certain I'm moments away from dying of a heart attack. "You know what he did?"

Alek nods slowly, nothing but sorrow shrouding him. I don't understand why. Why does he care if Kenny hurt me? Isn't he doing the same thing? But an epiphany hits. Alek has never hurt me the way Kenny has. This is an example of showing me he...cares.

Bile rises, and I lurch forward, intent on throwing up my dinner.

This is my surprise. My stepfather on a silver platter for me to do with as I please. Zoey hurt me, and to express his fondness for me, Alek is allowing me to rid this earth of the monster who plagues my dreams.

"How do *you* like being gagged, you worthless piece of shit? Bragging to your "friends" about what you did to a teenage girl wasn't a smart move," Alek says, leaning back in his seat. It appears he *has* done his research after all.

Kenny hasn't taken his eyes off me, which infuriates Alek.

"Lev, take out his gag." The moment he does, Kenny gnashes his teeth together, lunging forward, intent on murdering me.

Alek loosens his hold on me, and I spring up from my seat, desperate to put as much distance between Kenny and me.

"You fucking slut!" Kenny roars, struggling against Lev. "I'm going to kill you! Come here, you bitch!"

His voice evokes the memories that have dogged me for years, and I back up until my ass hits the wall. I know Alek wants me to use that knife in front of him, but I can't. That will make me no better than Kenny.

"No," I sob, wishing this would all go away.

I need a lifeline, and for once, the universe cuts me a break.

"What the fuck is going on?" Saint's question is laced with pure venom.

Lifting my eyes, I blink past my tears to see him. I need to focus on something that makes sense. Relief I have never felt before crashes into me, and I feel like I can breathe again.

Alek shatters that reprieve. "I told you to take the day off."

"And I told you I don't need the day off," Saint counters with rapid speed, his eyes never wavering from mine. "Who is that man?" He addresses me, beseeching me to tell him what's going on. But to vocalize it will mean I have to decide what to do next.

"Your momma was right. You are poison. Look what you've done."

The room grows even smaller as things are about to turn dire...for my stepfather.

Saint closes his eyes and tips his face to the heavens, breathing deeply as Kenny has just signed his own death warrant.

"Believe me, her pussy ain't worth the trouble."

Just like always, Kenny doesn't know when to shut up, but unlike then, when I had no one to protect me, now...I do.

Saint movements are lithe as he walks over to Kenny, and without warning, he punches him in the face so hard, his head snaps back with a nauseating crack. He staggers backward, the blood pouring from his nose, indicating Saint has broken it.

I yelp, muting my cries behind my hand as I watch on, wishing I could feel something other than this paralyzing fear. I've dreamed of the day I got my revenge. There are so many things I want to do like incite terror in him just as he did to me.

But I can't.

That would make me just like him, and I am *nothing* like him.

Alek springs up, not wanting to get blood on his chinos. He suddenly seems annoyed that Saint is here, raining on his good Samaritan parade. "Well, this just got messy." He reaches for the white napkin to dab at the splatter of blood on his shirt.

My hands are splayed out against the wall as I need

something to anchor me. And when Alek reaches for the knife, it's clear why he made the toast he did.

To new beginnings, indeed.

"дорогая, the choice is yours." He extends the knife my way while I shake my head in horror. "But he doesn't leave here alive."

"What? *No*. Y-you c-can't. I w-won't." I'm on the cusp of hyperventilating because this is wrong. No matter which way I look at it, if I kill Kenny, I will kill a piece of myself as well.

"Kill him!" Alek exclaims, waving the knife. He is clearly annoyed that I don't like my surprise.

Kenny suddenly realizes he's in deep shit. "Look, man, just let me go, and I won't tell anyone about this."

Alek laughs in response.

Groveling was never in Kenny's DNA, but desperate times call for desperate measures. So he tries another method. "Willow, your mother needs me. Don't let them do this to her. If you kill me, the blood will be on your hands! You kill her too by doing this!"

The mere mention of my mom opens the floodgates, ones which have been watertight for years, and I wonder if I'll ever come back from this in one piece.

"Mom?" I whisper; my voice sounds alien like a lost daughter calling out to her mother.

Kenny senses she's his get out of jail for free card and plays on it. I know what he's doing, but it doesn't matter. Regardless of everything…she's still my mom. "Yes, your mother loves you. She never forgot about you. If you let me go, I will leave her for good. You can have your mom back. You'd like that, wouldn't you?"

Suddenly, images of Mom and me shopping together and laughing over something stupid as we stand around the kitchen counter eating pink frosted cupcakes assault me because I never got to do those things with her, and I wanted to. So badly.

These normal mother-daughter things that most take for granted or you'd see in a Hallmark movie are things I wanted to experience with her but never did because she was too busy forgetting I existed. But now Kenny's giving me a second chance. He's offering me something which would patch over this giant hole in my heart.

"Yes," I finally reply softly, pushing off the wall. "How is she?"

"She's good. We live in South Carolina now. You would love it there."

"I've never been," I say in a faraway voice, staggering slowly as I walk on autopilot.

I am hovering over myself, watching on in anger. I can see what he's doing—luring me in with false promises—but I can't seem to stop. The excitement of living happily ever after outweighs my good sense.

"We have horses and four dogs."

"How many horses?" I ask, continuing my dazed pace.

"Three. Your mom wanted to get one for you. She knew you'd come back."

"She did?" A single tear trickles down my cheek, and a happiness I haven't felt in so very long overwhelms me.

Kenny nods quickly. "Yes. She never stopped loving you.

Neither of us did. So, you're going to be a good little girl, aren't you, Willow, and you're going to set me free?"

The world stops spinning, and I inhale to catch my breath.

A white noise fills my head, and something tilts, setting me off course. I try to sound out the ruckus, but I can't. It beats against my temple, demanding I stop being so fucking stupid and open my eyes.

"No," I whimper, pressing my hands over my ears. "Make it stop." But it doesn't, and it never will.

You're going to be a good little girl, aren't you, Willow? Let me fuck that tight virgin pussy. You're gonna come for Daddy.

Those repulsive words paved a world in which I didn't want to live, but I did. I had no other choice because *she* abandoned me. *She* chose this motherfucker over me. *She* is the reason for all of this. I suddenly realize this is all on her, not me. *She* chose to walk away, and now…it's *my* turn to do the same.

Deadpanning the man who took away my innocence, I say goodbye to the scared little girl who still lives within me, and I welcome this new me.

"No," I say, relief wrapping me in her arms. "I will not."

For the first time in a long time, I stand tall and am not afraid to look into the depths of hell.

"No?" Kenny spits, his tobacco-stained teeth grinding together. "What do you mean no? So, you'll let them kill me?"

Alek stands on the sidelines, watching me closely. Saint stands ready to spring into action. I only have to say the word. And I do.

"Yes." A single word has the absolute power to change

the course of one's life, and for someone like Kenny, it's come about twenty years too late. But better late than never.

"Go on." Alek presents the knife in both his hands. "Kill this pathetic excuse of a man. His life is yours."

As tempting as the offer is, when I peer down at my own hands, turning them over and over, I know that I can't. And Saint knows it too.

Alek wanted a bloodbath, though, and he won't be satisfied until blood is spilled. "If you don't kill him, I will make you." His threat isn't empty.

Kenny thrashes wildly as Lev's barely able to hold him back. "You whore! You filthy whore!" he screams, showing me that he hasn't changed.

Saint's fists clench by his side as he's waiting for me to give him a sign, to tell him that it's okay…to tell him that I'm okay with him being what he is.

"You wanted my cock. You still do. You wanted me to fuck you, didn't you? You wanted to feel your daddy's cock deep inside you."

He is disgusting, and I curl my lip, sickened.

"You are *not* my daddy," I snarl, squaring my shoulders, not at all intimidated because I am not afraid anymore. The manacles holding me prisoner suddenly snap, releasing me from the shame and guilt that's weighed me down for years.

And when I see Kenny's fear, when I witness him cowering because the power he had over me is no more, I nod at Alek because this is the greatest gift anyone could give me. Regardless of who he is, I will never forget this because, in a fucked-up way, he's right.

This is me taking back my life. Just as he did his.

"You are nothing." Those are my parting words to Kenny Smith, the last words he will ever hear because Saint swipes the knife Alek holds and drives it straight into Kenny's heart.

I don't whimper or cry. I simply stand still, watching the life drain from Kenny. His eyes bulge as he gasps for breath. But it's in vain because Saint never misses…except for the one time. The time he shot me to save me, just as he's done time and time again.

Kenny drops to the ground with a thud, and there is no encore. He's dead. The knife sticking out of his chest is a sure sign of it.

I thought I'd feel something, but I don't.

The room is silent except for Saint's heavy breathing. He's standing over Kenny's body, looking like he wishes he could kill him again.

Alek clears his throat, as I'm guessing he was not expecting tonight to unravel the way that it did. "Saint—"

But he cuts him off. "I've got it. Ангел, go to your room." His back is turned, but I don't need to see him to know this isn't negotiable. And for once, I do what I'm told.

"Yes, мастер."

Alek's eyes widen, but our ruse is up. He knows that Saint killed Kenny…for me. He knew that I couldn't, and he could. And he did. And for that…I love him all the more.

A love-struck Juliet smitten with her bloodstained Romeo.

Many hours have passed since I saw Kenny take his last breath.

Alek escorted me to my room, and I was surprised when he left me alone. I'm guessing he had some business to take care of because one of his men mentioned Chow. They were speaking Russian, so I'm not sure exactly what the business entailed, but I can't imagine it would be good.

Once I showered and changed, I thought I'd fall into an exhausted heap after the night's proceedings, but I didn't. I was charged.

I couldn't sit still, and I knew why that was.

I needed to see Saint.

Once the house fell quiet, I crept from my room and kept to the shadows, avoiding detection by the cameras by skulking in the black spots. He told me his bedroom was the only room not monitored, which is why I'm sitting on the edge of his bed, biting my nails as I wait for him to return.

I don't know what I'm going to say to him, but just being in here makes everything better.

When I see a sudoku book on his nightstand, I think back to the island. Things, in an ironic way, were a lot simpler there. I'd give anything for the simplicity of it because here, although I can have any luxury I wish for, there is one thing I can never have.

My freedom.

Even though I was Saint's prisoner, I never felt that way because how can one be a prisoner when they keep coming back for more?

"Ангел?"

With the slowest of movements, I lift my eyes to take him in because it feels like a lifetime since I last saw him. The bedside lamp provides hardly any light, but I can see enough. Flecks of blood splatter his handsome face and thick neck, and when I continue downward, I focus on his hands, the hands which ended a monster's life. They're clean now, but once upon a time, they were not.

He quickly attempts to wipe away the evidence of where he was, but I jump up and walk over to where he stands, gripping his hands. It's evident he doesn't know why I'm here, so he allows me the time to examine him closely.

"You...you killed him without remorse," I whisper, peering up at him through my lashes.

Saint swallows, his Adam's apple bobbing with the movement. "He deserved it. And that's what I do."

But I don't believe that. The tattooed armband proves otherwise.

"Wh-where is his b...bo—" But I can't finish the sentence.

"I took care of it," he says, shaking his head. "He will never hurt you again."

My heart fills with...relief, and Saint mistakes my silence as disgust.

"Are you angry with me?"

I blink once, completely confused. "*What?* Angry with you?"

He nods. "I'm sorry. I took the right away from you. *You* should have killed that bastard. It wasn't my fight. It was yours."

"Saint—"

But he doesn't let me finish.

"You've known nothing but death since meeting me. You've seen me kill. I understand if you want—"

However, this time, I'm the one who cuts him off.

Standing on my tippy toes, I press my lips to his, savoring in his sweetness, his trademark scent. "The only thing I want...is you," I whisper against his mouth, my breath hot against his. "Thank you. Thank you for doing what I could not."

"You want me even after everything you've seen?" His surprise is clear.

"Yes."

"Why?" He pulls away, running his fingers through my hair, familiarizing himself with the shorter cut.

"Do you want me?"

"Yes," he replies without pause, which confirms what I'm about to say. "Always."

"Well, how can you want me when I am so fucked up?" And I am. I know that now. My stepfather's blood covers Saint, and all I can think about is pressing my naked body to his, desperate to wipe away the last trace of Kenny from this earth.

He doesn't deny my claim, and for that, I'm glad. We've stripped back the smokescreen until all that remains are Saint and Willow. The way it should be. "Because...your demons dance with mine. They always have."

And it's that simple. What we always knew to be true.

I don't know who lunges for who first, but it's a flurry of lips, hands, and bodies as we tangle around one another, tearing at clothes that just get in the way. When I feel Saint's flesh beneath my fingertips, a guttural whimper breaks free.

He is soft and hard all in the same breath, and I want more.

My nightgown is ripped from my body, and I'm left standing in my underwear. Saint is shirtless, but I need everything between us gone. With deft fingers, I unbuckle his belt while he kicks off his boots. When his zipper is unfastened, we both yank down his pants.

His cock springs to life between us, pressing me deliciously low.

Our lips are still locked in a frenzy, kissing madly without taking a breath. But who needs air when Saint is my life source. He walks me backward to the bed, tossing me onto it and falling with me. He breaks our kiss only to trail hot kisses down my arched neck as I open my legs.

He bites and suckles, and each time he does so, I want him all the more. My underwear are coated with my arousal as I have never been this roused before. He dips lowers, kissing between the valley of my breasts, before detouring to my left and tonguing my pearled nipple.

My back bows from the mattress as it feels so good.

He does the same to my right as he walks his hand between us. When he feels the outside of my underwear, he hisses with pleasure. I boldly place my hand over his, coaxing him to go further.

He does.

He grips the waistband and tugs sharply, ripping it apart in his hand. It's such a barbaric thing to do, but I love it. I love that he doesn't wrap me in cotton wool. I want him to want me as much as I do him. With my breast still deep in his mouth, he works two fingers into me, stretching me wide.

I am so turned on, he slips inside with ease.

"Oh, fuck," he groans from around my breast, pumping his fingers in and out of me. "I want you."

I know why he seems to be in a plight, but I don't care. I arch into his touch, moaning because he is ingrained into me. "I don't care," I breathlessly confess, writhing against him.

But of course, he does.

"We can't." But his resolve is slipping.

He continues sinking his fingers into me, all the while tonguing my heavy nipples and driving me wild.

"If he finds out you're not a virgin, he'll kill you. It's the only thing keeping you alive."

I've heard it all before, but I still don't care.

"This *is* me, feeling alive." I open my legs wider, crying out when he flicks over my ripened clit.

"Oh, ангел," he pants, lifting his head and slamming his lips against mine. "You will be the death of me."

Even though he doesn't mean that in the literal sense, he's right. Alek will know Saint took my virginity, which will end in his death. I can't live with that reality, so I bite his bottom lip before flipping us over.

On his back, Saint looks beyond epic as he trusts me,

awaiting the next move. I take a moment to examine him because he is a vision. His wild and unkempt long hair, and those tattoos and the barbell, I can't stop myself from devouring every inch of him.

I bite his chiseled chin, then work my way down his chest. I lick a path down between his pecs before detouring to his nipple. I've wanted to do this since I first saw it. I flick my tongue over his barbell, then take his nipple into my mouth.

A cavernous moan leaves him as he arches into my touch. He threads his fingers through my hair, not appearing to mind my new style. I don't want to hurt him, but I can't help myself as I bite his piercing, before sucking softly.

"Fuck," he curses, pulling my hair. "Harder."

No surprise that he likes pain, so I do as he requests.

Once I'm done working over his piercing, I work my way lower, marveling at his rock-hard abs. I tongue each ridged plane, growing wetter with each lick. I glide my hands up and down his torso, fingering each raised scar.

Some would think his wounds mar his perfection but not me; they just add to who Saint really is.

His muscled V is heaven, and I trace the defined lines, unbelieving how incredibly sexy he is. I slither down his body, stopping at his impressive cock. I'm definitely no expert in this department, but when I push my reservations aside and take him into my mouth, I suddenly feel like a goddess.

He cries out loudly, thrusting his hips. When he hits the back of my throat, I instantly gag. "Shit. Sorry," he pants, gripping my chin and positioning me so he can look down at me.

"It's okay," I whisper, mewling when he runs his thumb over my bottom lip. He gently lowers my head back down, but I don't need encouragement. I want him all over me.

I work my head up and down, licking his shaft before taking him in deep. I can't take him all in, so I wrap my hand around his base and begin to pump. The motion combined with my bobbing seems to work because before long, he cups the back of my neck, urging me to move faster.

Hollowing my cheeks, I frantically work his dick. With each stroke, the fire within me burns brighter, leaving me so wet, my arousal coats my sex. I am so turned on by pleasuring him, and if I don't ease some of this pressure building in my core, I'm scared I might explode.

I begin to move my hips against the comforter because it rubs my clit in just the right way. I move my hand along his shaft in sync with my mouth, and when I tongue the slit at his head and a saltiness hits the back of my throat, I moan loudly. As does he.

The comforter acts as a poor substitute for what I want, but what other choice do I have? I want to come, but I'm frustrated because my orgasm will be lackluster. The only thing which will pacify this yearning is feeling Saint inside me.

Saint reads my thoughts and presents me with an option which blister my cheeks red raw. "We, we can do something else."

My curiosity wins out in the end, and I pull back, him slipping out of my mouth. "Something else?" I have no idea what he's talking about until he gently squeezes my ass cheek.

A winded gasp leaves me. "Oh? Oh!"

He knows the answer, but asks anyway as he doesn't want to assume. "Have you done that before?"

"No." I shake my head timidly.

He lifts me up, dragging my body along his so I'm straddling him. "We don't have to do anything you're not comfortable with."

He rests his large hands on my hips, stroking the flesh on my flank softly as he waits for me to reply. But I don't know what to say. I'm terrified at the proposal because he barely fits in my mouth. How will he fit in my…?

"Turn around," he huskily commands, coaxing me to spin so my back faces him. When I do, he gently pushes on the small of my back, positioning me to lay down. His generous cock bobs inches from my lips, and I instantly want to take him in my mouth again.

He arranges my legs to straddle his face. He grips my ass cheek before rearing up and suckling over my clit. I cry out and collapse forward, but I soon get my head or, rather, my mouth in the game and wrap my lips around him.

I begin to move slowly, bucking onto his face as I suck him deeply. The angle allows me to take more of him, and soon, I am working his shaft with speed as Saint eats me out ferociously, ensuring no part of me remains untouched.

This becomes my new favorite position because we are able to give the other pleasure at the same time. I take; he gives. He takes; I give. Saint then adds a finger to the mix, dipping into my heat and making me cry out around him.

I don't realize there is a reason for this until he circles that finger coated in my arousal over my back entrance. He gently works it between my cheeks, then fingers over my puckered opening. On instinct, I tense, but Saint's hot breath slaps against me.

"Relax, ангел."

But this is so taboo. No one has seen this part of me before.

"Do you want me to stop?"

And that's the million-dollar question. Do I?

When he works his tongue deep into me, all the while circling that finger, I know the answer is no. I don't. I want more. And to show him what I want, I slowly drive my hips backward. Saint hisses but never stops his tongue as he begins to work the tip of his finger into me.

My eyes bulge from my head because this feels so foreign. My instinct is to clench, but I relax, allowing him to enter me. It hurts, but Saint distracts me from the pain as he continues licking, sucking, and tonguing my needy sex.

I continue going down on him, but my movements are jolted because when he buries his finger in deep, I'm certain I'm about to turn to mush. He's halfway in when he begins to pump in and out slowly. I can feel myself tightening around him, and before long, I am rocking back on him.

"More," I pant, my breasts dangling between us as I arch my back, moaning. Never have I felt so full as I bounce against his face with his finger sinking in and out of me.

And he gives me what I want.

He increases the speed and depth, and before long, he slips in with ease. "I want you." And I do. I know it will hurt, but I want to experience this with Saint.

I don't know what position to take, so I wait for him to tell me what to do. It's what he's good at, and in this case, I don't mind.

With one final lick of my sex, he gently removes his finger. "Come here."

I don't need to be told twice, so I turn around, crawling up his body. I frantically press my lips to his, not caring that I can taste myself on his mouth. We kiss like starved animals, which only evokes a deeper burn within me.

He breaks the connection, only to roll me onto my side. He kisses the side of my neck, all the while spooning behind me. He positions my legs so they sit forward, opening myself up to him. I feel so safe with him at my back as he cocoons me in his arms.

"I don't have a condom. I'm sorry. I just, I haven't needed any," he confesses, his embarrassment clear as sleeping around isn't high on the agenda for a hitman.

This is incredibly irresponsible of me, but I don't care. I want to feel him in the flesh. Nothing between us. "It's all right. Just go slow."

Saint hums low, reaching around my hip and inserting two fingers into my sex. We both hiss at the connection, and I move slightly so he can deepen the penetration. This position is perfect as I am so relaxed. So when I feel Saint shift his hips and spread my arousal around my puckered entrance, I grow lax and brace myself for whatever is about to come.

Just as he did with his finger, he gently tests the waters, so to speak, ensuring my muscles are relaxed. I know I'm tight, and this will be an impossible fit. "God, I want you. But tell me if you need me to stop."

He kisses just under my ear as he presses his blunt head to my entrance. My arousal acts as the perfect lubrication, and with a deep breath, he slowly sinks in an inch.

"Stop!" I cry out, because I am certain he's about to split me into two.

He freezes and curses, angered at himself. "I'm sorry. I've hurt you." When he attempts to pull out, I reach around and place my hand on his hip, stopping him.

"You haven't," I assure him, catching my breath. "I just... you're not going to fit."

"Do want me to stop?"

"No." My fears have stopped me from experiencing something I want. And I am done living in fear.

"You control how deep I go," he says softly. "I won't move."

He reaches around me and begins flicking my nipple with his thumb, then cupping my breast. He adds his lips to the mix, kissing along my neck and biting over my pulse, helping me to forget about my reservations and just let go.

He's still rooted inside me, so when I arch back slowly, he inches in farther. I gasp, surprised that he slips in with ease. The pain soon lessens and is replaced with pleasure as I move my hips, taking his cock into me.

When he's a quarter of the way in, he buries his face in my neck, shuddering. "Can I move?" He's barely holding on. And it turns me on to know I am eliciting this desire from him.

"Yes," I whisper, inhaling because I feel so full.

But that is nothing compared to what comes next because

when he shifts my leg to deepen the angle, I'm convinced I will come apart in his arms. He pushes into me gradually, groaning as he sinks into me deeper and deeper.

"Do you want me to stop?" he asks again.

"No," I whimper, leaving my body and dancing with this depraved bliss.

"Does it feel good? The pain?" he adds, reading my wickedness loudly.

My cheeks blister because God strike me down, it does.

"Yes," I reply in a small voice.

Saint hums hoarsely, his approval sending goose bumps all the way down my spine. "We're one and the same. The pain is our heroin, reminding us that we're human."

And he's right. I never knew I toed the fine line between pleasure and pain until I met him.

"Move with me," he commands, wrapping his large body around mine. And I do.

I arch backward, crying out when he's fully embedded. He pauses, breathing harshly as he allows my muscles to adjust to his size. My channel grips him, milking him because I suddenly want so much more.

I don't know what I expected it to feel like, but this is indescribable. We are joined as one. Two hearts. One body. And I want to stay this way forevermore.

We begin to dance in unison, Saint moving inside my body as the pain disappears and all that remains is this unadulterated desire. His moans crash into me, blanketing us in a world meant for only him and me. He reaches around and begins to stimulate my ripe sex. He is everywhere, all over me, in me, and it's everything I want.

A string of Russian leaves him as he begins to move faster, stretching me wide. He pulls all the way out before gliding back in. His movements are lithe, making this feel so fucking good. Covered in perspiration, we are slippery and wet, helping him slide in easier.

He pulses inside me, and each thrust is my undoing. "Harder," I whimper, rocking my hips.

"Lift your leg toward your chest," he breathlessly instructs.

The moment I do, I whimper because the penetration is so deep, I can feel him all through my body. "Oh, my god. Saint." I don't even know what I want to say. I am lost to this feeling. I am lost to him.

I arch my back as he continues sinking his cock into me, all the while playing with my clit. It's sensory overload, and before long, I'm shamefully riding him hard. "You are… everything to me, ангел."

I don't know if those words are said in the heat of the moment, but I'll treasure them either way. Saint doesn't express his feelings openly, so to hear him say this has me chasing my orgasm quickly. He continues to rub my clit, all the while taking my ass and making it his.

He slams into me, splitting me into two as he wraps his arm around me. I let go and surrender, gasping for breath as Saint claims me as his evermore.

"I-I…" I want to tell him how I feel, but no words are needed.

He grips my chin and arches my head back so he can kiss the ever-living fuck out of me. His tongue moves in sync with his cock and fingers, and I am helpless to the pleasure of being owned by this man. My screams are muted by his lips as I come hard.

He moans into my mouth and pumps his hips fiercely before following me in a wild, sticky mess. His cries are hoarse and hot, and knowing he has come inside me has me whimpering, my body shuddering in debauchery.

We are breathless, both vibrating with the pulsating energy thrumming between us. In the minutes it takes us to come down, we never stop kissing. Our kisses grow sluggish, but they're a reflection of our utter bliss.

Saint suckles my bottom lip before breaking the kiss. "Let me get something to clean you up." I don't protest but can't help but feel a loss when he slowly pulls out of me.

I can't move. My body is Jell-O. I am comfortably numb.

Saint returns a moment later and gently turns me onto my stomach, then cleans me up. I can't help but draw the parallels as the warm water washes away everything we just did. My captor is now my savior.

Once upon a time, he inflicted wounds, and now, he's tending to them gently. When he rubs the washcloth over my behind, I flinch because I am sore. Saint leans down and places a soft kiss over my ass cheek. "You can stay here if you want. I'll wake you up early so you can go back to your room before Alek comes back."

I nod sleepily because I wasn't planning to leave anyway. *Where did Alek go?* I wonder.

Once I'm clean, he pulls back the blankets so we can nestle under them. I settle against the pillow, sighing happily as Saint snuggles in behind me. I'm on the cusp of sleep when I feel the mattress dip.

"Where are you going?" I can't keep the panic from my voice.

"I was going to take a shower. I probably stink."

Gripping his arm, I drag him closer to me so he's spooning me tightly. "You smell like you, and I like it," I groggily confess. "Besides, you can't smell any worse than you did on the island."

His hoarse laugh stokes a small fire within.

"That's true. I would give anything to go back there," he confesses, running his fingers up and down my arm.

"Me too. We'll be okay, Saint." We both need the assurance because all of this can't be for nothing.

"Sleep, ангел." He strokes the cross at my throat.

I'm too tired to fight him, so I do as he says.

I fall asleep in his arms, and for the first time ever, my nightmares are silenced, thanks to the man who continues to save me time and time again.

CHAPTER SEVEN

Each day I spend with her, I know that to save her...I will have to let her go. But how can I do that? She is as much a part of me as I am myself.

Day 53

"Remember what I taught you?"

I can't keep the grin from my lips because Saint Hennessy has taught me a lot of things. My cheeks flush a bright red, giving away my perverse thoughts.

He steps forward, facing his broad back to the camera. "Don't make me take you over my knee."

"Is that supposed to be a threat?" I challenge, folding my arms smugly.

He growls low in his throat, which doesn't help the

predicament in my pants.

How times have changed.

Since the night Saint explored my body in ways I never imagined, things between us have shifted. Our touches and kisses, although covert, have been far more open. Whenever no one was watching, Saint was dragging me into a dark corner or pressing me up against a wall.

Each night, I crept to his bedroom where he devoured my body and also my soul.

I am lost to him, and each second I spend with him, I fall deeper and deeper under this spell. Alek has been in and out, but overall, he's been making himself scarce. Saint claims there is nothing to worry about, but I can't help but feel this is the calm before the storm.

Saint and I are back in the gym training because I still want to learn how to defend myself, especially after what happened with Zoey. I've asked Saint how she is, but he said she doesn't want to see him. I didn't ask anything else because it's clear her anger toward him upsets him. All he wanted to do was help her, but now, things are just so messed up.

"Ангел," he cautions with no bite.

"Fine." I mock sigh. "I remember."

Saint gets into position, raising the gun toward me. It's not loaded, of course. He has taught me how to disarm someone with a gun, and now, he wants me to show him how it's done. I center myself, then reach out quickly and grab the barrel of the gun with my left hand before knocking his hand away with my right.

The trick to not getting shot is to ensure a fast approach.

And I am.

Saint nods with a smirk. "Very good. What about now?" He gestures for me to give him the gun. When I comply, he walks around behind me, placing the barrel to the back of my head.

I raise my hands in the air, higher than the gun, and move them from side to side, distracting Saint so his peripheral vision will focus on my hands. In one swift move, I turn quickly, grabbing the gun as I twist Saint's wrist. If I apply enough force, I could break his finger.

Once he's disarmed, I bend my knees and mimic punching him in the throat.

All of this is done in under a second.

"I'm impressed," Saint says, his hands raised in surrender.

"Thank you. I have a good teacher," I reply, passing him the gun. "Who taught you how to do this?"

"I took some martial arts classes when I was a kid," he reveals. "My parents thought I'd benefit from them, seeing as I was so scrawny growing up."

"Do you miss them?" We don't speak often of his past as I know it's a touchy subject for him.

So he surprises me when he answers. "Every single day. Do you miss LA?"

I shrug because that life seems an eternity ago. "In some ways, I do. But after everything…that all seems so…"

"Insignificant?" Saint offers as I search for the right word.

"Yeah." Because he's right.

On the island, he told me he could never go back to living a normal life. I didn't understand why that was, but now, I do.

"I most definitely don't miss modeling."

Saint smiles, and the sight is truly epic. With his good looks, he could grace any magazine cover or billboard. "Really?"

"Yes, really. It's a cutthroat industry, but it's also a lonely one. And besides, my look isn't exactly ideal anymore." When he arches a brow, I pull down the strap of my crop top, revealing my scar from the bullet wound. "Any imperfection is one's downfall, and believe me, there are ten other girls more than willing to take your place."

Saint steps forward, rubbing his fingers over my wound. I know he still feels guilty for shooting me. "It's not an imperfection."

My skin breaks out into goose bumps because his hands on me always provoke this response. When he shifts slightly so we're out of camera range, he lowers his lips to my shoulder and kisses the scar. "It shows the world how strong you truly are."

I whimper, unable to mask my desire for him. "Saint, don't," I whisper because I don't have the strength to stop this if things escalate.

"I can't stop," he exposes hoarsely, tonguing over my scar leisurely.

Although we are out of camera range, we both know someone can walk in at any time. But when he grips the back of my neck and kisses my throat, I suddenly don't care. In this fucked-up place, being with him is the only thing that makes me feel alive.

And I want him to know that.

I still haven't told him how I feel because saying it aloud is so…daunting. But there is no denying my feelings for him as they grow every single day. What I feel is unlike anything I've ever experienced before, even with Drew. But thinking back to that relationship, I realize how naïve I was.

I thought what I had with Drew was real, but in reality, I can't even remember what it felt like being with him. It's like I've replaced his memory because, in the end, he wasn't worth remembering. But with Saint, he is someone I will never forget.

"Saint," I gasp, arching my head backward, offering myself to him. "I want to tell you something."

"What, ангел?"

The soft bristles of his beard make it near impossible to focus on anything other than his lips on my skin, but I focus because it's time he knew.

"I…I…" But my admission will have to wait for another day because when his cell chimes, indicating he has a text, he groans against me.

"Hold that thought." He lays a single kiss over my racing pulse before pulling away.

Saved by the bell, I muse as I watch him retrieve his cell from the bench. When he sighs heavily, I know that is, in fact, the case. "Sara just text me. Alek is headed this way."

Sara has been keeping to herself since Hans's death. I didn't want to pry because we all deal with death differently, but I've let her know I'm here if she needs to talk.

Saint quickly reaches for the focus mitts, and we get into position. As I'm mid swing, the door opens, but we both ignore it and I continue training. Alek is watching us, which has Saint pushing me harder. He forces me to deliver some quick punches, but nods, indicating he's going to trip me.

He doesn't want Alek thinking I can defend myself because that would put an end to our training.

I punch high, bracing myself for a fall, but it still doesn't prepare me for when Saint sweeps out his leg, sending my ass to the mat. A whoosh of air escapes me because he didn't hold back.

"I told you to block," he scolds. "Get up."

Before I have a chance to move, Alek glides over like a knight in shining armor and helps me to my feet.

"Thank you," I say breathlessly while he smiles.

"Alek, I didn't see you come in," Saint says, slipping off the focus mitts before turning off the music.

He seems to buy it. "I didn't want to interrupt your training session," he replies, his fingers still wrapped around my bicep.

Saint's gaze drops to our connection, but he's soon to recover. "I would hardly call it training. Maybe if she listened, she wouldn't be on her ass half the time."

I hate that he speaks about me like I'm not in the room, but I know why. We both have to pretend, but it's getting harder and harder each day.

Alek lets me go, but he's here for a reason. My mouth suddenly grows dry. "I'm glad you're both here. I've been thinking about this for the past few days."

"Thinking about what?" Saint asks casually, sipping his water.

"You've been good to me, Saint. Regardless of the circumstances of how you came to work for me, I have never seen someone excel at their job like you have."

Not exactly a compliment, but I have no idea where he's going with this.

"Which is why I've made this decision with a heavy heart."

Heart? That's rich.

"I'm a man of my word, and the terms were clear—you were to deliver Willow to me on the proviso that I grant Zoey's freedom. As well as your own."

Even though I know what he's about to say, it still doesn't prepare me for the bombshell.

"So it's now time that I delivered. You are free. Both you and Zoey." He spreads his arms out wide, like he's liberating a nation, but all he's done is ensured my imprisonment in this place forever.

Saint, for the first time ever, seems to be caught off guard as this has come out of nowhere, but has it? We were stupid to think we had Alek fooled. This entire time, the only people we were fooling were ourselves.

"Alek"—Saint pauses as it seems he needs a moment to gather his thoughts—"I am grateful for the offer, but she needs more training. She isn't—"

But Alek elucidates that this isn't a choice. It's a warning. Saint leaves now with his life intact, or he never leaves at all, meaning his life will end within these prison walls. "You've done your job. I thought you'd be happy. You've fought so hard for your freedom; what could be more important than that?"

And there it is. A test.

"I am happy. But who will protect you? You need someone you trust, now more than ever with Chow gone." Saint is grasping at straws because it's clear Alek has made his mind up.

He sees us for what we are. He sees that I...love him. Saint is a roadblock, and Alek doesn't want anything standing in the way. But I will never, *never* love him, and if he sends Saint away, he may as well kill me now.

"I thank you for your loyalty, but I can't have Zoey here anymore. I am done with her." And with a flick of his hand, he has cast Zoey from his life forever. She has served her purpose, and now that she is no use to him, he will discard her like a piece of trash.

"I will take Zoey away and ensure you never see her again, but I will return." Saint steps forward, and the room suddenly grows smaller.

But Alek isn't intimidated. He came prepared for a fight. "And why would you do that?"

No matter how badly I want to hear him say it, I won't let those words be his last because that's what they'll be if he tells Alek the truth. Saint has forever been my savior, but we both knew it would end this way.

We were on borrowed time.

"Because I—" Saint storms forward, as does Alek, but he's finally been rewarded with what he's always wanted.

His freedom.

And I won't let his loyalty stand in the way of that.

Knowing he's safe away from this life is, in a way, my

freedom as well. I may be trapped here forever, but he isn't. I want him to live. To be happy. And every so often, if he thinks of me, well, that will make all of this worthwhile.

To love someone, you have to be prepared to set them free, and now, this is me letting Saint go.

Stepping between them, I press a hand over Saint's chest. I can feel his strong heart thrashing against my palm. He peers down at it, confused. The sight breaks the final piece of me; the piece which was held together for him. "Goodbye, Saint."

His mouth parts open slowly, his eyes wild. "Will—"

But I cut him off. This is my gift to him. "You got what you always wanted. You're free." His freedom has come with a price, but I'd happily sacrifice everything for him because that's what you do for the people you love.

Saint turns his cheek like I've slapped him. "No, I—"

But this isn't negotiable. Alek is the gamemaster, and he's changed the rules. We were always his pawns, waiting for the next move.

"You heard her. She doesn't need you anymore." Alek is at my back, but I don't need to see him to know he is smugger than a pig in shit.

I'm set alight by Saint's glower because it's game over.

Alek has won.

"Such a shame. You'll miss the masquerade ball I'm organizing for Willow's big unveiling." He is such a patronizing asshole. It takes all my willpower not to turn around and knee him in the balls.

I close my eyes, desperate to keep the tears at bay because I need him to know that I'm okay. No matter what Alek does to me, Saint will always, *always* have my heart.

When I reopen them, the last sliver of hope floats to the wind, leaving me with an emptiness so great, I don't know how I will survive this without him. But I must. And I will.

"You can pack up your things. And take whatever you think Zoey will want."

"You're not going to say goodbye to her?" I ask him, but my eyes are locked on Saint's. Is this our goodbye?

He is furious with me, and I am fearful he's seconds away from exploding. But when Alek presses against my back, threading his fingers through my hair and tugging softly, we know if we don't play by the rules, Alek will ensure we suffer and suffer greatly.

"No." He offers no further explanation because a single word speaks volumes.

Saint stands deathly still, and I know he wrestles with what to do. But this is really it this time.

No matter how strong I'm trying to be, a single tear traces a path down my cheek. Saint follows its movement; his expression not just breaking my heart, but he fucking destroys me. I commit him to memory, memorize the man who changed my life forever.

"I'll ensure you're paid everything you're owed."

"Keep your money," Saint snarls, his fists curled by his side.

"No. As I said, I'm a man of my word."

Waves of anger roll off Saint, and they only intensify with every jagged breath he takes. I need to end this. For once, I need to be the strong one.

"Come, дорогая. Let's leave Saint to gather his things." He isn't even going to let me say goodbye.

Panic grips me because this is really it. I'll no longer feel his touch or be comforted by his trademark scent. Everything we experienced will soon be a distant memory because to survive this place, I will have to do so under the guise of whatever drug I can find.

Or better yet.

When the time presents, I will finish what I started on that yacht because what sort of life is this? Without Saint, it feels like I'm living half an existence anyway.

I want to say so many things, but what would that achieve? I will keep my secret under lock and key and allow myself to slip back into the past when I miss him, which will be every single moment of every single day.

He launches forward, uncaring that Alek stands feet away, and buries me into his arms. He squeezes me so tightly, I can barely breathe, but what a way to go. He strokes my hair as he presses his lips to the top of my head.

The game is up, so Saint can touch me so openly. What is Alek going to do? He's already done the worst possible thing he can. If he were to kill me, he'd be doing me a favor.

I sob into Saint's chest as the world shatters around me. But I mute my whimpers because he is free. Finally, he can step out of the shadows and live where he belongs—in the light, which is why I gently break our embrace and...let go.

I turn on my heel and walk toward Alek, taking his extended hand. Saint curses behind me as I hear something shatter against the wall, but I don't look back...and I never will.

I'm curled in a ball on my bed, fixated on the swirls on the wall. My tears have long dried up because there aren't enough to express the utter anguish within me.

Alek detailed all the things he has planned for me—shopping, parties, trips around the world. It was clear what he was doing. He was hoping to buy me so I would forget about Saint. But how can I forget about someone ingrained in my very core?

A piece of me is missing, and it'll never heal. But I focus on what's important, and that's Saint's freedom.

I wonder what's next for me. I've been living each day at a time, but the truth is, in part, I was living for Saint. For us to leave this place and start afresh together. I don't regret my decision, not one single bit. I just wish I could have said goodbye.

But would it have lessened the ache within my chest?

I think not because nothing ever will.

Clutching the cross around my neck, I squeeze my eyes shut, not knowing what to do next. Saint was my compass, my true north, but now, I'm so fucking lost.

"Shh, don't cry." My mind, the cruel, sadistic bitch isn't satisfied until I'm rocking in a corner it seems because when I hear his voice, I know it's just a trick.

But when the bed dips, and I feel him. Smell him. I know that it's not. "Ангел…"

Who knew a voice had the ability to take the pain away, and like a magic salve, I'm suddenly myself again.

Brushing the hair from my eyes, I sit up slowly, almost too afraid to look. But when I turn and see Saint, that fear turns to relief, and I burst into tears.

He scoops me into his arms, and I sag against him, intent on staying this way forever. "Ho-how are you h-here? I thought you'd be go-gone be n-now."

"You really didn't think that was goodbye, did you?" he says, pressing his lips to my head, my temple, and my cheeks, kissing away my tears.

"I didn't know," I confess. "I know you're mad at me."

"Yes, I'm fucking furious." But his tone holds no bite.

"You have to go," I press, wrapping my arms around his nape and nuzzling into the crook of his neck. No matter how angry he is, he knows I'm right.

"I know. But I fucking hate this is the only way. The stolen moments, it's not enough time." Being in here, we're both being watched. But with Saint out of these walls, he has a fighting chance to set us free. "I'll come back for you," he whispers into my ear. "I promise."

My skin breaks out into goose bumps from the vow alone. I gave him the option to take his freedom and run, but it seems he wants something more…and that's me.

"I know you will."

"I'm only leaving"—he inhales slowly, akin to being in pain—"because I know you can look after yourself. You're not the princess who needs rescuing." He pulls away and cups the back of my neck. With fire burning behind his eyes, he declares, "You're fucking fierce. And you're no one's victim. You never have been. Never forget it."

Unable to hold back a second longer, I paw at him madly as I smash my lips to his. He drags me up his body so I'm straddling him so tight, not a wisp of air can pass between us. Our kisses are messy and frantic, but they're perfect. They remind me that I'm alive.

I want him with every frenzied breath I breathe into him, but this kiss is a stolen one in time. He bites my bottom lip, before our tongues duel, fighting for top spot. I rub myself against him, his hard erection hitting me in just the right way.

I want him so much, consequences be damned.

Slipping my hands under his T-shirt, I run my fingers down his chest, relishing in the way his skin prickles under my touch. When I reach his nipple piercing, I circle the metal before tugging lightly. Saint moans into my mouth and bucks against me.

His abs are the next thing I caress.

Saint reaches between us, rubbing over my shorts roughly. I am so aroused it will only take a few quick strokes, and I will come. He lowers his head to my neck, biting over my pulse. Helpless to him, I bounce against his fingers, all the while stroking his hot, hard body.

He snaps the waistband of my shorts, diving into my underwear and sinking two fingers into me. I am lost to the feeling, and shamelessly, as I arch backward, riding his hand, I come within seconds. Saint moans into my neck, robbing me of every last tremor.

When I've come down, I want to return the favor, but

Saint removes his fingers, the ones buried deep within me, and puts them into his mouth. He suckles, humming in utter bliss. Weeks ago, I would have turned a beet red, but now, I just get slicker between the legs.

When he's done cleaning his fingers, he wraps his arms around my waist and draws me close. "Here." With one hand, he reaches into his backpack and produces his journal. "I want you to take this."

I eye it like he's just given me a live grenade. "Why?"

"It's my journal," he explains. I know what it is, but I need to know why he's giving it to me. "There are notes on the people you will most likely meet. The Circle."

My mouth hangs open in understanding.

"To beat your enemy, you need to become them. This will give you everything you need to know. If something were to happen, use this to save yourself."

I gulp because it's all so dire, but I know he isn't being melodramatic. When he offers it to me, I resist the urge to flip through it right then. I place it under the pillow and promise to guard it with my life.

"I don't have much time." He sighs, running his fingers through my hair. "I will be in touch. I have a plan."

Of course he does.

I know he can't tell me, seeing as my room is bugged and under surveillance. Odds are Alek's men have already seen us, but we just don't care anymore.

He hunts through his backpack once more, and when the silver of his switchblade catches the light, I shiver. He places it in my hand, nodding subtly. "Use it if you need it."

The metal feels heavy, but I know it's only my mind playing tricks.

"Don't hesitate," he orders, running his finger along the apple of my cheek.

"Okay." I lean into his touch, closing my eyes.

He takes his time because just as I did earlier, it's now his turn to commit me to memory. He traces down the slope of my nose before caressing over my parted lips. I am so lost to him that not even a roadmap could guide me to any other road but him.

"Love and fear, I've come to learn, are one and the same. It makes you feel the same. Your heart rate increases. Your palms sweat. And most of the time, you want to die. That's how I feel whenever I'm around you."

My eyes pop open because his analogy is absolutely perfect.

"I fear what I feel for you, ангел. For the first time in my entire life, I'm afraid, and I think that's because"—he wets his lips while I remain completely still—"I fear love. But in the same breath, I love fear. I thought I was destined for only one, but then, I met you, and you changed everything.

"You are the only thing I fear in this world because I…I…lo—" He shakes his head, expressing how hard this is for him. And I understand.

So, for now, this will have to do. I will hold his imperfectly perfect analogy close to my heart.

Placing a finger over his lips, I silence him. "I fear you too."

It's unorthodox, but I was struggling to find the right

words for how I feel about Saint, and now, I've just found them. I fear him because I love him too. But my fear is because I am scared of losing him. I am scared of the way he makes me feel because I am so in love with him. Being without him is the most terrifying thing I've ever had to face.

To most, it doesn't make sense, but to me, I have never felt more certain than I do right now.

Saint presses his forehead to mine. "I have to go."

Those words leave me a whimpering mess, but I nod quickly, holding back my tears. "Okay."

"Be safe, Willow. You do whatever you have to, to survive."

Gasping, I pull away gently, locking eyes with him. "You too, Saint."

At this moment, I understand why they say the eyes are the window to one's soul. Saint's soul seems to be in mourning with mine. We've spent fifty-three days together—a mere drop in the ocean compared to the endless hours of our lives—but I will never forget this fraction in time.

"I will send word as soon as I can."

"Mmm-hmm." It's taking every ounce of strength I have not to break down and beg him to stay. But knowing he will be free has me pressing my lips to his. The kiss is chaste, and it's how I want him to remember me.

"This isn't goodbye," he says because he can read straight through me.

"Then what is it?"

He ponders my question before he wraps his fingers around the back of my neck. "This is our new beginning." And those words are his legacy because he kisses my forehead softly before untangling our bodies and standing.

There is so much more I want to say, but I can't. So I will keep it under lock and key until we meet again.

There is a soft knock on the door, hinting it's not Alek. When Sara enters, she looks back and forth between Saint and me, her eyes filled with sorrow. "The car is downstairs. Zoey is in the back. Alek made sure she wasn't waking up anytime soon. I guess he isn't one for goodbyes." There is nothing but venom behind her words.

Saint nods, his jaw clenched. "Thanks, Sara."

"I'll miss you, Saint," she says, tears welling, but she quickly wipes them away with the back of her hand. "You were the only person who was kind to Hans. Thank you."

He clenches his jaw. "There is no need to thank me for being a human being. I'm sorry I couldn't save him."

I understand why she feels the need to express her gratitude. She is a lover scorned, and she reveals just how much so. "I want in. Whatever you're planning, that bastard has to pay."

Saint appears stunned by her aggression, and I am too.

"I know you would never leave Willow here alone without a plan."

His chest rises and falls as it seems we weren't as discreet as we believed.

"So whatever scheme you have up your sleeve, count me in."

It feels nice knowing I can trust at least one person in this place.

"Okay, I will be in touch soon." His lips twitch. "Look out

for her. She tends not to listen."

I scoff but don't argue because it's true.

"I've noticed."

"Goodbye, Sara." Saint reaches for her hand and squeezes it. Why is he saying goodbye to her? He said this wasn't goodbye for us, so what plans does he have for her?

"Goodbye."

The air is thick with unspoken promise, but Saint has to leave first because I am a coward and can't say goodbye. He turns over his shoulder, and just as he's done countless times before, he steals my breath.

"запомни, я всегда рядом."

I don't know what he just said, but a single tear betrays my inner turmoil.

He watches me closely, and does something which tears me into two.

He smiles.

It's not something I see often, but I will treasure forever his parting gift.

He nods once, exhaling, then opens the door and leaves me to deal with this torment within. For the first time in fifty-three days, I am truly alone. Only when his footsteps grow faint do I wrap my arms around my middle and let the tears fall.

Sara rushes forward and hugs me tightly as we both weep for the men who have left our lives.

I thought I knew what pain felt like, but right now, I feel like a switch has been flipped, and my life has been shrouded in nothing but darkness.

"Wh-what did h-he say?" I stumble over my words as I sob into Sara's shoulder.

She rubs my back, her tears reflective of my own. "He said, remember, I'm always next to you."

But honestly, how could I forget?

CHAPTER EIGHT

Day 54

Your journal sits in my lap where it's been since you left. You told me it holds the answers I seek, but I'm afraid because I know once I open it, I will have to face this— alone.

Running my fingers over the leather-bound cover, I wonder where you are and if you're safe. All of this can't be for nothing, so with that as my mindset, I take a deep breath and open the book to the first page, which is our beginning.

Unable to help myself, I stroke over the paper. The indents from your handwriting have me remembering the last words you spoke to me.

Remember, I'm always next to you.

How I wish you were here now, but having this with me gives me the strength to persevere and focus. The first entry is a flowchart of sorts, and in the center, the number three has multiple circles around it. Branching from this are arrows with words that mean nothing to me.

The fairest of them all is underlined twice. An arrow extends outward from this puzzle with *six dwarfs* written in block letters. Saint needs to touch up on his Disney because Snow White had seven dwarfs.

The next arrow simply says *Shaken, not stirred*, which is a James Bond quote, and *seven deadly sins* with *+2* is the next thing circled.

What does this all mean? From memory, there isn't a movie called Seven Deadly Sins with a sequel.

The last arrow is something I actually recognize.

A good friend will always stab you in the front.

It's an Oscar Wilde quote. But what does it mean? These are connected to Alek and The Circle somehow, but I may as well be reading Russian because none of it makes a lick of sense.

More notes are connected to these points, but I decide to flip to a different page because the harder I think about it, the more confused I become. However, when I turn the page, I wonder if Saint was high when he wrote this because I find a hand-drawn sudoku puzzle, but the numbers don't correlate.

Saint doesn't make mistakes. I've seen him complete these puzzles with ease, so why is this puzzle riddled with errors?

The next page and the one after that are just rows and rows of numbers. They seem to be divided into sentences, which is ridiculous, seeing as there are no words. What is he trying to tell me? I flick through page after page of similar riddles. Some with numbers and the others with quotes or simple words underlined. And some are just symbols I've never seen before.

He told me this journal contained notes on The Circle, and to beat my enemy, I need to become them, but right now, all I'm becoming is delirious. Groaning, I stretch my neck from side to side as I'm sitting at an odd angle on the bed. My back is to the cameras, so anyone looking in remains clueless to what I'm really doing.

I wish Saint could explain this to me because I'm honestly baffled by what all this means. I toss the journal onto the bed, but when it opens to a page, and I see writing, sentences I can comprehend, I reach for it quickly, hoping to make sense of something. But nothing can prepare me for what I see.

> She won't break. No matter what I do, she will not submit. Each time I punish her, I feel whatever small shred of humanity I have left slip away. I know this is wrong but so is delivering her to that soulless asshole.
> I don't have a choice. God save my soul.

Looking at the date, I see this is when we were on the yacht. Day six of my being held captive, to be precise. I read over his musings with my heart in my throat because he has detailed everything. My fumbling fingers can't keep up as I flick through the pages, gasping when I see he has written down everything—from beginning to…now.

I start from the day that kick-started this entire nightmare, which seems like a lifetime ago.

Page after page, I am privy to Saint's most inner thoughts and feelings, which is ironic because, at the time, I was certain he wasn't capable of the latter. But as I continue to read, I experience our story through his eyes. I've lived it, but seeing me how he does is just extraordinary.

I'm not sure how long I sit, reading over each journal entry because the further I get, the blurrier the words become, thanks to my tears. At first, he is angry, angry with the world, but that soon turns to confusion, as it did with me.

When we were shipwrecked, I would have given anything to know his thoughts, but when I read a particular entry, I realize I knew what he was feeling all along because I felt it too.

> Being with her erases the pain, and I will move heaven and hell to protect her. I will figure out another way to save Zoey, but I can't give her to Popov.
> She is mine.
> She always has been.

Unable to stop the avalanche of tears, I hug the journal to my chest and sob silently. I wish I'd known this then, because now, all I can do is remember those memories and clutch onto them tightly. Saint knew I would read this when he gave me his journal. He wanted me to know just in case…

A breath catches in my throat at the thought.

If something were to happen, use this to save yourself.

That's what he told me. I now know it was a double-edged sword. Knowing he feels this way about me, that he's felt this way for so long, has me quickly wiping away my tears. I will save us both because everything I just read…I want to hear them pass through those lips I've come to love to kiss and intend to kiss for the rest of my life.

I spring from the mattress and rush into the walk-in closet, hunting through the endless garments I've never cared anything for. But now, they will help me get out of here. Alek wants to dress me up like a prized pig and parade me around to his friends, and thus far, I've fought him. But no more. As Saint said, to beat my enemy, I need to become them, and what better way for that to happen than to dress up like the doll Alek wants me to be.

I shower, ensuring to use the lavish body gels and lotions Alek has provided for me. Once I'm scrubbed clean, I dry off and begin the laborious chore of getting ready. I lather my skin in cream and perfume before slipping into a sheer black bra and matching thong.

Next, I work on my hair and makeup, putting as much care and effort as I would if getting ready for a show. Usually, I would have endless makeup artists and stylists on hand, but not now. There is only me, and that's okay because to survive this, that's the only person I can rely on.

It takes me over an hour, but once I pull back from the mirror and look at my reflection, it was time well spent. With the shorter hairstyle, there isn't much I could do other than sweep my bangs to the side and give a little body to the length. However, the ribbon headband encrusted with rhinestones and pearls adds to the look, and when adjusted in just the right way, it appears I'm wearing a crown, which is why I chose it. To pull this off, I have to act like a fucking queen.

My makeup is smoky, and I've tinged my cheeks a subtle rose. My lips are painted a bright blood red, which matches the dress I've chosen to wear. I've opted for one shorter than anything I've worn around Alek.

Leave a trail for a scavenger, and he will follow. Alek said that when referring to Kenny, and I intend to do exactly that but for Alek.

Alek wants me to submit to him and doing so will give me the upper hand. It's clear Alek believes he has feelings for me. One only has to look at what he did to Kenny, to Zoey for me, so I will play him at his own game.

Alek doesn't trust me. He believes with Saint out of the picture, I will succumb to his "charms" like all the other women before me. So I will behave how he wants me to, like the docile little lamb he paid a quarter of a million for.

And when he lowers his guard, because he *will*, I will strike. To get what I want, I will have to play dirty and do things I may not want to do, but I refuse to end up like Zoey—a shell of the woman I once was. This is the only way I can ensure I get what I want, and that's my freedom.

Taking a final look at myself in the mirror, I slip into my heels and hold my head high. Deciding to leave the switchblade under my pillow, I pretend I'm on the runway as I strut out into the hallway on the hunt for Alek. No surprise a guard stands at my door, but that will soon change. I'll make sure of it.

"Where's Alek?" I ask the man in the most innocent voice I can muster.

He grunts in response before gesturing with his head that I'm to follow. That's all I seem to be doing of late but not for much longer. He leads me through this labyrinth while I scope out every door, every corner we turn because I will need to know these halls like the back of my hand. The trapdoor in the kitchen is still my best way out, but I have to bide my time.

We walk up the grand staircase and turn left toward an area that has been out of bounds until now. I've always wondered what was up here because we've always turned right when I was escorted here. The first thing that strikes me is how quiet it is. There aren't as many rooms as there are downstairs.

When we get to a double door at the end of the hall, my guard grunts once again. I assume that's to indicate Alek is inside. I'm clueless to what I'm about to face, but remembering my game plan, I knock softly.

Alek says something in Russian, which I'm guessing means enter because the man opens the door for me. He then leaves me alone to face the devil himself.

Alek sits behind a large desk, typing away on a computer without lifting his head. I close the door behind me and wait for him to speak first. When he finally lifts his eyes, I quash down my elation because it's evident my plan has worked.

He hisses in a deep breath through his teeth as he leans back in his black leather chair. He devours me from head to toe, his tongue sweeping out to lick his bottom lip. This is the first time he's seen me dolled up, and judging by the way he gawks at my breasts, it's safe to say he likes what he sees.

"H-hello." He clears his throat while I focus on the task at hand.

"Hi. I hope you don't mind me coming in here. I was lonely."

When he raises a brow, I wonder if maybe I've gone too far, and he can see through my ruse. But when he shakes his head and gestures with his hand that I'm to come closer, my worries subside. "I'm sorry I haven't come to see you. I've been busy with work, and I figured you needed some time to…"

Grieve? Calm down? Stop envisioning him on fire?

"I understand," I settle on as I walk toward him. A good submissive would kneel, but I don't want to rouse suspicion. So I stop on the side of his desk.

The perfume I applied generously has worked a charm because he sniffs the air and smiles. "You look absolutely breathtaking. That dress was made for you." I don't know if he means that literally because my wardrobe is creepily donned with clothes in exactly my size.

But I smile shyly in response. "Thanks. I wanted to dress up. I was hoping it would cheer me up."

"Oh?" Alek frowns, waiting for me to elaborate.

I take a moment because I don't want to appear too eager. "I know it makes no sense, but Saint has been my… мастер for so long, I feel lost without him."

One wrong move and Alek will have my head, so I play it cool. "I wanted to be honest with you."

He nods as a slow grin spreads from cheek to cheek. "I know it must be hard for you. You've come to rely on him."

"I have," I confirm, my lower lip trembling.

"Which is why I had to let him go. You understand that?"

"Yes, I know."

"Because you're mine. Not his." This is a complete power play for Alek to feel like a big man. So I give him what he wants because it means I will win in the end.

"I am yours," I say, blinking once. "And I know you want to make me happy…which is why you brought…Kenny here." His name gets lodged in my throat, but I persevere. "I never thanked you for doing that for me."

Alek tilts his head to the side as he strokes his chin, deep in thought. He is clearly gauging my sincerity. But when I think about Saint, about him telling me to do what I must to survive, I play the role Alek has wanted me to this entire time.

"Thank you."

He continues watching me as he rolls back in his chair, leaving a small space in front of him. "Come."

I walk toward him without hesitation but with baby steps. Up until a few minutes ago, I was fighting Alek every chance I could, so I need to do this slow. He wants me to kneel, just as I've seen Zoey do many times before.

With Saint gone, he is now my мастер, and I am to treat him that way. But submitting to this asshole stoops me to a new level of shame.

Alek is testing me because I know it's going to take a lot more than a wiggle of my ass and a few sweet words to win him over. So, without choice, I lower myself beside him and kneel. I do exactly as Saint taught me.

Head bowed. Eyes downcast.

I wait for him to see straight through me and send me to wherever he sent Zoey to be punished, but he does neither. Instead, with a touch I could almost mistake as tender, he runs his fingers over my hair.

"A crown," he says in a faraway voice, stroking over my headpiece. "It's fitting. For my queen."

A sadness overcomes me because although it seems I've achieved what I wanted, what price do I have to pay?

"Do you miss him?" There is no need for him to elaborate who.

"Yes," I whisper with sincerity because god, I do.

"That's expected," he says, not at all angered. Which is the reason I kick-start my plan into action.

"I know it's a lot to ask, but—" I pause with intent, enticing Alek.

He takes the bait. "What? You can ask me anything."

With my head still bowed, I softly reply, "Would you allow me to move into Saint's old room? I think it will help with the nostalgia. I must learn to move on, but he was all I knew."

I measure my breathing, not wanting my nerves to show.

Alek takes his time as it's clear he was not expecting me to ask him this. But there is a reason, and it has nothing to do with nostalgia and everything to do with Saint's room being camera free. If I'm to do this, then I need free rein. I can't be watched 24/7.

Just when I think he's going to say no, he surprises me and has me wondering if maybe this will work. "Of course. It makes sense. Saint was your мастер. You will always share a connection with him."

I nod slowly.

"Very well. If this will make you happy, then I will see that your things are moved into his room immediately."

I'm waiting for a catch, but there doesn't seem to be one, which surprises me.

"Thank you."

"You're welcome. See, all I want to do is make you happy," he says, cupping my chin and coaxing me to look at him.

When I do, I try my hardest to appear appreciative.

"Let's go out for dinner. You look far too lovely to waste it by staying indoors."

"Okay." The only way I can survive this will be to keep contact to a bare minimum. Besides, Saint was trying to achieve this all along; to make me behave.

Alek smiles, and if I didn't know any better, I'd say he was genuinely happy. But his happiness is spurred on by the fact he believes he has won with Saint gone and will be able to morph me into whatever he wants me to be.

Ignorance is bliss.

"Mr. Popov. It is lovely to see you again," the server greets us at the front door of some classy restaurant in town. When he runs to assist us, it's clear everyone knows who Alek is.

"Hello, Robert. Is my usual table available this evening?"

Robert's glance flicks to the secluded area on the second floor reserved for people like Alek. It's evidently full, but you don't say no to Alek.

"Of course. Follow me." He touches the earpiece and says something into the headset he's wearing. I'm guessing it has something to do with relocating whoever dared to sit at Alek's table.

Alek leads me through the very elegant restaurant with our arms linked. Golds and rich blues decorate the large room, and the white plates and sparkling crystal have been polished to perfection. A soft piece of classical music plays over the speakers.

Overall, this place seems to be a haven for people like Alek because it exudes wealth and superiority. Alek nods to a few people in passing while others turn to look at who ventures into their domain.

Robert removes the black rope from across the bottom of the staircase so we're able to go upstairs. It feels so snobbish to be segregated this way, but I follow Robert as he leads us to a small white booth toward the back. This table must be the best in the house because it allows us a superb view of our surroundings.

No one can sneak up on us as our backs are to the wall. It appears Alek's paranoia extends to his dining.

As we take our seats, Robert places the menu down in front of Alek, not me. The move makes my blood boil as it seems Alek has brought other women here before. Therefore, Robert knows Alek's women are his property who don't even have the right to order their own food.

However, before Robert has a chance to pour us some water, Alek grips his wrist, startling him. "She will have a menu also."

Robert's eyes widen in horror as Alek releases him. "Of course, Mr. Popov. Apologies. I didn't think—"

But Alek cuts him off. "That's right. You're not here to think. You're here to serve me and my girlfriend."

Now my eyes widen. Girlfriend? Is that what I am to him? He definitely never treated Zoey like a girlfriend, but it appears I'm different because I'm permitted the luxury of ordering my own meal.

Sweat gathers along Robert's brow despite the cool temperature. He passes me a menu, which I accept. "Would you like to order the house wine? It's a beautiful red imported from Italy."

I'm perusing the menu, which is thankfully in English, when Alek asks, "Would you like wine? Or something else?"

I slowly lift my gaze, wondering if he's really addressing me because since when do I have a choice? But when he waits for me to answer, it seems I do when eating. "Sure," I reply in a small voice. "Wine sounds good."

Alek nods while Robert exhales, then scampers off. He's most likely thankful he's leaving here in one piece. I continue reading over the menu, but nothing stands out because eating is the last thing on my mind.

"Do you need any help deciding?" Alek asks, appearing to want to please me. "I highly recommend their beef stroganoff."

His kindness is so foreign to me because I would never use that word when referring to him. But I hate to admit he does show tiny glimpses every now and again, leaving me feeling conflicted. If he were always the coldhearted bastard I know he is, hating him and plotting his demise would be so much easier.

But when he shows his humanity, I almost feel guilty for wishing him harm.

"I don't think I could stomach something so rich." Which is true as I've eaten next to nothing since this ordeal began. Eating wasn't high up the survival chain. "I think I'll have the cabbage soup."

Alek nods, pleased with my selection. "Good choice. The food here is really superb."

"So you come here often?" I innocently ask, reaching for my water.

"Yes," he reveals casually. "A lot of my friends and I have used this place as a…" He quickly backtracks. "We enjoy their infamous pelmeni. Speaking of which, you must try them. I think you may know this dish as dumplings."

Alek never backpedals. He's always guarded with what he reveals. But his mistake has cost him as he let it slip that he and his friends frequent this place. Could some of those friends be a part of The Circle?

"Will I meet more of your friends?"

Alek smiles, gently reaching for my hand on the tabletop. "Yes, you will. You will be introduced to my world because now, you are a part of it."

I blink once, stunned by his admission. If anyone bar a psychopath were to utter those words, I would be swooning, but coming from Alek, I can't help but think he has an ulterior motive. "I will take care of you. I know all of this is very…" He searches for the right word. "Weird. But you will soon come to think of Russia as your home. As well as me."

The evident sincerity in his tone once again throws me for a loop.

"I will try my best, but it'll take some time."

"I understand. I wouldn't expect it any other way. Saint was right about you."

I gulp, as hearing his name still hurts.

"He said you were different. And you are."

"Is that why you treat me differently?"

Alek arches a brow, tightening his grip on my hand. "Differently?"

I have to watch my words. "I can't help but compare your treatment of me to how you treated Zoey. You're…kinder to me." I choose that word to praise him because what egomaniac doesn't like their ego stroked?

It works.

"You and Zoey are miles apart. You are a fine wine while she is…street food."

This food analogy turns my stomach. Street food? Common? Easy? Basic? Is that how he sees her?

"I thought…what is the term you Americans use? Slumming it?" he proposes, looking at me for confirmation.

I nod slowly, insulted for Zoey.

"Ah, excellent. Slumming it would be fun. And it was at first. But Zoey was uncouth, and in the end, I wanted a lady. Besides, you are a challenge, and I like challenges. There is something quite extraordinary about you."

His compliments are meant to leave me with the warm and fuzzies, but they only have me more confused. "Thank you. I think."

My comment wasn't supposed to be funny, so when a low chuckle leaves Alek, I stare at him like he's an alien. "You are really one of a kind."

Robert returns with our wine and carefully pours our drinks. "Have you decided what you'd like to order?"

Alek releases my hand. "Yes. Thank you. We will have a serving of the meat pelmeni. And I will have the steak. Rare. And the red beet salad." He closes the menu and passes it to Robert.

I don't know why I assumed he would order my meal for me, but him allowing me to do something simple like place my own order feels liberating. "I'll have the cabbage soup. Thank you."

I pass my menu to Robert who nods with a big smile. "Wonderful choice." It seems we're suddenly best friends because I am someone of "importance." From his reaction earlier, I think it's safe to assume he hasn't seen one of Alek's "girlfriends" before.

He makes himself scarce, leaving me alone to make small talk.

But what does one say to someone imprisoning them against their will? How's the weather seems completely ludicrous.

A small thought scratches at the surface that once upon a time, Saint was also my captor, yet I had no issues talking to him.

"I wanted to talk to you about the masquerade ball," he says casually. As if devirginizing me in front of a bunch of strangers isn't a big deal. "I know what you heard sounds awfully…confronting. But I wanted you to know that I will make it as comfortable for you as possible."

"How?" I spit with heat. It's out before I can stop myself.

Alek reaches for the glass and swirls the wine around before taking a sip. "The way my friend Oscar explained it probably has you thinking I'll throw you down on the floor and fuck you senseless while everyone cheers me on."

My cheeks heat at the description. "And aren't you?" I challenge, folding my arms across my chest.

"You mistake my affections for you. I would never do that. Not to you," he adds as my next comment would have asked if he's done it before. "We will be in my bedroom with only a few close friends in the room."

No guessing who these friends will be.

"You will be under the covers. It will be discreet. This isn't something new or perverse. It's been happening for centuries throughout many cultures."

His flippant explanation pisses me off. "I assume a white sheet will be laid down so your 'close friends' can ensure your bride is a virgin?" I air quote, annoyed. "This is completely barbaric."

I don't care that my docile act has slipped. There is no way this is right. And nothing Alek says will ever change my mind.

"I don't expect you to understand. We are from different worlds. And I realize how hard this is for you." But he doesn't realize jack shit.

"You have no idea what it's like in my position," I rebuke, shaking my head. "It's easy for you. All you have to do is roll on top of me, wiggle around for a few seconds, and then get a pat on the back for a job well done."

My voice is raised, and I am shooting daggers in Alek's direction, so you can imagine my surprise when I witness a small smirk tug at his full lips. "Is that what you think of me?"

His question catches me off guard, but I soon recover. "You *really* don't want to know what I think of you right now."

No doubt my act is up, and Alek will guarantee my soup is poisoned so he can wipe his hands clean of me. But I'm beginning to see that I should never expect anything when Alek is involved. "On the contrary, I want to know everything."

He shuffles closer toward me in the booth so our knees touch.

"If you think that's what sex is like"—his voice drops an octave lower as he leans into me—"then I am so pleased to be your first. I will worship every inch of this glorious body, ensuring no part is left untouched."

I swallow in disgust but can't hide my embarrassment when I feel my cheeks flush.

"And only when you're begging for me...is when I will show you what making love is."

I'm expecting him to press his lips to mine, give me a sneak peek of what he promises, but he doesn't. He simply pulls away and reaches for his wine like he didn't just speak sweet nothings into my ear.

I need a moment to gather my thoughts because what the hell was that?

How dare he assume he can win me over with a seductive voice and some empty promises? Does he expect me to bat my eyelashes and drop my panties now that he's fed me some bullshit lines? He has another thing coming if he does.

And I want him to know it.

"I will never beg," I promise.

Alek leans back in the booth, extending his arm out to rest on top of the plush leather. "Never say never, дорогая."

"What does that mean?"

He smiles and it's genuine, which startles me. "A number of things, but to me, it means precious, which is what you are."

I'm thankful when a lady saunters over to say hello because I need a breather from this conversation. However, when I peer up and meet her icy blue eyes, that gratitude turns to dread. Something shifts in Alek, and he appears regretful she caught him in a vulnerable moment.

"Alek, you didn't tell me you were coming here this evening. And with a friend, no less." Although her words are playful, nothing about this woman is lighthearted.

Her monster heels add to her already tall stature. Dressed in a black jumpsuit, she has a gold laurel leafed headband positioned perfectly in her long ebony hair. Something about her feels…familiar, but not in the sense that I've seen her before.

She must feel me staring because she focuses her attention my way. "I'm Astra," she says, her gold bracelets jingling as she gives me a small wave. "Alek and I have been longtime friends. Isn't that right?"

Her gaze flicks to Alek, who nods, although something

about his demeanor has me wondering why he's suddenly so uptight. "Yes, that's right." He's quick to recover, but I didn't miss him clamming up. "This is Willow."

She purses her ruby lips and examines me closely. "Oh, it's great to finally meet you. I have heard so much about you."

She has?

It's the most bizarre feeling. Why does it feel like I should know her?

She begins to toy with the ruby pendant around her neck, sizing me up. Something turns lethal in Alek as he watches her fingers closely. "I'm so pleased to finally meet the guest of honor. We all can't wait for the ball. Alek has been keeping you, among other things, a secret."

My cheeks heat as I clutch my thighs to stop from throwing my knife at her head.

She clearly knows the real reason for this ball, which means she's one of the "close friends." Could she be a part of The Circle?

She definitely looks the part of wicked witch with her long black hair and ruby lips…

The fairest of them all…

An epiphany hits, leaving me winded. Oh, my god.

Alek and Astra make small talk while I frantically skim over Saint's journal in my head. I didn't understand what he was trying to say because I was looking at it the wrong way. He has left me breadcrumbs, clues he knew I would eventually work out because what he left me was a…code.

The incorrect sudoku puzzle should have been enough of a clue because Saint doesn't make mistakes. The sentences made of numbers decipher like a Morse Code as each number represents a letter. And the sudoku puzzle is the key to figuring out what each number means.

I can hardly contain my excitement.

I then remember the ambiguous flowchart. They are people. Three people, to be precise. And Astra is one of them.

But I need to be sure.

Saint said six dwarfs. I glance around the room, looking for any clues, something which will confirm my hunch. And when I see it, I stop myself from leaping from my seat and screaming amen.

In a larger booth a few tables down, I see six men. From their look alone, one can see they aren't here to enjoy the fine dining. They are here to protect their…queen. They keep a very close eye on Astra, which confirms they are here for her.

"Let's talk about these matters another time," Alek says, a clear warning that Astra is crossing a very thin line.

His caution has me snapping from my thoughts to focus on what's going on around me.

"Gladly, but you're too busy, it seems, of late, to discuss anything with your friends."

He is? This is news to me.

"And we have much to discuss." Astra may be smiling, but a grievous threat lurks beneath. She isn't a woman who appreciates being ignored.

"Chow—"

The moment I hear his name, a tremble passes through me. Alek senses my discomfort and quickly shuts Astra down. "Now is not the time." He is seconds away from ripping off her head.

I'm watching the ultimate standoff because Astra doesn't seem like the type to back down. She eventually nods even though her anger is palpable.

"Very well then. I'll see you very soon, Willow."

Astra's grin should fill one with warmth, but it does the complete opposite for me. She appears to be sizing up her prey.

I nod in response.

She saunters back to her table, waving to a few people along the way.

Robert arrives with our food, and although it smells delicious, eating is the last thing on my mind. I need to get back "home" and decode Saint's journal.

Alek reaches for the napkin, offering to plate up a serving of pelmeni. "I'm sorry about that. She doesn't know when to quit. Bon appetite."

His apology surprises me.

"Bon appetite," I reply, but unbeknownst to Alek, I am hungry not for food but, rather, for uncovering what the hell is going on.

CHAPTER NINE

Day 56

"Ugh," I groan, falling back onto the pillows. Massaging my temples, I wonder if the action will help me see through the fog clouding my brain for the past two days.

Saint clearly gave me more credit than I deserve because I'm no closer to decoding his journal. After dinner, I moved into his old room. It surprised me how quickly he was replaced because apart from the wallpaper, the bedroom looked completely different.

It saddened me that my things were brought in because I would have preferred to sleep in a room where his scent and presence still lingered. But Alek wouldn't have it. It seems out of sight, out of mind, but Saint never strays far from my thoughts.

I haven't heard from him yet. I assume he has a lot to take

care of. Zoey, for one. I wonder if he'll take her back home or rehabilitate her here, saving their parents further heartache. I have so many questions, but sadly, those answers will have to wait because until I hear from Saint, I'm left guessing.

I scoured the room for cameras, and when I was pretty certain I was not under surveillance, I perched myself on the bed with Saint's journal on my lap and went to work. It didn't take me long to work out that The Circle has three game players.

Astra is one.

The Oscar Wilde quote had me guessing that Saint was hinting Oscar, the vile man I met nights ago, was another imperative piece to the puzzle.

Which just leaves me with one more person.

I have stared at Saint's clue for endless hours but am at a complete loss at what seven deadly sins +2 means. The numbers in the sudoku box are even more cryptic. It's so frustrating because I know the answer is there, but I just don't know what it is.

When a knock sounds on my door, I quickly spring into action and hide the journal under the mattress. The switchblade sits in my back pocket. I'm ready. But when it opens and I see Sara, I sigh in relief. She enters and softly closes the door behind her.

"Sorry, I didn't mean to startle you. We need a secret knock."

I smile because, in light of everything, it's nice to have a comrade in arms.

"I have to be quick, but I have a letter. It's from Saint." I watch as she hunts through her pocket to retrieve an envelope.

"You saw him?" I ask, my trembling voice betraying my happiness.

She nods and walks over, passing the note to me. "He's still in Russia. In a safe place. With Zoey. He told me to give you this. It'll help with figuring out his journal."

"Yes!" I exclaim, unable to hide my excitement.

Unable to wait, I rip the envelope open and unfold the sheet of paper. The moment I see Saint's handwriting, a nostalgia hits, and I slump onto the end of the bed, afraid my feet won't hold me up. I scan over it, and even though it doesn't make any sense, I clutch the paper to my chest, needing a minute. "Ho-how is he?"

Sara appears just as nostalgic as I am. "He's Saint." Her response elicits a playful scoff from me because I know what she means. "He wanted me to tell you he made a new friend."

I pale, bracing for the worst, but what she says has me laughing.

"Harriet Pot Pie the Second?" She phrases it as a question because to anyone but Saint and me, it doesn't make a lick of sense. "He said you'd know what that means."

"I do," I confirm, unable to stop smiling. "It was the name of my pet chicken when I was shipwrecked with him."

Sara nods with half a grin.

"Chicken would mean he's probably out of the city then?"

"Yes, he's hiding somewhere remote, no doubt, but he didn't tell me where. He knew where I was because this time every week, I pick up Alek's shirts from the dry cleaners. Just like clockwork."

"Thank you, Sara. I know this is dangerous for you."

She shakes her head. "I will do anything to see Alek go down. He has to pay for what he has done. I have to go. I'll check in on you later."

When she closes the door behind her, I slowly peer down at the note, which is the alphabet divided up into four grids, similar to the sudoku boxes. I stare at them, completely puzzled. Beside them is the alphabet, but beneath each letter are symbols I have never seen before. Some have dots in them.

Underneath that is just a row of numbers, reaching twenty-five. Beneath that are sums. And a lot of them. I decide to start with them because they are your basic equations.

0+3=3

7+1=8

And so on.

I know Saint loves math, but this is ridiculous. There is a pattern, but why couldn't it be as easy as ABC...

However, when I take a closer look, I see that it is.

Unable to keep up, I quickly finish the answers and then match them with the letters in the alphabet because each answer correlates to a letter.

0 is A

1 is B

2 is C

When I match the answers, they read:

Ahren, I'm sorry for the secrecy. I couldn't risk anyone intercepting. I

had to do it this way in case they found my journal. The above code is pigpen cipher. It will help you decode the journal. The sudoku box works in a similar way.
Stay safe.
Saint.

I read the note endless times because never have I been so happy to see a bunch of numbers in my life. You expect to see something like this in a James Bond film. I wonder which actor would pull off this ploy best, seeing as there have been many actors who have…

Oh, my god.

Scampering off the bed, I drop to my knees and reach under the mattress to retrieve the journal. I flick open the pages crazily, and when I reach the sentence I'm looking for, I holler in excitement.

Shaken, not stirred. Seven deadly sins +2

I know the seven deadly sins like the back of my hand as they were drummed into my head at Sunday School. They are: pride, greed, lust, envy, gluttony, wrath, and sloth. Could plus two mean the second sin, which is greed?

It makes sense.

Could Saint be telling me that my James Bond likes to gamble? Or is just plain greedy? But there are a million other famous James Bond phrases he could have used. What's the importance of using this particular one?

From memory, Sean Connery was the actor who first said this famous catchphrase. So what's the importance of that? That mystery will have to wait, however, because I have about a hundred or so pages of secrecy I still have to crack.

Settling against the pillows, I reach for a notepad and pen, determined to put James Bond to shame.

I've spent the entire day combing over the journal, and I haven't even made a dent yet. But I won't allow that to deter me because what I have uncovered has me desperate to unearth it all.

From what I can tell, there is no fixed number of members in The Circle. The "club" is exclusive and only known to trusted friends. However, there are four main members, and Alek is one of them. I have figured out three of the four.

Astra, otherwise known as The Ice Queen, was born in Ukraine, though I wouldn't have guessed it as I didn't hear an accent. But just like Alek, these people are chameleons and fly under the radar to remain undetected for what they really are.

Saint was a little light handed with the information on Oscar, which leaves me wondering why. I can't shake the feeling that something between them is personal. He made it clear he is interested in Saint, and I think if he were to pick, Saint would be his number one.

There are notes on where they meet, who they deal with, and how they keep their little club a secret. All members have something to lose if their dealings became public because the shit they've done is truly horrific.

Human trafficking. Sex slaves. Embezzlement. The list reads like something out of a true crime novel.

These people are far more dangerous than your average criminal because not only do they have power, but more importantly, they also have money. And money talks—no matter your crime.

I have the addresses, occupations, and the connections these people have, but there is still so much more to learn. Saint said this journal would save me, and he's right. Once I decode everything, I will have enough dirt on all of them to bring them down.

I just need to find the weakest link.

I can't stop looking at the quote Saint used for Oscar.

A good friend will always stab you in the front.

Could he be trying to tell me that Oscar is, in fact, just that?

Needing a break, I decide to raid the refrigerator to hydrate before I go back to the books. I have no idea where Alek is as he hasn't checked in on me, and I don't know if that's a good or bad thing. Once I've hidden the journal, I walk down the quiet hallway, wondering where everyone is.

Finding the kitchen empty, I can't help but glance at the hidden trapdoor. I wouldn't get three feet before I was dragged back by my hair. I will just have to wait for further instruction from Saint.

I hunt through the fridge, grabbing a bottle of water and what looks like leftover potato salad. I don't actually know how many people reside here because I rarely see the same face twice. Most people come and go in this place. Sadly, I'm not one of them.

As I'm gulping down my water, a man enters, and judging from his black combat getup, he's one of Alek's guards. "I was told to come and find you."

His English is exceptional.

"You found me," I quip, instantly disliking him.

"You're to come with me."

"To where?" I ask, capping the water bottle.

"You will see soon enough."

All this ambiguity makes me nervous.

"I'm not going anywhere with you," I state, ready to lunge for the knife block if he takes a step toward me. "Where is Alek?"

It's ironic that I'd feel safer with him here because something about this man makes my skin crawl.

Clearly not one for small talk, he says, "Look, you may have fooled everyone else, but I see you for what you are. So you either come with me willingly, or I make you."

I wet my dry lips. "I haven't fooled anyone," I argue. "If I had, would I still be here as a prisoner?"

He has the gall to laugh. "Prisoner? Is that what you call it? Zoey was never allowed the privileges you have."

Oh, shit. This is personal for him because he speaks her name with affection. Then a thought hits me. Does he know where she is because if he does, then he will know where Saint is too?

It's a long shot, but I'll try anything.

"Fine then. Lead the way." I wait for him to turn around so I can hide the paring knife in my pocket, but he reads me loud and clear. Without a choice, I move forward, and he only begins to walk when we are side by side.

I'm regretful I left the switchblade behind.

I have no idea where he's taking me, but it's evident wherever Alek is, he isn't here because he leads me toward the garage. A black SUV waits for us. He opens the door and shoves me into the back seat.

"Hey!" I yell, shuffling over as he slides in after me. He remains unaffected as he tells the driver where to go.

We pull out into the dead of night, which is when I take note of the time. It's after eleven p.m.

"Where are we going?" I ask, but it's in vain as I'm ignored. The driver turns up the stereo while the psycho beside me taps away on his phone.

Sighing, I wonder if I can pull on the handle without detection. Yes, I may fall to my death, but it's a risk I'm willing to take.

But he beats me to it. "Don't even think about it. The child lock is on. Seems appropriate."

"What's your problem?" I snap, glaring at yet another captor of mine.

"I have no problem. I just don't like you."

"I'm sorry," I sarcastically quip. "Have we met?"

"Believe me, I've tried to keep our interactions to a minimum. But when Alek calls…"

"Then what beef could you possibly have with me? I'm sorry if Zoey was your friend, but it's not my fault she's gone."

"Enough talking!" he says in a raised voice. "This *is* all your fault. Zoey was discarded and punished horribly because of you. She doesn't deserve that."

"And I deserve this?" I question, spreading my arms out wide. "I don't want to be here."

"That's what they all say," he mutters, turning to look out the window. "But you're different. Alek allows you this... freedom, and I don't understand why."

"Freedom?" I scoff, unable to contain my anger. "Is this what you call freedom? Being here against my own will? I will happily, *happily* leave. Just give me an out and I'm gone."

He doesn't entertain me further. We travel the rest of the journey in silence.

I've become accustomed to traveling in the darkness. Like a thief in the night, that's how I live my life these days. We drive out of the city and into a clearly upperclass neighborhood. My palms begin to sweat. Why does Alek want me to meet him out here? I'm hardly dressed for a late-night gathering.

If we are to reach our destination soon, I need to act now. "What's the problem? Now that Zoey's free of Alek, you can visit her anytime you like," I say to the man whose name I still don't know.

He tenses when he hears me utter her name. "I don't know where she is because, thanks to you, Alek threw her out like some street whore. Does that bother you in the slightest?"

Damn, there goes that idea. I thought he may have disclosed her location.

Putting my game face on, I shrug as I can't draw attention to my interest in Saint. "No. She can go to hell for all I care. She's the reason I'm here. Maybe if she wasn't such a crazy bitch, Alek would have kept her around."

I hear the whack before I feel the stinging pain in my cheek.

"Don't you ever speak that way about her again!"

I move my jaw from side to side as I cradle my face. How dare this motherfucker put his hands on me.

Without thought, I cup my hand and jab him in the throat. A strangled wheeze leaves him as I've caught him unaware. Saint's training has come in handy.

Even though he gasps, face turning a deep crimson, he reaches out, ready to throttle me, but I'm prepared and am about to strike out again.

"Touch me again. I dare you," I challenge, primed on gouging out his eyeballs.

"Max!" the driver exclaims, looking at us in the rearview mirror in horror. His warning settles the war—for now.

No matter how much I am despised, Alek's men know better than to lay their hands on me. But it seems Max's affection for Zoey knows no bounds. And I can use that.

My assailant, Max, has just become a pawn. He doesn't know where Zoey is, but I may be able to find out from Sara if Saint reveals where they are. Just what would he do for this piece of information?

But now is not the time to barter with him because when a tall steel double gate slowly opens, it seems I've reached my destination. I look from left to right as this mansion has to belong to someone of importance.

The gardens are green and vast, and the imposing house looms in the distance. To anyone else looking in, they'd be impressed with what they see, but to me, I just see yet another jail. The driver parks the car and speaks to Max in Russian.

"Let's go." Max is still breathless, thanks to me punching him in the throat, but he grips my bicep and drags me out of the car.

"Whose house is this?" My question remains unanswered. He continues hauling me around until we reach the front door. It opens without him ringing the doorbell.

The man who stands before me reveals I am in so much trouble.

"Ah, you made it." Oscar stands in the doorway, wearing a red velvet robe and holding a cognac glass. He looks like a fucking cliché.

On instinct, I shrink back, desperate to flee, but Max still grasps my arm in a punishing grip. I'm not going anywhere.

"Is Alek inside?"

Oscar hasn't taken his eyes off me, and I can't shake the feeling that Alek has no idea that I'm here. "Let me go." I wiggle against Max, but the action spurs Oscar to move from the doorway, granting us entry.

I'm dragged into what I presume is Oscar's home, struggling every step of the way. Both men ignore me and chat among themselves. I need a weapon. Or an exit. Anything. I examine my surroundings, but everything passes me by in a blur as Max continues to manhandle me.

When we venture down a long hallway, I dig my heels into

the carpet, not liking the sudden devious vibe. Oscar opens a door to what looks to be a dining room. However, I have the sneaking suspicion we're not here for food.

No one else is present inside, alerting Max to what I already know. "Where is Alek? You said he'd be here."

Oscar smirks, the sight not at all pleasant. "I did?"

Max's face falls as he knows his oversight will cost him. He attempts to reach into his pocket for his cell, I assume, but two men appear out of nowhere and stop him. Now he's the one to be manhandled as they drag him from the room, kicking and screaming.

When they shut the door, I rub over my arm where my flesh stings from Max's fingers digging into me and look around. A large table holds a silver candelabra burning candles brightly, setting a mood which turns my stomach.

"I'm sorry for all the mystery, but Alek wouldn't let you out of his sight. I thought we could get to know one another without any distractions." Oscar finishes his drink and places it onto the mantel.

"Why?" I ask, genuinely curious.

He gestures for me to take a seat. But I'd rather stand.

"Something about you intrigues so many. Alek. Saint." I'm unable to hide my response when he says his name, and Oscar reads it instantly.

He circles me, just as a shark would of their prey. "The moment I saw you two together, I knew he felt something for you that I didn't think he was capable of ever experiencing."

"Excuse me?" There is no need for him to explain who he speaks of.

"He watched your every move. You moved. He moved. He was drawn to you like a moth to a flame," he explains, coming to a stop in front of me. "He cares for you."

My chest rises and falls, betraying my nerves.

"So I need to know what makes you special."

I'm so sick of hearing this. "I'm not special. I'm just me."

Oscar shakes his head slowly, reaching out to brush a strand of hair behind my ear. "I need to find that out myself."

In a quivering breath, I ask, "How?"

When he takes two steps back and snaps his fingers, I know I'm about to regret my question. The door opens, and a man and woman, who I've never seen before, enter. They are both absolutely breathtaking.

The man looks like a Greek god and the woman a blond goddess. The man only wears what I can describe as baseball pants, and they don't leave much to the imagination. The woman wears a sheer sarong dress tied around her neck. The transparent material reveals she's naked beneath.

Instantly, I turn my cheek, embarrassed to be looking at them when so scantily dressed. I can't imagine they enjoy being paraded around half naked this way. However, it's a different story for Oscar.

"Please, there is no judgment here," he says, gently coaxing me to look at them. "This is Dominic and Ingrid."

Those names caused Alek to freeze. At the time, I remember wondering who these people were, but now that I've met them, they are no doubt Oscar's playthings. Just as I am Alek's.

Still, the question remains…why am I here?

"What do you think of them?" Oscar asks, sweeping his hand out toward them.

They stand motionless with their eyes straight ahead.

"They look terrified," I reply, stating fact. I may be bound to Alek, but I owe nothing to this asshole.

"Terrified?" he questions, cocking his head to the side. "I doubt that. How about we ask them? Ingrid, come."

Without hesitation, Ingrid walks over to Oscar, head bowed as she awaits further command.

"Is it true? Are you terrified?"

Ingrid slowly shakes her head, but it's clear she's lying.

"You see, you heard it yourself. No one is terrified." Oscar grins, daring me to challenge him. "I'm not sure what household Alek runs, but here, we're all friends. Aren't we?"

"Yes, sir," both Dominic and Ingrid mumble.

Sickened, I close my eyes, needing a moment.

"Why am I here?" I'm done with the small talk. If there is a point of me being here, I'd rather he put me out of my misery now.

Oscar pats his leg, as a master would to a dog, motioning for Ingrid to drop to her knees. "I told you, I want to know your worth."

As he pats Ingrid's head, I glare furiously, so sick of these people thinking they have any right to degrade another human being. "Well, let's get it over with then."

Oscar's lips twitch. "Dominic, I want you to tell me if she's as sweet as she looks."

Time stands still, and my bravado suddenly fizzles.

Dominic meets my eyes with nothing but regret as he

steps to command.

Instantly, I back up, feeling around for a weapon, but it's useless. "What are you doing?"

Oscar stands on the sidelines with Ingrid at his feet as he watches his sick dreams come to life.

"No, please don't," I beg Dominic, but he's just as much a prisoner as I am. "Why are you doing this?"

"Because Alek owes me," Oscar replies. "And you have what I want."

Dominic stalks me as I dance around the table, pushing chairs in his way, hoping it'll buy me some time. "What do I have?" I exclaim, sick and tired of these games. "I have nothing!"

"That's where you're wrong. You have the one thing I want and can't have."

The game of cat and mouse ends as Dominic lunges for me and grips my wrist, dragging me toward him. "No!" I cry, thrashing wildly. I try to use my self-defense training, but Dominic is strong, and I'm panicking, forgetting everything Saint taught me. "Whatever it is, you can have it!"

Oscar clucks his tongue, a look of genuine loss passing over him. "I wish that were true."

"What is it?" I am hysterical because when Dominic clears the table with his forearm, sending china crashing to the floor, I know there is no escape this time. No matter how hard I fight him, I'm doomed. He throws me onto the hard surface, fumbling with my zipper as I desperately try to slap, punch, and kick him. I get in one punch, but he barely feels it.

The fight in me dies when Oscar reveals why we're here.

"Saint. I want him, but I can't have him… because of you."

"He isn't mine to give!" I exclaim, kicking and flaying my arms to keep Dominic off me. But he continues to pin me to the table with ease.

"You're right, but maybe he'll change his mind with you gone."

"You're fucking crazy!" I spit, turning my face to look at Oscar. "You can't buy people's love. You earn it. But I wouldn't expect a monster like you to understand that! So do what you will. It won't change the fact that you're right." I stop fighting, narrowing my eyes. "You can't have him…because he's mine. And he always will be."

Oscar's mouth parts in utter shock as I've just confirmed his suspicions. But I don't care. He's about to destroy me anyway. So this is my final fuck you.

I stare up at the ceiling as Dominic yanks off my jeans. My underwear is next to go. I'm lax, detached from my body as he removes my tank. When he removes my bra, he lowers his body down onto mine and whispers a hollowed, "Sorry," into my ear.

But I understand. It's either him or me.

"Fuck her," Oscar demands, knowing how humiliating this is for me, seeing as my first time will be with a stranger as I'm pinned down.

There is a tremble to Dominic's touch as he grips my chin and presses his lips to mine. He kisses me, attempting to coax me to reciprocate, but I'm numb. He begins touching my naked body, over my breasts and down my stomach.

A single tear slips free, but I accept my fate. I am tired, so fucking tired of fighting. Is this how Ingrid and Dominic feel? Is their spirit broken too? After a while, the fight in one will die because how many times can one get back up after being knocked down time after time?

I brace for my innocence to be shattered once and for all…but it never comes.

"What's the matter? Do it!" Oscar screams, but to my surprise, Dominic shakes his head and slowly rises off me.

I don't know what's happening? Is this yet another cruel joke? A false sense of security before they destroy me for good?

"I-I can't. Forgive me, but I can't." He meets my eyes and nods an apology as he bends to pick up my T-shirt.

I stare dumbfounded, not sure what's going on.

But Oscar storms over, beyond livid as he punches Dominic in the stomach, resulting in him buckling over with a pained grunt. "If you want something done, then you've got to do it yourself."

Dominic tries to roll away but is too late as Oscar kicks him in the side, stomach, back. Wherever he can strike him, he does. Ingrid screams, rocking backward and forward, pulling her hair as she watches the horror unfold.

I spring up, still very naked, ready to take this bastard down with my bare hands, but he turns and slaps my cheek. The force is so great, I stagger backward, trying to catch my breath.

"We will see what Saint thinks when I send you back to him in teeny-tiny pieces." The threat isn't empty, and I run for my life, clutching my side as I'm winded.

The door suddenly bursts open, and when I see Alek, I am actually thankful he's here. When he sees my very naked state, his confusion turns to absolute pure rage. "дорогая?"

I can explain everything later because right now, I just want to flee.

"Let's go," I pant, intent on running out the door. But the two men who subdued Max stand guard. They don't mask their leering, which has me covering my modesty with my hands.

"Oscar, what is the meaning of this?" Alek shouts, standing in front of me to shield me from prying eyes as best as he can.

Oscar is breathless, and his usual cool demeanor has slipped as he brushes the tousled hair from his eyes. "I was just getting to know your дорогая. That isn't a problem, is it?"

I peer at Oscar from around Alek's taut frame. Of course, it is. So why isn't Alek stringing him up by the balls?

Oscar reveals why. "Because I didn't have a problem when you did the same to my Ingrid. Isn't that right?"

I gasp, unsure what I'm hearing.

"This is hardly the same thing," he spits, shaking his head. "She wasn't running from a room, fearing for her life."

Alek quickly removes his jacket and turns, offering it to me. As much as I want to tell him to go to hell, I accept it and quickly slip it on. It comes mid-thigh and covers everything, seeing as he's triple my size. He nods, his eyes full of apology.

"Regardless, you had no qualms taking what was mine."

Alek swallows deeply, appearing…remorseful for the fact. He turns back around to face Oscar while I shift toward the wall to watch this all unfold. "Yes, you're right. It was wrong of me. But that doesn't warrant you terrorizing Willow."

Ingrid's tears have stopped as she looks at Alek with nothing but affection. What the hell is going on?

"What makes her so different?" Oscar asks, gesturing his head my way. I use the wall as my shield and press my back up against it. "How does what I did differ from what you did? Didn't you take what was mine and do with her as you pleased?"

"Enough," Alek warns, the air thick with tension.

But Oscar doesn't take the hint. "No, tell me. I want to know."

Alek storms forward, towering over Oscar as he bellows, "I actually care about Ingrid's well-being! You are doing this merely out of spite. *That's* the difference, *friend*. Willow means more to me than you'll ever know! Touch her again, and we'll have a problem."

The room falls deathly silent while I blink once, winded by his confession.

I have no idea what's going on, but could it be Ingrid and Alek were a thing? It sounds like it. He did say Alek owed him. So kidnapping, raping, and murdering me were his way of getting even?

But Oscar didn't take me to get back at Alek. He did it because of Saint. My eyes widen because he now knows about Saint and me. Oscar seems to read my thoughts and meets my terrified stare. "You're right. I'm sorry, Alek. I don't know what came over me. Please accept my apology."

Alek looks like he'd rather eat glass, but he eventually

nods. "Let's never mention this again. We don't want anyone else to find out about this indiscretion."

It's a threat. If Oscar doesn't back off, Alek will ruin him.

"Very well. Water under the bridge."

Like hell it is, but when Oscar trains his eyes my way, he makes it clear he has the upper hand as he knows my secret. He knows without a doubt that Saint is coming for me now that he's free.

"Can you forgive me, Willow?" The arrogant bastard. He knows I don't have a choice. If I make a fuss, he will tell Alek about Saint and me. "If there is anything I can do to make it up to you, please let me know."

This will end in one of our deaths. That is the only way. But for now, I nod. "Let's go, Alek."

Alek stands rigid as I can only imagine him leaving is a sign of weakness. If he'd gotten here a second later, god knows what he would have found.

When he doesn't move, I gently reach for his bicep. "Please. I just want to go home."

The word is out before I can stop myself, and it's the first time I have referred to my prison in such a way. Alek's shoulders eventually drop before he turns around and nods. "Okay."

Ingrid sniffs, reminding us that she doesn't have the luxury of leaving. She and Dominic are trapped in this hell forever. Dominic's back rests against the wall as he clutches his side, breathing deeply through his bloody nose. I can't leave them to the mercy of Oscar especially after what Dominic did.

He could have been a monster, but he showed humanity.

And I have to do the same.

"There is one thing," I say, hoping this doesn't backfire. "Don't punish them."

Alek is taken aback as I've spoken out of line, but he allows it.

Oscar swallows, not happy with my request, but he's in no position to argue. "You have my word."

Dominic peers up at me and nods his gratitude. I may have saved him this time, but who will be there the next time and the time after that? Ingrid weeps, covering her beautiful face with her hands. Alek grips my elbow and leads me out the room.

Max stands by the front door with his tail between his legs. He fucked up—epically. When I meet his eyes, if possible, there is more hatred than before. But he opens the door and leads us down the stairs to the idling SUV.

I can't get in fast enough. Alek slides is after me while Max takes the wheel. The moment he puts the car into drive, I sigh in relief, sagging against the seat. I have never been happier to leave a place. There is silence, but it speaks volumes.

"Are you all right? Did he…" There is no need for him to elaborate.

"No, he didn't. Dominic didn't do what he wanted."

"Son of a bitch," he mutters under his breath. "So typical of him. Making others do his dirty work. I'm so sorry this has happened. None of it is your fault." He makes clear who is to blame as he glares at the back of Max's head. "Luckily, Max was able to do one thing right and called me when he did."

Max avoids looking at us in the rearview mirror, and

instead, he focuses on the road. But that soon changes.

"It's not Max's fault," I say, which has him meeting my eyes with nothing but curiosity plaguing him. "He thought he was doing the right thing. No doubt Oscar lied to him, making him believe you were waiting for me. Oscar is a manipulator. I've seen it myself."

One might ask why I'm saving the ass of the man who delivered me to the devil. The reason is, I need as many allies as I can get now that Oscar knows the truth.

Alek sighs, running a hand down his face. It's the first time I've seen him rattled. "You're right."

Max nods, expressing his gratitude. But this doesn't come without strings attached.

"Goddamn him! I'm so sorry you got caught up in his sick games." He grips the leather seat beneath him, causing it to squeak under the force. If I didn't know any better, I'd say he actually cares. But he isn't capable of such a human emotion.

Then why did he save you? says a voice, which I quash down quickly.

"Will he hurt Ingrid and Dominic?"

Alek shrugs, unfastening a button on his shirt as it seems he is having trouble breathing. "No, I don't think so. They are safe. For now. That was very noble of you to ask for their clemency."

"Did…did you really do what he said?" I know I'm treading dangerous waters, but what have I got to lose?

Alek turns to look out the window, but he eventually replies. "Yes. I was wrong to do what I did. Ingrid was not mine, yet when she slipped into my bed, I didn't say no. Oscar has every right to hold a grudge."

"What kind of world is this?" I whisper, so broken and alone. A tear runs down my cheek.

"Please don't cry." He sighs heavily. "I'm...sorry."

Sorry? He's apologizing for what, exactly? He's done so much.

"When will this end?"

I'm expecting Alek to give me the same spiel I've heard a million times before—that this is how they do it here—but he doesn't.

He doesn't say a word.

CHAPTER
TEN

Day 60

The masquerade ball is in two weeks. That's all I have. Two fucking weeks to get the hell out of here if Saint doesn't pull through.

I'm proud to say I have finished decoding the journal, but now, the question is, what am I supposed to do with this information? I could blackmail Alek because the dirt on him spans for years. But after he came to my "rescue," doing that feels almost…wrong.

Compared to the other game players, Alek's crimes are far less callous. Yes, he's Russia's number one drug lord, mafia boss, and all-round bad guy, but unlike Oscar, whose cruelty I witnessed firsthand, Alek's crimes are all about power and money.

The people he's in possession of came to him either voluntarily or they were used to settle a debt, like me. But apart from Sara and me, it seems after a while, these people don't want to go. Look at Zoey. She did everything in her power to stay.

Because he will worm his way into your soul.

Her words still echo loudly because when they were first spoken, I scoffed, believing that would never happen to me. But I can't deny that being around Alek doesn't…repulse me like it once did. He's almost pleasant at times, making it hard to plot his demise.

However, I only have to remember why I'm here, and such nonsense soon disappears.

When I hear a knock on my door, I quickly hide the journal in its usual spot and wait for whoever to enter. It's Alek.

"Hi, I haven't caught you at a bad time?" he asks. I'm standing in the middle of the room not really doing much of anything.

"No, it's okay. I was going to read." I gesture with my head to the newspaper on the nightstand. "But it's in Russian, so you know…I don't read Russian."

Alek's lips twitch. "I was wondering if you'd like to accompany me for lunch. I have some business to attend to in town." He looks a little casual for a business meeting in khaki pants and a white button-down shirt.

I arch a brow. "Business?"

He nods but doesn't disclose what that business is.

The last time he had business to attend to, I witnessed a lot of bloodshed. I can't stomach a repeat performance.

He must read my apprehension. "It's a business meeting

with the mother superior who runs the local orphanage. I am a benefactor and like to check in from time to time."

My mouth hinges open as I can't hide my utter surprise.

Alek laughs in response. "Thought I was just a bad guy, right? I know what it's like to be hungry. And to not have a home."

I'm speechless because I wouldn't expect him to do something like this. Giving money to an orphanage is thoughtful, kind, and generous, and I would have never associated those qualities with Alek—until now.

"Sure, I'll come. Thank you for asking me."

Alek smiles, catching me off guard again. "I'll wait for you outside. Take your time." And with that, he closes the door, allowing me to get ready.

Once he's gone, I stare into space, unsure what just happened. I suddenly feel off center as though everything I thought I knew has been tipped on its side. Sure, the money is dirty, blood money, but does that make the food it buys or the shelter it provides for the children any less substantial?

I hate that the answer is no.

Those children have no home and no family, so that money provides them with a small comfort most of us take for granted. Thanks to Alek, they can go to sleep with food in their bellies and have a safe place to lay their heads for the night.

Exhaling, I wonder why Saint failed to mention this in his notes. It shouldn't make a difference, but it does. And I don't know why that is.

Shaking my head to dispel such thoughts, I quickly

slip into a pair of jeans and boots. I have on a light knitted sweater which seems appropriate for a meeting with a mother superior. Ensuring the journal is tucked away securely, I open the door and see Alek standing outside, scrolling through his phone.

He looks up and smiles.

All this smiling throws me for a loop.

"I thought I'd drive us today."

"Really?" I ask incredulously. "You know how to do that? Drive, I mean."

I'm not trying to be funny, so when Alek chuckles, I look at him like he's grown a second head. We walk to the garage in silence, and only when the lights flicker on the flaming red Ferrari, deactivating the alarm, is the silence broken.

"I certainly do," he says, referring to my comment as he opens the door for me. "Buckle up."

The inside is sleek but also ostentatious. This car's worth could feed a small starving nation.

"Don't you like it?" Alek asks, getting into the driver's side.

"It's okay."

"Okay?" He smirks, reaching for his seat belt. "Most wouldn't refer to riding in a Ferrari as just okay."

"I'm not most," I counter with lightning-quick speed.

Alek nods, adjusting the mirrors before kick-starting this beast to life. "I'm beginning to see that."

I don't have a chance to reply because he tears out of the garage, the tires squealing to keep up. I squeak and ensure my seat belt is fastened because he wasn't joking when he said to buckle up. He drives the road with ease, his steel blue eyes focused ahead.

"Where are your men? You never leave home without them," I say, turning over my shoulder to see no cars are following us.

"On some occasions, I venture out alone."

I scoff in response. "Up until a few days ago, you had a personal bodyguard. That's not exactly venturing out alone material." Now that the topic is breached, I ask, "Are you getting a new one?"

"New what?" he questions, his eyes never leaving the road.

"Bodyguard. Hitman. Whatever you want to call it." I don't know the right terminology.

Alek takes his time to answer. "Saint was one of a kind. It'll be hard to replace someone like him."

I keep a straight face, not wanting my emotion to show.

"If that's the case, then why did you let him go?"

"Because it was time. He's served me well. But I gave him my word." There isn't a lick of deceit in Alek's words. He truly means them.

Regardless of their relationship, it's evident they both respected the other. I remember Saint once told me that Alek was a man of his word. It's all so primitive. And fucking weird.

"Do you miss Zoey?"

Alek turns his chin slowly to look at me. "No," he replies flatly. "You can't miss something you never had."

I ponder on his statement as I'm unsure what he means. "And what was that?"

His breathing is shallow, but when his fingers tighten around the steering wheel, I know my question has stirred something in him. "I never loved Zoey."

"Oh," I reply, swallowing deeply.

"She was a...satisfying companion but not a game changer."

"How can you speak about people that way?" I question, shaking my head in disgust.

"I'm honest, Willow. Unlike most, I speak my mind. I don't have time for pretenses." He shrugs as though that is a valid response.

"You dispose of women," I argue, cutting through his holier than thou crap. "When you grow bored, you trade them in for an upgrade. Something faster. Fancier. Less complicated."

"Is that what you call yourself? Less complicated?" he questions with an amused grin. "If that were the case, I would have disposed of you the moment we met."

Turning in my seat to glare at him, I state, "I make no apologies. My husband, who actually only married me to trick me, sold me to you. Like a cow at market. I think that warrants my behavior, don't you?"

"Your husband is a weak waste of space. Don't punish us all for his cowardly actions."

"That's rich! *You're* the reason for his cowardly actions." I turn back around and slouch in my seat with a huff. How dare he try to see himself as anything but a monster.

He gives me time to stew, but as usual, he has to have the last word. "You may think that, but I never forced his hand. He knew the stakes when he agreed to play that game of poker."

"I'm not a bargaining chip," I spit, refusing to let this go. "Accepting payment was your choice. No one forced *your* hand."

Alek opens his mouth but closes it soon after. He focuses on driving instead of engaging in an argument I will never back down from, which surprises me. He could punish me for my insolence, but he doesn't.

I don't care what he says; nothing will ever excuse what he did. Yes, Drew is also the villain in this story, but Alek could have said no. Yet he saw this as an opportunity to accumulate another pretty thing for his collection.

When we pull into an older part of town, I realize that the business will be taking place at the orphanage. I thought it would be over lunch in a restaurant, but it appears Alek likes to keep me guessing.

He parks the car in front of a large white building. Although longstanding, it radiates sincerity and strength. Tall brick walls wrap around the premises, allowing privacy and safety for the children inside.

I now understand why Alek drove here without any backup. This place is hardly dangerous. But not only that, it also isn't the appropriate place for his men in black. It would scare the children, and they have had enough fear in their lives.

We walk toward the steel gate, where Alek presses the intercom. Someone speaks to him in Russian, laughing at something he says in a low, flirty voice. The gate then opens.

I can't stop my eye roll. How can someone be so smooth?

He's a murderer, liar, not to mention a drug lord, yet he has all these people fawning over him. It's sickening. His charisma knows no bounds.

Children of all ages laugh and scream as they play ball games and tag behind a silver fence. When they see us, the commotion stops, and they run toward their prison bars, looping their tiny fingers through the wire. It brings tears to my eyes as they watch us in hope. Is today their day?

Alek waves to them kindly, saying something in Russian. The nuns shoo the children away from the fence, encouraging them to continue with their games.

The place reeks of sadness but also hope. A perfect oxymoron.

I follow Alek as he walks toward the ramp leading to the double white doors. An older lady with kind green eyes in a full habit waits for us, smiling broadly. When we are feet away, she speaks in Russian.

"English, if you don't mind, Mother Superior. This is Willow. She has yet to learn our language."

Mother Superior nods with a smile. "Of course. It is nice to meet you," she says in broken English, but I appreciate her effort.

"You too, Mother Superior. Thank you for having me."

"Any friend of Aleksei is a friend of mine. Please, won't you come inside." She gestures we're to enter. Alek signals for me to go first, so I do.

The interior matches the exterior. Although old, it's not impoverished or dirty. It's bright and filled with colorful pictures painted by the children. Mother Superior leads us down the hallway where I look into the windowed doors of the children's rooms.

Painted in pretty pastels and filled with toys and well-made beds, it appears each room holds four children. As we advance farther, I see the nurseries, which hold about twenty or so newborn babies. Nuns rock the crying children or feed them a bottle. They are so tiny. So helpless.

Alek waves at the nuns through the glass, who smile and return the gesture.

I suddenly feel so…sad. So out of sorts. How can someone like Alek who inflicts so much pain also be able to show such humility? It doesn't make any sense. But it's clear the nuns, who are pure and only wanting to do good, are happy to see Alek.

I feel sick to my stomach as my world is once again tipped on its side.

Mother Superior opens the door to her small office and welcomes us in. "I am so happy to see you, Aleksei. How have you been?"

"Good, Mother Superior. Always busy, but good."

We take a seat in front of her desk, waiting for her to speak.

"I wanted to thank you for your latest donation. It was—"

But Alek stops her with a sharp shake of his head. He doesn't want gratitude. "Please, let's not talk about that. Tell me how the kids are doing."

"Considering their circumstances and where they are, they are as good as good can be. We've been able to add many books to the library as well as purchase new toys. Did you notice we painted?"

Alek nods. "I did. It looks wonderful. How are the adoptions going?"

"Slow," she confesses. "But it's God's will. We have to trust Him as He has a plan for everyone." I notice her gaze drifts to the cross around my neck, similar to the one which hangs over her habit.

"Willow's father was a religious man," Alek explains. "A minister in America."

Mother Superior smiles. "What brings you here?"

I'm expecting Alek to answer for me, as he wouldn't want me to spoil his reputation, but he doesn't. He sits back and awaits my answer.

"I—" I clear my raspy throat. "I'm here, helping a friend." Not entirely untrue.

"Well, thank you for visiting us. Aleksei is a wonderful man. This place wouldn't exist without him."

I don't know what to say as I wonder if Mother Superior's attitude would be different if she knew who Alek really was. But maybe she already does? It's a small sacrifice to turn a blind eye to where Alek's money is coming from as long as it's for the greater good.

However, in this circumstance, do two wrongs make a right?

It's a question for God.

But when a young nun pops her head around the doorway, declaring lunch is served, my questions will have to wait.

After we had lunch with the nuns and the kids at the orphanage, we bid them farewell. The kids seemed to know Alek well, and after watching him interact with them, I couldn't help but feel something other than hatred toward him.

He wasn't acting. His feelings were sincere. He spoke to them and even played ball. I stood watching, unsure what to make of all this. Hating him when he's a monster is easy, but when that mask slipped, I saw something I never thought Alek was.

A human being.

His childhood was the reason he threw millions of dollars into this place. He said he knew what it felt like to be unloved and hungry. But with his profession, does he not realize that by dealing drugs, he is inadvertently destroying the lives of children outside these walls? Or he may even be the reason some were in there in the first place.

My moral compass is screwed. It can't choose which way is north anymore.

Needing a moment to process today, I was silent on the way back to Alek's. However, when something popped and our chariot veered to the left, it seemed we needed a detour. A tire had blown, leaving us sitting in a tow truck on the way to some Ferrari dealership to have it replaced.

Alek knows the driver, and they're speaking fluent

Russian, but I don't mind. I don't have the energy to make small talk. We pull into an industrial area and head for the enormous Ferrari workshop. Alek hasn't pressed, but he knows something is on my mind.

The driver parks the truck and goes about unhooking Alek's car and pushing it into the garage. "I'm sorry we had to take a detour. My mechanic said it wasn't as easy as just changing the tire. He wants to make sure no damage was done mechanically."

"It's okay."

"I hope it won't take too long," he replies, exiting the truck and offering his hand to help me down. I can't bear to touch him right now, so I shuffle along the seat and hold the doorframe as support to jump down.

He steps back, allowing me the space I need. I know I'm testing his patience, but I can't pretend.

A man in oiled jean overalls walks over to us, wiping his greasy hands on a rag. Alek and he speak for a few moments before Alek translates. "He thinks it should only take about forty-five minutes. There is a lounge if you'd like to wait in there."

Alek, being the control freak that he is, clearly wants to oversee the repairs. Or maybe he is giving me the space I need. Scoffing, I eradicate that thought because Alek doesn't do anything unless it benefits himself.

"May I use the bathroom?"

The man must understand me because he points at an isolated building behind the garage with a smile.

"Спасибо."

Alek's mouth parts, revealing his surprise that I just thanked the man in Russian.

I don't stick around for any praise, however, and make a quick dash for the restrooms. The moment I'm inside, I lock the door and lean up against it, taking three deep breaths. My heart beats wildly, and I'm shaking uncontrollably.

I don't know what's come over me.

I catch my breath and decide to use the toilet while in here even though it was just an excuse to escape. The cubical is small, but the confinement helps calm my nerves. Once I'm done, I wash my hands and peer at my reflection in the mirror above the basin.

Today has shifted something inside me, and I don't like it. Everything was clear-cut. Take Alek down, ensure he pays for what he's done, and leave this country with my freedom in hand. But now, I can't stop thinking about the faces of those unfortunate orphans and the impact that will have on them.

If I end his life, I will inadvertently be ending theirs too because Mother Superior hinted that Alek's generous donations keep the orphanage afloat. If they stop, then the work they do will be hindered, and hundreds of children will suffer because of the vengeance of one.

It's not fair…to any of us. I'm stuck at a moral crossroad once again.

A sharp knock sounds on the door, hinting that another customer needs to use the amenities. I splash some water onto my flustered cheeks, hoping to wash away some of this remorse I feel. Another knock follows, more desperate this time.

"Just a minute!" I call out, quickly drying my hands on the paper towels.

The person at the door is clearly desperate as the knocking grows more frantic. Not wanting to impede their call of nature, I quickly unlock the door and am about to apologize, but a hooded figure bursts through the door, pushing me back inside.

Panic overcomes me.

It happens so quickly, I don't have time to process what's happening. However, my fight or flight suddenly takes over, and I make a mad dash for the exit, desperate to flee. But when the cloaked figure slowly removes the hood from his head, revealing their identity, I stagger backward, blinking frantically.

It can't be…

"Ангел."

"S-Saint?" My brain can't seem to accept the fact that he's here, he's really here, and plays it off as some cruel trick. It wouldn't be the first time. However, when he advances forward and passionately presses me into his chest, I know this is really happening.

"Oh, my god," I cry, unable to stop the tears when I breathe in his scent. "You're really here?"

"Yes, I'm really here," he confirms, pressing his lips to the top of my head. "I had to see you again. Even if for just a moment."

I want to say so many things, but I can't. Words escape me, so I simply feel. We hug one another so tight, I can barely breathe, but it's still not close enough. I can't get enough of him, and I bury myself deeper.

"Are you all right?" he asks, frantically stroking over my hair before cradling the back of my neck.

"I am now," I whisper, squeezing him tightly. "How did you know where I was?"

"I'm the reason the tire blew." I don't care how he made that happen; I'm just so glad he's here. "Has he hurt you?"

"No," I reply, inhaling deeply as I can't get enough of his scent. "Are we leaving now?"

Saint gently breaks our connection so he can look at me. His chartreuse eyes spark to life, and I sizzle under the intensity. I wish I could look at him forever, but I know we're on a deadline. "No, not yet. I don't have a solid plan, and I won't risk your safety that way."

I can't hide my disappointment.

"Hey," he says, cupping my cheek. I instantly melt into his touch. "I promise, soon."

"When?"

"The night of the masquerade. I'm working through the finer details, but soon, I'll have everything organized."

"What organized?" I place my hand over his.

He inhales deeply. "Alek has really pissed off Oscar."

"What?" I almost lose my footing as I sway backward a step. I'm shocked to discover he's in contact with that monster. "You know what happened?"

Saint's jaw clenches as he exhales steadily. "Yes. That motherfucker is lucky I didn't kill him for what he did to you. But I made sure he knows not to touch you again."

"What did you do?" I gulp.

"Just gave him a taste of his own medicine," he honestly states, which means he beat him within an inch of his life. "I'm so sorry he hurt you."

"It's not your fault."

"Yes, it is. But I need him for this plan to succeed."

I arch a brow. "I don't like the sound of this. Oscar can't be trusted."

Saint sighs, running a hand through his mussed hair. "I know, but he is the key to getting you out of there."

"And what does he get in return?" I hate to think what his payment will be in exchange for helping us.

"You let me worry about that. I will use him to get into the house undetected. I will be his plus one," he explains while I pale. "He isn't happy with Alek coming into his house and disrespecting him and is more than happy to see him pay."

"He didn't disrespect him," I argue angrily. "He saved me from being raped and god knows what else."

Saint's dark brow arches as he cocks his head to the side. "Saved you?"

I quickly backpedal when I realize what I've just said. "I didn't mean it like that."

"Then how did you mean it?" he counters, folding his arms across his broad chest. "Because you still remember he's the reason for all of this, right?"

"Don't patronize me," I snap. "Of course, I do. I am just stating the facts. If it weren't for him coming to Oscar's house, I probably wouldn't be here."

Something changes in Saint. "There are no redeeming qualities about that man. Don't ever forget that. He came to your rescue because he sees you as nothing but property. Do you know what he did to Ingrid?"

I shake my head as I don't know the full story.

"He saw an innocence in her which he had to pollute. He charmed her behind Oscar's back. And when she fell under his spell and he had his way with her, he discarded her, just as he does with the others every single time he grows bored."

I can't forget the look in Ingrid's eyes, however, and the fact Alek claimed he cared for her. She didn't look at him with repulsion. She looked at him with a lover's gaze.

"Don't fall for his bullshit. He will do the same with you once he's grown tired." There is a desperation to Saint's tone.

I don't like it. I want to leave. Now.

"Why can't we go now? Alek is distracted. We can make a break for it and not look back." I beseech he sees reason in my plan. But he doesn't.

"No," he exclaims, clenching his fists. "He has to pay for what he's done."

The room suddenly grows cold, and I have the urge to rub the chill from my bones. "By pay, you mean…k-kill him?"

"Yes. There is no other way." He doesn't miss a beat in his emotionless reply.

I knew it would come to this, but the thought sits heavily in my stomach. It shouldn't, but it does. "What about the kids in the orphanage? They rely on him for—"

Saint hisses sharply before stalking toward me. He grips my cheeks in his hands, forcing me to look at him. "Never forget where that money comes from. How many lives has he destroyed?"

"I know, but can't we just leave? I am so sick of…death and vengeance. It's all I've been surrounded with. I just want to forget."

His manner softens as he strokes the apple of my cheek with his thumb. "And you will. But I have to do this. Please understand."

"So this isn't just about my freedom. It's about revenge as well."

Saint averts his gaze, which is all the answer I need. "Please, trust me. I will atone for my sins for the remainder of my life, but I will never be able to rest until he gets what he deserves."

There is no compromise. This is set in stone. To attain my freedom, Alek has to die. An eye for an eye— but how can I live with myself knowing someone had to die to set me free?

I want to say so many things, but there is no changing Saint's mind. The night of the masquerade ball, he will make sure Alek pays for his crimes with more bloodshed and more pain. I don't know how, and maybe it's better he keeps me in the dark.

"I'm doing this for you. For the both of you." Regardless of what Zoey has done, Saint will avenge her.

Unexpected tears arise, but Saint shakes his head, wiping them away. "Don't cry. This will all be over soon. I promise."

I open my mouth, but Saint swoops forward and passionately claims my lips with his. He kisses me with a force so wild, he steals the air from my lungs. But who needs air when I've got this? I thread my fingers through his long hair, pulling his face toward me.

He groans into my mouth, lifting me to wrap my legs around his waist. He walks us backward until my back hits the wall. A whoosh of air escapes me, but his aggression is exactly what I need to feel alive. Our tongues contest, but each flick of his has me whimpering, turning into mush.

He suckles my bottom lip as he cups the back of my head, angling me so he can dominate every inch of me. Our kisses have always been filled with passion and need, but an urgency to this embrace has me holding him tightly in fear he will fade away.

His thicker beard strokes me, the coarseness setting my senses alight. I'm straddling the line between pleasure and pain, but with Saint, the two seem to go hand in hand. He rubs against me, growling when I gasp.

I want him with every inch of my body, and my pearled nipples pressing against his hardened chest attest to my needs.

"Oh, god," he pants from around my lips. He begins to work his way down the column of my neck, biting softly. "I am going crazy picturing him with you. Is he sleeping in your bed?"

"*What?*" I whimper when he suckles over my pulse. "Of course not. I-I'm in your room." Being coherent is a sudden issue as he works my body into a frenzy.

"You still want me?" His question drips with torture.

"Yes. Always." I throw my head back when he strokes over my aching center through my jeans. "Please…I need—"

I don't even know what I need. I just know I need and want more.

Saint reads me just as he always does. Yanking open my

jeans, he thrusts his hand down the front of my underwear. He isn't gentle, but it's exactly what I want. He inserts a finger into me, hissing when he feels how wet I am.

He holds me effortlessly as I buck and writhe against him.

"Tell me you're mine," he groans against my throat.

"I'm yours," I pant without pause, knowing why he needs to hear this.

He inserts another finger, stretching me so wide, I cry out in intoxicating pain. "I dream about what a life with you would be like. Away from all of this."

"Me...too," I manage to gasp as I chase my release.

His fingers are relentless as he coaxes me to come. "You give me something to look forward to. You eclipse my darkness and make me want to embrace the light."

"Oh, my god," I cry, clawing the back of his neck as I anchor onto him, afraid I will fall.

"I never thought there was an after...until I met you." He bites my chin before claiming my mouth as his because that's what I am. I am his.

He continues working me skillfully, circling over my ripened clit with his thumb. I shamefully ride his hand, getting lost in this feeling of utter bliss. He strains against his zipper, but this is for me.

"Come, ангел. Give me something to hold on to until I see you again."

His demands are reminiscent of when it was just him and me, lost in our own paradise and locked away from the world. What I'd give to go back to that island. What I'd give to be with him again.

When he moves his hand backward and forward, rubbing every part of me in just the right way, I grow lax and allow him to be my puppeteer. He buries himself deeply, fucking my mouth in rhythm with his fingers.

A string of sweet Russian leaves him before he flicks over my core with a delicious smack. It's suddenly too much, and my orgasm bursts from me with a strangled sob. Saint holds me tight, wringing every last tremor from me until I flop forward, totally and utterly spent.

I am breathless, and my heart threatens to spill from my chest. But I embrace this feeling because he's the only one who makes me feel alive.

However, this can't last forever. I know Alek will come looking for me soon.

When I stop trembling, Saint gently lowers me to my feet. Our eyes lock as he removes his hand and licks his fingers with delight. My cheeks blister, but I can't stop the feral whimper from escaping.

"You are so beautiful," he whispers sadly. We both know it's time to part once again. "I'll be in touch as soon as I can."

My head bobbles like a springy toy as I don't want to say goodbye.

He caresses my cheek, then lays a final kiss over the corner of my mouth. "Dream of me. I'll see you soon."

I reach out, clutching his shirt, desperate for him to stay. But he can't. He grips my fingers, nodding that it'll be okay. "I'm coming for you. I promise."

Saying goodbye shouldn't be this upsetting, but it's because I know the next time I see him, so much will change.

He gives me one final look, his chartreuse eyes luring me in and promising me the world. He opens the door, and just as quickly as he appears, he disappears, leaving me once more.

I stare at the door, hoping it'll open, but it doesn't. I'm alone again.

His scent lingers as does his touch on my skin. Each time he says goodbye, he takes a piece of my heart with him. But I will do what he says and dream of him until we meet again.

Quickly fastening my jeans, I wash my face and reapply some makeup, hoping to conceal the fact I was just entangled in my lover's arms. Once I look semi decent, I take a deep breath and compose myself. Saint is nowhere to be found as I step out from the bathroom.

I walk back to the garage, keeping my nerves in check as I see Alek talking to a man. When he notices me, he says a quick farewell and walks over. "Everything all right?"

"Yes," I reply in an even voice. "I probably shouldn't have had all that chili with lunch. I don't have any antacids. Can we please get some on the way?"

"Of course," he replies, eyes narrowed as he watches for any signs of deceit. But there aren't any. Saint taught me well. "The car is almost ready."

"Great. I really need to lie down." I leave out the reason that is.

Alek senses something is off, but he nods nonetheless. "I will make you some of my special broth when we get home. It'll help settle your stomach."

But it's not my stomach that needs settling. And when he reaches out to tenderly stroke my cheek, it just confirms the fact that I'm so screwed.

CHAPTER ELEVEN

Day 73

Tomorrow is the night of the ball, the ball that will change so much.

My dress hangs from the back of the door, and although it quite possibly may be the most beautiful dress I've ever seen, it taunts me. The pure white shade is no accident, no doubt implying my chasteness beneath.

The sweetheart neckline bodice is encrusted with shimmering jewels. The skirt balloons out layer upon layer of ruffled material. The quinceanera-style dress is rather lavish and over the top, which is exactly the point.

I don't know what tomorrow holds, but it can't be good. I haven't heard from Saint, but I guess that's because his plan is set in motion and there is no changing his mind. This time tomorrow, I will be free and Alek...Alek will be dead.

Since the day he took me to the orphanage, he's been pleasant, nice even. But I can't stop thinking about Saint's warning. Never forget just who he is.

However, when I hear a soft piece of music float across the still air, it contradicts everything.

From what I know, Alek and I are alone after the house has been bustling with commotion for the past two days. Caterers, party planners, gardeners, you name it, have been here as no expense has been spared to ensure tomorrow night's celebrations go off without a hitch.

I've dared not ask about the proper protocol regarding the "ceremony," and Alek hasn't mentioned it either. He has been quiet, and I can't help but think something is bothering him. I overheard him on the phone a few days ago chewing someone's ear off.

Although the majority of the conversation was in Russian, for the parts that weren't, he made it clear that he wasn't someone to be fucked with. I wondered why the person on the receiving end would ever question his authority in the first place. Wasn't it common knowledge that he was the top dog?

I then began to wonder if maybe there was a shift in power. Had someone challenged his throne? It all seemed like a storyline out of a bad mafia movie, but I can't stop thinking about Chow's last words.

You're going to regret this.

Has Alek's time come? Someone stronger, someone more powerful is always biding their time. If someone did challenge him, who would remain standing, loyal by his side? This is a dog-eat-dog world where loyalty is few and far between.

My thoughts drift to Astra. Something about her

encounter with Alek has played at the back of my mind. She mentioned Chow, but he immediately shut that conversation down. Why?

This entire thing grows far more complicated by the second, and even though Saint has a plan, I can't help but believe that getting out of here seems close to impossible. I can't shake the feeling that something wicked is coming this way.

And the melancholy of the piano keys only confirms this thought.

Deciding to find the source of the poignant music, I walk the quiet halls in the direction of one of the living areas where I've seen a piano. I peek my head around the doorjamb to find Alek lost in the music. His fingers work skillfully over the ivory keys as he plays a sorrowful yet beautiful piece.

I watch him for a moment, wondering what emotion he's tapping into to play something clearly from the heart. Which is ironic because I'm doubtful he has one. But seeing him this way, with his guard lowered, and the way he was at the orphanage, I'm beginning to see that Alek has many sides.

"Hello, дорогая."

His voice jars me from my thoughts, and seeing as my ruse is up, I step into the room without a word.

Alek continues playing, exhibiting his true talent as he closes his eyes and allows the music to take him over. As much as I hate to admit it, seeing him this way is…fascinating. There is something about seeing a man of his stature being this way. Being vulnerable.

He continues playing for minutes, each note even more

desolate than the one before it. It pains me, but he is a superb pianist. Some people are musically gifted, and he is one of them. When he's done, he hangs his head low, his chest rising and falling steadily.

"I didn't realize you played," I say, needing to break the sudden silence.

He exhales, then lifts his steel blue eyes. "All my life. It's the only thing that brings me peace."

I blink once, stunned by his honesty. "You are really talented."

"Thank you." A gentle smile splays across his weary face. It's only now do I realize how exhausted he appears. "I have something for you."

He rises from the polished piano, and I watch on with curiosity as he walks over to the mantel and retrieves a blue box. A white ribbon is wrapped around it.

"I-I don't want anything." I know I sound awfully ungrateful, but I don't want his gifts.

"I know, but please, just open it." He offers me the box while I peer down at it like it's a live grenade. "It's something I'd like for you to wear tomorrow."

"I definitely don't want it now." I take a step backward, shaking my head as images of obscene items come to mind.

Alek sighs, his last tether surely about to snap. I am actually surprised he hasn't reprimanded me sooner. God knows he wouldn't have let Zoey get away with being so disobedient. But with me, he seems to make an exception, which leaves me wondering why.

"It's not what you think. It's something to remind you just

who you are."

I arch a brow, a little curious. "Who I am?"

"Go on. Humor me."

Goddamn my inquisitiveness.

He shakes the box, coaxing me to take it. With a heavy sigh, I accept.

I untie the ribbon, astounded at how soft the silk feels beneath my fingertips. Whoever tied it did so with the utmost care. Deciding this is best to do quick, I yank open the lid, but what I see leaves me speechless.

I can feel Alek watching me, attempting to gauge my response. "Do you like it? I know it's a little over the top, but I thought it was fitting."

"H-how?" I ask when I finally find my voice.

"Nothing but the best for my queen."

And he means that in the literal sense because enfolded beneath the ivory tissue paper sits a gold tiara layered with red rubies. Matching drop earrings lay close by.

"How is this supposed to remind me of who I am?" The lights catch the vivid sparkle to the jewels as if eager to hear his response also.

Alek places his hands into his pockets, taking a moment to examine me. I stand unbending while he softens. "I know tomorrow is going to be… difficult." I scoff, unable to keep my contempt at bay. "But no matter what you think, never forget that you are now royalty. You are with me; therefore, you will always be respected and feared."

"I don't want to be feared," I state defiantly.

But Alek stands firm. "You will. You will soon learn that

fear gives you power."

And the egocentric asshole I've come to know has returned. "Is that all this is to you? A power play?"

It's supposed to be an insult, but it rolls off him. "No. I do what I have to, to survive. Like you."

Touché.

But I won't be compared to the likes of him. "We are *nothing* alike."

Alek takes a step toward me, pinning me with those intense eyes. "You may think that I'm a heartless bastard, but I'm a lot nicer than others who would do anything, and I mean anything, to be on top."

Now I've heard it all. "Really? Well, what have you done to get to where you are because from where I stand, you aren't exactly the moral upstanding citizen?"

Alek turns his cheek, appearing wounded by my comment. "If you think that of me, then I'm sorry I've given you that impression. The people you'll meet will soon change your mind because you'll come to learn that I'm not the big bad wolf. Someone is always crueler. Others will sacrifice everything to be in control."

A shiver passes over me because I suddenly don't think Alek is speaking in hypothetical terms.

"No matter if you believe me or not, I wish you could grow to at least like me before I take what's sacred."

My eyes widen, and all words escape me when he brushes the back of his fingers down my cheek.

"But things are expected of me. And to remain in control, I can't show weakness"—his eyes soften—"no matter how weak I feel when it comes…to you."

His admission throws my mind into a tailspin, leaving me feeling…confused. He can't actually mean it. This must be just one of his ploys to blindside me. But I see nothing but sincerity as he brushes a lock of hair behind my ear.

"If what you say is true"—I swallow down my nausea—"then you won't go ahead with tomorrow night. You will tell all those sick, twisted bastards to leave and never come back."

Alek sighs, his fingers gently caressing the shell of my ear. "I wish I could. But it's too late. If I were to do that, we both would be dead."

"I don't understand," I say, stepping away from his touch.

He seems saddened by the disconnection. "You will soon enough," he replies, indicating this conversation is over with. "Please think about wearing your gift. It will make me most happy if you did."

The box tingles in my hand.

"As much as I wish tomorrow could go a million other ways"—he pauses, inhaling deeply—"I am counting down the minutes, the mere seconds until I make you mine. I will ensure you enjoy every moment because I meant what I said."

Swallowing deeply, I question, "You've said a lot of things."

He smirks, thankfully keeping his hands to himself as he states, "You'll be begging for me." His comment isn't cocky. It's simply fact.

My cheeks heat for so many different reasons. "That'll *never* happen," I spit, sickened by his confidence.

He shrugs, placing his hands into his pockets. "We'll see. Stranger things have happened. Good night, дорогая."

I brace myself for a kiss or a touch, but he surprises me when he turns his back and leaves me standing like a dumbfounded fool.

The box in my hands rattles as I squeeze the sides, my body trembling in rage. The jewels stare back at me as I recall Alek's words. All of them.

I am not his queen. Nor will I *ever* beg for him to touch me. But something has shifted inside of me. I don't know what it is, but I don't like it. It has no right being there, and the need to flee suddenly suffocates me.

Without thought, I toss the box onto the floor because it makes me feel...dirty. The tiara rolls across the polished flooring, seeking refuge under the piano. It spins and comes to a stop, standing upright and regal, taunting me with what it represents.

But I will never be Alek's plaything because that's all I will ever be to him—his property. In light of his words, his actions will always speak louder, allowing me never to forget what he's done.

Tomorrow is too far away. I need to leave. Now.

Consequences be damned. I race out into the hallway without looking back as I only have one place I need to be. Thankfully, Alek is nowhere to be found, but even if he was, it wouldn't stop me. Better he kill me than feel this, this sympathy within.

The hatred I had for him is slowly ebbing away, and I am becoming what Saint, Zoey, what everyone predicted. He's worming his way into my soul and making me feel...this, whatever this is. And I hate myself for it. I should want him dead, but I don't. And something is very wrong with that fact.

My bare feet skid along the floor as I am focused on only one place, and that's the kitchen. I'm getting the hell out of here. Tonight. If that means breaking open that trapdoor, then so be it.

There is no one inside, which allows me to frantically remove the carpet over the secret doorway and try the handle furiously. Of course, it's locked. And no matter how hard I pull, it won't budge.

"Come on!" I cry out in frustration, peering around the room for a key.

Springing up, I open every drawer and cupboard, tossing everything out of the way as I desperately try to find my way out. There is no key, which has me focusing on the razor-sharp knives sitting innocently on the magnetic holder above the blender.

The metal of the cleaver shimmers like an arrow pointing me home. Without hesitation, I yank it down and race back to the trapdoor where I drop to my knees. If I can't open this door with a key, then I will break my way through it. I know Saint has a plan, but I can't wait. I'm fearful for my soul if I do.

The old wood splinters as I raise my arm and bring it down, cutting into the sturdy material. I am running on pure adrenaline, unsure what I plan on doing once I get through. But none of that matters. I just want to be free.

I hack into it over and over as sweat drips from my brow and collects at the small of my back. The sharp knife hardly makes a dent in the thick and durable wood. But I don't allow that to deter me. Each strike brings me one step closer to fleeing this betrayal within.

"Willow! Stop it!"

Sara's rattled voice cuts through my panic. However, I can't stop, even when she latches onto my arm to halt my motion. I am suddenly possessed, blinded by my self-loathing.

"I can't!" I shrug her off me and continue swinging the cleaver, each strike claiming back a small piece of my integrity. "I need to get out of here."

"You'll wake the house. Please. Stop." Her whispered pleas are filled with so much fear, alerting me to how selfish I am being.

I'm not just endangering myself. If Alek found the journal, if he knew Sara had been helping me, he would punish her and ensure Saint was found and dealt with in the most painful way possible.

Tears of anger stream down my cheeks because I am furious for being so fucking weak. "I don't hate him, and I should," I mumble in a jumble of hysterical words. "Saint wants to kill him, but the thought of him d-dead...it doesn't sit right with me. What's the matter with m-me?"

The cleaver tumbles to the floor with a defeated thud as I wrap my arms around my middle and curl in on myself, ashamed. I don't deserve Sara's comfort, but she gives it to me anyway.

"Shh, nothing is wrong with you," she whispers into my ear, drawing me into her arms. "Alek has a way of making you question everything. That's what a master manipulator does. It's just one more night. Saint is coming tomorrow."

This human contact, one most would take for granted,

centers me, and my heart rate begins to slow.

"You will be rid of this place soon enough. It'll be okay."

I stay cocooned in Sara's arms, allowing her to comfort me even though I don't deserve it. "How can I feel…sorry for him?" I whisper, needing someone to tell me I'm not crazy.

"Because you're not a monster," she replies softly, rubbing my back.

"But after everything he's done, how can I feel any kind of empathy toward him?" I don't understand any of this, and the only person who can explain it to me is god knows where, trying to set me free.

"I wish I could answer that question, but I don't know. But if it makes you feel any better, I understand." Wiping away my tears, I gently pull from her embrace so I can look at her.

She timidly brushes a lock of hair behind her ear. "After everything he's done to me and Hans, I still can't hate him."

"Why? What power does he have over us?" I don't understand.

"Because when you have so little, something small means so much, and in our case, that something small is kindness. Like a starving dog, waiting under the table to get thrown a scrap, we are thankful when we are shown any kind of mercy.

"Alek is our tormentor, but he's also the person who can make the pain go away. He is cruel, but when he's kind, he makes you forget how malicious he can be."

Saint said something similar long ago.

"What have I become? Before all this, I used to be a… saint." That word holds so much meaning to me, and it has nothing to do with my religious childhood.

Sara frowns, weighing my response. "Well now, you are a…fallen saint. But unlike a fallen angel, you were never given a choice to sin."

Her analogy appeases me somewhat.

"We need to get out of here." Now more than ever.

But when Sara lowers her eyes and tugs at her bottom lip, I grab her wrist. "He's coming for you too."

She shudders. "The possibility of freedom scares me."

I wait for her to explain.

"What do I have out there anymore? A family who forgot about me, that's what. The only person who cared about me is dead. I'm fighting so hard to break free"—she sniffs softly—"but nothing awaits me on the other side."

"Don't say that. Anything is better than here. We are getting out of here. Together," I add because I mean every word.

A ghost of a smile plays over Sara's lips, and maybe, even if it's a mere second in time, she believes it. "Saint really cares about you. I've never seen him with anyone the way he is with you. It gives me hope that someone will look at me that way again."

When tears stream down her cheeks, I'm the one to console her, and we sob together for our lost innocence. But hopefully one day soon, we'll find it again.

CHAPTER TWELVE

Day 74

I've done this countless times before. Dress in fancy clothes. Paint my face. Ensure not a wisp of hair is out of place. But this time is different because when I shed my skin, my future will be changed forevermore.

Once this silken garment pools at my feet, will it mean I am free? Or will the outcome have me wishing to never disrobe again?

Sara arranges the tiara in my once again long hair, thanks to the extensions she painstakingly clipped in. "You didn't have to put in the extensions. I'm happy with the way my hair is."

I peer at Sara's reflection in the mirror I'm sitting in front of, wondering what's going through her mind. She's a lot quieter than usual.

"But thank you, Sara. Thank you for everything." I reach for her wrist as she adjusts the hairpiece. "I suppose our hair looks a little alike now."

She instantly averts her gaze while biting her bottom lip. The gesture has me raising an eyebrow, and I get the feeling she's hiding something.

"You look beautiful," she says, changing the subject as she slips from my hold.

"What will you wear?" I ask as she's still dressed in her ratty maid's outfit. I wish she'd take something from my closet. She can have it all.

"I'm not invited," she replies, avoiding eye contact.

"That's bullshit," I cry, turning over my shoulder to look at her.

"I don't have anything to wear anyway." She tugs at her white apron, ashamed.

"Sara," I chastise. "You can wear anything from my wardrobe. You know that. I insist."

I attempt to stand, but she shakes her head. "I couldn't stomach being in the same room with those monsters anyway. I'd rather stay up here."

I don't press because I can't blame her. If I had a choice, I'd join her. But I don't.

Inhaling, I look at my reflection. I shooed away the makeup artist Alek sent to glam me up. I refused to be dolled up because to do this, I have to be as comfortable as I can be in my own skin.

My eyes are dusted with a shimmer and winged with a black liner. My cheeks are rosed. My porcelain skin boasts red lips. It's simple, but the rubies in my ears and hair are enough.

In what feels like another lifetime ago, I paraded clothes

and jewels like this without a second thought, but now, all of this feels so…superficial. So insignificant in the greater scheme of things. So much will change if—no, *when*—I leave this place.

A knock sounds on the door, rapping in time with my heart. I know who it is, but that doesn't make what I'm about to do any easier. Sara squeezes my shoulder in support. I place my hand over hers, unsure when I'll see her again.

"Tonight is our night," I whisper, nodding in assurance.

She swipes away a stray tear.

Coming to a slow stand, I examine my full reflection, wishing I didn't look how Alek wanted me to. But there is no denying that, coupled with the elaborate dress, opulent jewels, and monster heels to make me stand tall, I look like a queen.

And when another knock sounds at the door, it's clear the king doesn't like to be kept waiting.

"Tell me it'll be okay." I inhale deeply, hoping it'll help with the nerves.

Sara smiles, but the gesture is so bittersweet. "Saint is coming. Of course, it will be."

Turning, I give her a tight hug, unsure what the circumstances will be when I see her next.

I will never be ready for what tonight holds, but when I think I'm as ready as I can be, I break our embrace and make my way toward the door. When I open it, Alek stands before me, looking immaculate in a tailored tuxedo that accentuates his defined body.

His fresh cologne wraps me in a bubble of citrus and pine. His slicked-back hair highlights his strong features and full lips. He too looks the part of royalty, and when his steel blue eyes float up to the tiara in my hair, he makes it clear he's glad I relented to his request.

"You look…stunning." His pause isn't for effect, and the fact he appears to actually mean it has me shifting uncomfortably on my feet.

The commotion below hints our guests are arriving by the droves.

I close the door behind me, leaving Sara inside as it's safer for her in there than it is for her out here. I make an attempt to move, but Alek stops me when he reaches into his suit jacket pocket.

"It wouldn't be a masquerade ball without this." He produces a beautiful white mask, decorated with shining diamonds and lace. "May I?"

The mask offers me a sense of anonymity, so I nod.

He walks behind me and positions it over my eyes. I hold the edges in place as he gently ties the ribbon in a bow. Once it's secured, he walks back around to face me.

"боже мой." When he sees my confusion, he quickly reveals what he just said. "My god, you really are an angel."

A hollowness sinks low because Saint called me that. Having Alek say it is…unsettling. However, when he slowly brushes away a stray piece of hair from my cheek, his fingers lingering, that feeling multiples tenfold.

Before I have a chance to recoil, he lowers his lips to mine and…kisses me.

The shock of feeling his warm mouth move against mine leaves me standing motionless, too dumbfounded to move.

He caresses my lips with his before gently pulling away. Every part of me retches in disgust.

"I know you don't feel that way for me yet, but I hope, in time, you will."

That won't be happening in this lifetime. Or the one after that.

I watch as Alek dons a mask of his own. When it's settled over his face, I can't help but think how fitting the gold wolf mask is because he is just that tonight—a wolf in sheep's clothing.

"Shall we?" He offers his arm, and I peer down at it.

My chest begins to rise and fall as I am unsure how to get through the night without having a heart attack. I have no idea what I'm walking into. Saint hasn't divulged what he has planned, but he hasn't let me down before. I know he would have sent word if something was wrong, so I just have to have faith.

With that thought, I slip my arm through Alek's and allow him to lead me down the stairs. With each step we take, I can't shake this ominous feeling that we're both stepping into the unknown, which is ridiculous. But something sinister lingers in the air. I can feel it.

And when we descend the staircase and are greeted by a sea of faces, some friendly, mostly scowling, it just heightens the sensation that both Alek and I are in trouble. However, he doesn't seem to be in tune with my premonition because he saunters down the last step with confidence.

He doesn't release my arm as he greets a couple hidden behind extravagant Venetian masks. I scan my surroundings with my heart in my throat because I wonder if Saint is already here. He said Oscar was the key to get him past the guards standing post at the front door.

I notice a line of elegantly dressed people, waiting to walk through what appears to be metal detectors. These are new.

"Your safety is my only concern," Alek whispers into my ear as he must notice me staring at them.

If he thinks I'm afraid of guns, knives, and whatever other weapons his guests are inclined to, he's wrong. The only thing that scares me is standing right beside me.

The guards attach tags to the barrels of guns before they place them into a divided shelf behind them. It's all so orderly and how most would have a cloakroom for coats; Alek just has storage for weapons instead.

Once the gun is stowed, they give the patron their ticket and wish them well.

The house has been transformed into a baroque-themed paradise with music to match. The debonair outfits also complement the vibe. The women are dressed in elegant dresses in all shapes and colors. No expense has been spared. The men are either decked out in tuxedos or fine silk suits.

Everyone hides behind their mask, which gives them an air of ambiguity, and will lead to scandal and mystery, no doubt, as the fine champagne runs freely throughout the night.

Alek leads me through the throngs of people. At a guess, I would say there are about a hundred guests here. He greets most, ensuring I stay by his side. He doesn't introduce me, which I find strange, but he reveals why a moment later.

"We'll greet our guests in the ballroom, which is where I will announce you. I want all eyes to be on you so you get the attention you so deserve," he whispers into my ear.

"I'd rather stay incognito," I reveal, meaning every word.

But Alek won't have it. "Nonsense. You've earned your place by my side. Besides, you're the guest of honor. All these people"—he sweeps his hand outward—"they're here to see you. Not me."

"I don't feel comfortable doing this." My voice is uneven.

He stops walking and turns over his shoulder to look at me. We are standing in the middle of the room, but Alek doesn't care. "This really leaves you unsettled, doesn't it?"

"Of course, it does," I reply without thought.

Alek shakes his head as he continues staring at me in awe. "You surprise me every single day. When I have"—he clears his throat and toys with his bow tie—"introduced other… women, they haven't minded. But you, you are so different. You truly are unlike anyone I have ever met before."

His comment has me wondering just how many women he's introduced. This is completely Zoey's scene as I can just imagine her parading around in her extravagant dresses and jewels, proud to be hanging off Alek's arm.

"All I ask is for one dance and then you can retreat to your room until—" His abrupt pause clues me onto what he intended to say. *Until he exploits me in a room full of perverts and sick human beings.*

I can't keep the horror from my face.

"дорогая—" But he is interrupted by a voice which turns my blood cold.

"Aleksei, my dear friend. Your home looks absolutely charming."

Both Alek and I turn to see Oscar pushing through the crowd to greet us. He looks impeccably dressed in a black suit with red velvet lapels, and his mask is a simple black design. My skin suddenly prickles in awareness, and I know it has nothing to do with Oscar and everything to do with the man who stands by his side.

The crisp black tuxedo hugs the man's refined frame. He is towering and imposing, and my heart skips a beat when I meet his eyes. Although his mask, which is separated into black and white halves, is full length and covers his face, I know without a doubt the masked stranger is not a stranger at all.

Those eyes, those hypnotic green eyes belong to Saint.

How can I not recognize him? Our first few weeks together played out similar to this. Him hiding behind a mask while I attempted to uncover what he was thinking.

An intake of breath escapes me as I try to compose myself. But seeing him does something to me, and my hands begin to shake. Saint's intense gaze burns a hole straight through me, and the need to run to him overwhelms me.

But as Alek peers down at me, taking note of my strange reaction, I rein in my desperation. I need to keep my head in the game.

"Oscar." Alek is curt as he addresses his so-called friend. When he looks at Saint, tilting his head to the side, I hold my breath. Is our ruse up?

Alek offers his hand. "Hello, Dominic."

I exhale in relief.

The corded veins at Saint's throat strain as he begrudgingly takes the offering. I can only imagine how hard it is for him not to snap his wrist.

"Dominic has taken a vow of silence until further notice," Oscar explains, looking at me with a smirk. He so knows I'm in on their little secret. "That's what happens when servants don't behave. Maybe you should follow the example, Aleksei."

The smug jibe has the desired effect as Alek rips his hand from Saint's, glaring at Oscar. But he won't make a scene in front of his guests. "If you'll excuse us."

He doesn't wait for Oscar to speak and escorts me away, fuming as he mumbles obscenities under his breath. I can feel Saint's eyes following my every move, but he refrains from acting out because tonight is all about timing.

Apart from Saint's eyes, I can't shake the feeling that someone else watches me. But who?

"You're shaking," Alek says, leading me toward the corner of the room. "I know seeing Oscar and Dominic after what happened is beyond traumatizing for you. I'm sorry. I should have revoked his invite!" The true anger in his tone surprises me.

A waiter zips past us, carrying a tray of champagne flutes. Alek stops him and reaches for two glasses. "Here, this will help take the edge off."

"I'm going to need a lot more than one glass." Nonetheless, I accept and gulp down the sweet liquid in one mouthful.

It's impossible not to seek Saint out because I am drawn to him. When we lock eyes across the room, I realize staying away from Saint is going to be nearly impossible. He calls to my very existence.

Even though he wears a mask, he reeks of fury. Oscar, on the other hand, appears causal as he leads Saint around the room like a trained poodle. It's his dream come true to have Saint at his beck and call. I can't help but feel guilty because he wouldn't be here if it weren't for me.

Saint nods subtly, a silent assurance that he's here and he won't let anything happen to me.

"Let's get this over with." Alek's irritated tone snaps me into the now as he leads me into the ballroom. His good mood has been dampened.

A flurry of excitement exists in the ballroom as people take their position, more than ready to have the festivities formally commence. I gape around at the sea of people, unbelieving that so many corrupt individuals exist.

I'm unsure who the official members of The Circle are. Surely not all of them. I can imagine Alek would invite your "nobodies" not to rouse suspicion and to fall in their favor. To the innocent, we are simply celebrating Alek's new bride.

"May I have everyone's attention?" Alek calls from the front of the room.

The moment they hear his commanding voice, a quiet falls over everyone. People in the foyer quickly enter the ballroom, shuffling into the room like lambs to slaughter. Oscar and Saint make their way through the crowd, standing against the far wall as they watch us closely.

When Alek has their attention, he draws me against his side so we're touching. The action doesn't go unnoticed by

Saint as he folds his arms across his broad chest exceptionally slow.

"I hope you don't mind, but I will speak in English," he says, not that anyone would dare object. "Thank you for coming. Tonight is about celebrating life and love."

I swallow down my nerves.

"And this woman who stands by my side represents both. It's because of her that all of this"—he sweeps his hand around the room—"is happening. I wanted to celebrate her existence with all of you because she means...so much to me."

Instantly, I gaze at Saint whose chest rises and falls in dangerously measured breaths.

"I never believed in love at first sight. I laughed, mocking those who believed in such childish nonsense. But my mind has been changed. Willow"—he hugs me closer while I stand as stiff as a board—"she has shown me that there is no shame in being vulnerable. It doesn't make us weak to lower our guards. It makes us stronger because learning to love allows one to see the world differently."

The room listens intently as Alek's speech has come as a surprise to some. Astra suddenly appears out of nowhere, and the sea of people part, allowing her to take front row, center. Her men flank her, but I'm surprised to see another addition.

However, he doesn't appear to be a guard. He seems to be someone...valued. She whispers into his ear, and his lips tip up into a slanted grin. Together, dressed in riches and gold, they are deadly, and the sense of foreboding suddenly returns.

Alek notices her arrival but soon recovers. "So I ask you raise your glass to my дорогая." A waiter quickly scurries to

Alek, passing him two flutes of champagne. He offers me one, staring at me with longing over the rim of the glass.

My cheeks heat because Saint's scorn burns me. But I accept with a small smile. The room raises their glasses, awaiting the toast.

Alek turns me so I'm facing him as he takes my hand. With nothing but devotion, he declares, "To you, my darling. I promise to cherish you and to hold you in the highest regard. I live only to make you happy. I pledge this to you. Always."

Unsuspecting guests gush over Alek's words as they shout out their approval. Astra and her mystery man raise their glasses at Alek and me, but in no way are they touched. I stand speechless, my mouth slightly parted, unsure what to say.

But speech isn't what Alek wants because when he bends forward and kisses me, he stakes his claim that I'm his. I attempt to recoil violently, but he loops his arm around my waist, holding me prisoner. The catcalls from the crowd echo around us while I focus on nothing but this ending forever.

The kiss isn't chaste, and when he nudges my lips open with his tongue, it takes all of my willpower not to bite down on it. But as he continues coaxing me to surrender, I finally open up to him, realizing this will be over a lot quicker if I comply.

His moans slip down my throat while I close my eyes, blinking back my tears. My heart aches because I can only imagine what this is doing to Saint. Surely, he knows I'm only doing this so I don't rouse any suspicion.

However, when Alek finally breaks the kiss and lets me go and I seek him out, his usual chartreuse swirls are narrowed and overtaken by a darkness that chills me to the very core. I never believed he was capable of such vehemence, but now, I do.

Everyone drinks to the happy couple while I look at Alek's red-stained mouth, disgusted at myself. I shouldn't have allowed him to kiss me that way. I should have pushed him away.

"You are everything and so much more," he whispers against my neck. "I meant every word. You have opened my eyes, and I hope, in time, I can do the same to you."

The walls close in around me, and I suddenly find it hard to breathe.

"Oh, Alek, I never took you for a romantic," says a voice, dripping with pure sarcasm.

Astra and the mystery man stand before us, smirking as if they're privy to a secret no one else but them knows. She looks stunning in a royal blue ballgown with a gaping neckline. Her ruby pendant dangles between her bountiful breasts, setting off her royal glow.

The man in a sharp tuxedo makes no secret he's examining me closely. "I'm Sokolov. Borya Sokolov. Nice to meet you." He lowers his voice while I wonder who introduces themselves by using their surname. It's not like he's James Bond.

He offers his hand while I notice Astra roll her eyes.

"You have outdone yourself with this one."

This one? I claw my palms to stop myself from slapping his cheek. His comment has me guessing he is a member of The Circle.

"She has a name, and I'd appreciate if you'd use it." Alek's quick retort stuns everyone, but he soon recovers. "And yes, I am most fortunate." He wipes his mouth with a crisp white handkerchief, and it comes away red with my lipstick.

Astra smiles, but she is, without a doubt, sizing me up. Her smile soon turns into a bitter scowl.

"Where is your wife tonight, Borya?"

The temperature drops to artic levels, and when a smug smirk tugs at Alek's lips, I wonder if he said this to get under Astra's skin. "She had to look after the kids. Our sitter took ill."

"Hmm," Alek replies, peering around the room, bored by his story.

"You still owe me a game of poker. How about we play a game? Are you afraid I'll beat you?" Borya states. It seems like an odd thing to say, considering we're at a party.

"Afraid?" Alek scoffs. "Of you? Mother Superior is far more frightening than you are."

I can't help the winded chuckle that leaves me because Astra's sour face is priceless. "Mother Superior is an old wench who should leave those children in the gutter where they belong."

Horror soon replaced my humor. How can she be so cruel? Alek's lips twist into a scowl.

"Then let's play," Borya challenges, ignoring Astra.

"You and your gambling will be your downfall, my friend." Alek slaps him on the back, then hooks an arm around my waist, hinting it's time to go. "It's a party. Have fun. We will play another time."

Just as Alek is about to usher us away, Astra folds her arms under her breasts, leveling Alek with an intense stare. "I know what will change your mind."

Her confidence piques his interest, and he waits for her to elaborate.

When she runs a hand down her throat and circles over the ruby around her neck, something in Alek changes. She not only has his attention. She owns him. "How about we use this as a wager? I know how much you want it…back."

Alek's body tenses as he glares at the necklace. She's implying it once belonged to him, and the way he's looking at it, I dare say it holds some value to him. But why would he give it away if it does?

"I suppose I can sneak away for a few minutes," he says, playing it cool.

"I thought you might," Astra replies. "Come find us when you're done playing house."

Alek's spine stiffens because her comment was a blatant insult. She clearly wasn't touched by his speech. But I suppose it's hard to touch a heart made of ice. She and Borya saunter off in victory while I wonder why it's so important to play a game of poker.

Unless Borya has a gambling problem…

I'm Sokolov. Borya Sokolov.

Oh, my god. Why didn't I see this sooner?

Saint's journal said *Shaken, not stirred*, which is a James Bond quote, and *Seven deadly sins* with *+2.* At the time, I was completely perplexed to the meaning of this all. But now, I know what it means.

Borya is the missing member of The Circle. His James Bond-inspired introduction was the first clue to unveil his identity. And the seven deadly sins come into play because the second sin is greed. And Borya reeks of it. Not to mention, Alek let drop he had a wife, but it's fairly safe to assume that he and Astra are a thing. No wonder Saint used that quote. Their union, like a shaken martini, is very, very cold.

"I'm sorry about that," Alek says, his jaw clenched as he watches his frenemies walk away. "I shouldn't let them get to me like that, but the wager is one I couldn't say no to."

"The necklace means something to you?" I ask softly, unsure if he'll answer me or not.

He inhales deeply, appearing to steady himself. "Yes. It was my mother's."

A whoosh of air leaves me as I am taken aback by his revelation. His mom's? From the story he told me about her, I thought there was no love lost between them. So why is winning back her necklace so important? And why does Astra have it in the first place?

My head begins to throb. "I need to use the bathroom."

"Are you all right?"

"No," I reply, not seeing the point in being coy. "I want nothing to do with these people. And neither should you."

Before he has a chance to get a word in edgewise, I lift my dress and excuse myself through the crowd. Thanks to his speech, everyone knows who I am, but I have no desire to converse with anyone because I need some air.

Once I break through, I race up the stairs, my feet barely able to keep up with my frantic steps. The hallway seems never-ending, but when I finally burst into Saint's room, I slam the door shut and lean up against it, catching my breath.

This is far harder than I thought it would be. For the greater good, I was certain I could play nice, but I don't think I can go back downstairs. The thought of pretending for a second longer turns my stomach. I need to find Saint.

God only knows what he agreed to, to be here. I can only imagine what sick and disgusting things Oscar made him do. He will get his pound of flesh, and it pains me to know that means in the literal sense.

"We need to get out of here," I whisper as a surge of adrenaline courses through me.

Without a moment to waste, I yank open the door but bump straight into a wall of divine smelling muscle. I bounce back, steadying myself as I grip the wall to keep from falling over. The masked man rushes into the room, slamming the door shut behind him.

His mask, divided into black and white halves, is the perfect analogy to describe him because even masked, I know him. Saint encompasses both, but right now, with his eyes sparking alight, it's evident he skates close to the edge. He grips the bottom of the mask and yanks it off his face, revealing the light in my forever darkness.

He looks dangerously pissed off, and the room suddenly shrinks, clouded by his fury. I wait for him to speak, but it seems he can't find the right words to properly reveal what he wants to say.

I've never seen him dressed up before, and I know this isn't the time, but I can't help but admire how good he looks. He doesn't look refined or gentlemanly. He looks like he's ready to eat me alive.

Instinctively, I take a step back, but that doesn't deter him in the slightest.

"You kissed him," he states in a low timbre, his blazing gaze rivaling the sun.

"I-I…I didn't want to rouse any suspicion."

My answer should appease him. It doesn't.

He prowls forward, engulfing me with his commanding frame. "I am going to rip him apart with my bare hands."

And I don't doubt him for one second.

"Saint," I coo. Placing an apprehensive hand to his cheek, I'm thankful he doesn't pull away. "It didn't mean anything. I did what I had to. Just as you have."

His nostrils flare.

"Tell me it's time to go," I whisper in a plea. "I can't bear to be here anymore. What's the plan?"

Inhaling, he closes his eyes for a few seconds, and when he reopens them, he seems focused, and the anger has dispersed. For now. "We leave when they sit down to play their game of poker."

My mouth hinges open as realization hits. "You know about that?"

He nods slowly.

Everything collides into me at once, and I gasp. "That, that means you're working with *them*?" All of them.

There is no need for me to elaborate on who *they* are.

"Better the devil you know," he says without emotion. It scares me.

"How?" It's all I can muster.

Saint looks over my shoulder. "That's how."

Completely baffled, I turn to see what has ensnared his attention. But when I do, I stagger back, shaking my head slowly. My gaze floats to a modest green ballgown and mask which lay on the bed. And then to Sara, who steps from the en suite, sheepishly. "No, absolutely not."

"This isn't negotiable," he states. "This is the only way I can get you out of here."

"I will not," I press, eyes filled with tears because I could never live with myself if we went through with what he proposes.

Sara nervously toys with her hair, hair styled identically to mine. I now understand why she was so insistent that I wear extensions because her hair and her makeup are a complete mirror image of mine. "Sara, I can't let you do this."

"I want to," she says in her soft voice, a voice which has carried me through this nightmare. "This is the only way he can pay for what he's done. We're the same size. He won't know—"

But I raise my hand, nausea rising. "No. I won't allow you to sacrifice yourself. He will…kill you."

Sara and Saint propose something so far beyond valiant, it could be called suicidal. Sara is willing to take my place and pretend to be me as I slip away into the darkness in that simple green dress. The poker game is a ruse because Alek will be focused on winning back that pendant. As long as someone who looks like me is by his side, he won't notice until it's too late.

But when he notices, Sara will be the one to take the blame.

"I won't," I cry, pleading with Saint because there must be another way.

But Saint doesn't have time for sentiments. "I won't let anything happen to her."

"And what happens if you fail?" Tears leak into my mouth as I gasp for air.

"Then I'm finally free." Sara's response makes this worse.

"No." I rush over to her, gripping her upper arms. "We go together. That was the plan."

"In an ideal world, that would work. But unless someone who looks like you is by his side, then no one will leave."

"How could you?" I turn to look at Saint, horrified. "By saving me, you're endangering someone else."

He flinches, and I instantly feel guilty for blaming him when he's only trying to help.

"It was my idea." I turn back around to look at Sara, my grip on her releasing.

"What? *Why*?" I manage to choke out, taking off my mask. "Why would you do that for me?"

Sara smiles, and for the first time ever, it's void of pain. "Because we're friends."

A sob escapes me as I place my hand over my mouth. This isn't negotiable. The plans are set in motion. I'm to abide by them, no matter how wrong they are.

Saint stands behind me, knowing better than to touch me. "Once the game starts, you make an excuse to slip away. Come up here and Sara will be waiting. You change into the dress and mask, and we slip out through the front door. No one will know."

Closing my eyes, I shake my head, but it's in vain. This is happening, and it will work because no one will suspect anything. Nothing will be seen as unusual about two people walking out the door, especially two people whose true identities hide behind guises.

"What did you agree to for them to work with you?" I don't want to know, but for this to work, I need to know every detail.

"You let me worry—"

"Tell me!" I exclaim, cutting him off.

His warm breath bathes the back of my neck as he exhales. "To kill Aleksei."

I always knew it would come to this, but it doesn't make the certainty any easier to accept. "And what do they get?"

"His empire," he replies without pause.

"And you believe them? You think they'll just let you live after everything you know?"

His silence is all the answer I need.

Saint's journal now makes perfect sense to me. The Oscar Wilde quote sums Oscar up to a T. He would betray Alek for something he wants—Saint—but this isn't a deal without strings. And as for Borya and Astra, they are two sociopaths who are sick of being second best. They want true reign—all hail the king and queen of the underworld.

"I think I'm going to be sick." Hugging my middle, I take a moment to compose myself because I know Alek will come searching for me soon.

"Ангел." Saint gently places his hand over the slope of where my neck and shoulder meet. "It's going to be okay. I promise. Someone will be waiting for you. You can trust him. I will come meet you as soon as I can."

I can't shake the feeling that he's not telling me something.

"As soon as you can?" I turn around slowly, hating that I feel this weight in the pit of my stomach. This was supposed to be our out, the moment when we were both reborn, but it's fallen short because leaving here will just be another blemish on my soul.

"You mean when Alek is dead? And god knows what will happen to Sara?"

I don't mean to be confrontational, but how can I do this?

Saint arches a dark brow, folding his arms across his chest. "And you have a problem with Alek being dead? I thought you wanted this to be over with as much as I do."

And that's the catch. I thought I did. But now, the thought of me having a hand in Alek's death makes me sick.

"Of course, I do. I just...I know it's personal because of what he did to Zoey. I'm not excusing his behavior but—"

Saint shakes his head, his cheeks billowing as he exhales. "But? It sounds like you *are* excusing his behavior. There is no but in this situation. I never thought you'd be so...naïve. He's gotten to you, hasn't he?"

"What?" I gasp, angered because...he's right. Not in the way he has to so many others, but I can't deny being a part of his demise doesn't sit right with me. And I know what that says about me.

I hang my head in shame.

"That son of a bitch!" Saint turns around, and with a roar, he punches a hole straight through the wall. His fist disintegrates the plaster like it's made of mere paper.

Sara yelps while I rush forward, stopping him from doing more damage. "Stop it!" I grip his forearm, begging him to stop. "It's not like that."

He shrugs me off, his fury burning me as he turns around quickly. "It's exactly like that, but listen to me, ангел." He lowers his face to mine, his tepid breath blowing the hair from my cheeks. "I will never allow him to destroy you too. I will do everything in my power to get you the fuck out of here. Even if you are kicking and screaming, you will be leaving here. Tonight. We clear?"

I stand my ground, gritting my teeth in frustration. "I'm not Zoey."

He inhales sharply, closing his eyes, appearing to ask for mercy from above. When he opens them, I gasp because the color consumes every inch of me. "I said are. We. Clear?"

Fuck him and his infuriating need to protect me. This is an argument I have lost. No matter what I say, Saint will ensure tonight's plan will go off without a hitch. "We're clear."

And that's what defeat sounds like.

"Good. Now go back downstairs and have your customary dance."

My eyes widen. How did he know?

"Oh yes, I know all his tricks. Don't forget who made me." Nothing but bitterness reflects in his tone as he stands before me broken.

Something ugly is transpiring between us. Saint was my safe place, but now, he can't stand to look at me.

"Saint—"

But he doesn't let me finish.

With a ferocious craving, he presses his lips to my forehead, a tremble to his touch. "You can hate me later, but now…just obey me. Please."

A tear trickles down my cheek. His admission reveals he doesn't grasp my true feelings for him. "Okay," I whisper. "But I will never hate you. I can't."

He inhales sharply, but I pull away, turning toward the door as I fix my mask. I smile at Sara, unable to say anything because there are no words to thank her for what she's doing. I open the door coolly and make my way down the hallway, embracing my freedom, whatever the consequences may be.

CHAPTER THIRTEEN

Day 74

All I can think about is Saint. I have hurt him in unimaginable ways. He sees my apprehension as weakness, but it's not. Killing Alek won't make the world a better place because there are three far crueler monsters ready to take his place.

However, it will make the world a better place for Saint because I understand this is about redemption for him. He can't move on until he ends this chapter in his life once and for all.

So what do I do?

Do I turn a blind eye and allow a man shadowed in darkness, but who has flickers of light shining through, die? My father would have said that everyone deserves a second chance. No matter what one has done, there is always room for forgiveness. If they are trying to change the path they are on, then how can I judge him?

If anyone should be judged, it should be me.

"May I have this dance?" Alek extends his hand, looking more than honored.

We are standing in the middle of the ballroom, the string quartet ready to commence. However, when I stand frozen, hearing whispers echo around the room, sweat begins to collect on his brow. I have never seen him nervous before.

Something catches my attention from the corner of my eye, and I know what or, rather, *who* it is. Remembering the heartbreak in Saint's tone, I slip my hand into Alek's, cementing another step to my doom.

The music plays right away, and I'm certain I can hear a relieved sigh. He places his hand on my lower back, drawing me close with a smile. "I'll try not to step on your toes," I jibe, needing to say something lighthearted before I burst into more tears.

Alek smiles as he leads us into a slow dance.

As everyone stares, and some whisper behind their hands, I wonder what they see. I still don't have the guts to look at Saint because after our confrontation, I don't know what to think. He's angry with me, and he has every right. But I can't help how I feel.

I can't take the life of another, no matter what they've done. I just can't.

"You seem distracted," Alek says, his cheek almost pressed to mine as he lowers his face.

"I do?" I need to be on my A game because the next few minutes are vital.

"I understand this is all a little much. You are most

welcome to go upstairs and rest after we're done here."

"What about your poker game?"

Alek's body grows tense. "I wish I'd never agreed. But you're right. I should get it over with."

The question lingers about when he intends to take me upstairs.

"Are you nervous?" he asks, in sync with my thoughts.

I shrug, unable to look at him.

"I…" His pause has me lifting my eyes. I see his uneasiness, which is ironic, considering I'm the one who should be nervous. "I wish it could be different."

"So do I." And I mean that in every sense of the word.

"You make me…happy, Willow." I look for any signs of deception, to confirm what Saint said, but I don't see any. He appears genuine, which makes what I know all the worse.

I wet my dry lips, overshadowed by guilt.

"It's something I haven't felt in a very long time. I can see why Saint was so spellbound by you."

Hearing his name brings on a sadness that crushes my spirit. I don't see the point in denying it because, once upon a time, he was. We were captivated by the other. But now, after all that's been said and done, Saint believes I have fallen victim to Alek's charms.

Peering into Alek's eyes, I know what I must do because all is fair in love and war, and with Saint, the two go hand in hand.

"I wish you would have ruled with your kindness because I know it's there."

He recoils slightly, appearing stunned by my revelation.

But that isn't possible. It's too late for him. And no matter how guilty I feel, I have to make a choice.

When I find Saint across the room with Oscar by his side, there was only ever one choice to make, and that is Saint.

He will always be my first.

With eyes still locked on his, I whisper, "How about you get that game out of the way, and then we can go upstairs?"

Time stands still for so many reasons.

For Alek, his mouth parts, clearly stunned by my openness and acceptance of him into my bed. And for me, I just condemned a man to death. I can deal with the consequences later because now, it's time I claimed back my life and deal with whatever the aftermath might be.

"Yes," he exclaims, leaning down and placing a chaste kiss on my cheek.

Saint looks ready to tear the flesh from Alek's bones, but when I nod subtly, everything changes. A wave of what appears to be relief washes over him. The black of his eyes slowly transforms into their mesmerizing green, and what I see confirms I made the right choice.

Saint looks...happy.

If presenting Alek to him will erase his darkness, then it's what I have to do. It's a sacrifice I'm willing to make because this is as close to freedom as I will ever get. For every action, there is a consequence, and I will have to live with that every single day.

But I'm ready.

The music comes to an end, and Alek twirls me around one final time. When we come to a stop, he pulls away and bows. It's all very gallant, which makes me feel like an even bigger villain.

"Come." He takes my hand and escorts me from the room, stopping to speak to a few masked guests along the way.

Saint never strays too far and knowing he's close by settles my nerves. Oscar gestures to Astra and Borya that things are about to start. It sickens me that everyone has a role to play in this twisted game.

Alek notices his three "friends" gathering, and without a word, he leads the way through the crowd who are none the wiser to what is about to unfold. We walk down the hallway, and only the stabbing of Astra's heels reveals they're all following in hot pursuit.

My hand is shaking in Alek's. I can't help it. He draws it to his lips and kisses the back of it. "It's okay," he assures, but it's really not.

Once we get to wherever they're playing this game, I would have played a part in Alek's demise. My father would be so ashamed of me. The cross at my throat burns, a psychological response to what's thrashing around my mind.

Alek opens the door to the den, where I first met Oscar. Stepping inside, I'm instantly assaulted with images of naked women and filthy men. Alek was one of those men. I need to remember that when he kisses me on the forehead and leads me to sit on a small sofa in the corner of the room.

Thankfully, it's not the same one Zoey sprawled out on as nameless men fucked her senseless.

The door closes, cementing the fact this is really happening. Saint follows Oscar, but when he makes a beeline to stand near me, Oscar shakes his head, his vile eyes glowing.

"Come sit with me. You're my good luck charm, after all." He pointedly looks at me as he rubs over Saint's crotch.

Saint stands unflinching, playing his part, while I swallow down my disgust at Saint being subjected to this because of me.

Astra and Borya are oblivious to Oscar's perversion because when they take a seat at the poker table, it's clear they only have one thing in mind. "Shall we start? I'm sure you want this over with as soon as possible."

Borya's eagerness has me shuffling in my seat, causing the leather beneath me to creak.

"Yes," Alek says, unbuttoning his suit jacket as he takes a seat at the table. "I do. Shall we set the rules?"

Astra makes a fuss as she arranges her layers of tulle so she can sit, and when she does, she appears like a queen, sitting on her throne. "Oh, Aleksei. You are such a stickler for the rules lately. But only when it suits you."

I gulp.

"The necklace if I win," he says, ignoring her quip. "And if I lose?"

Astra turns to look at Borya who sits at her right. "If you lose," she purrs. "You give us the name of your new contact."

Alek remains cool, but the tic under his eye reveals his shock.

"I liked Chow, but then you had to go and..." She accentuates her point with a wave of her hand in the air. "Without our consent or knowledge."

And now I understand. They are angry with Alek for

making a decision without consulting them first. And if that wasn't enough of an insult, he has not yet told them who the new supplier is.

"Enough," Alek snarls, setting the mood. "Fine. Your terms are accepted."

He reaches for the deck of cards and shuffles them with skill as he glares at Astra. Because they aren't playing for money, the chips are pushed aside. Oscar finally leaves Saint alone and joins his comrades.

Saint stands between me and the table, and I know he's done so with intent. They will have to go through him before they get to me.

Surely, Alek can sense something is amiss. It's fairly obvious it's three against one. But when he focuses on the rock around Astra's neck, it seems to blind him and he throws good sense to the wind. He deals the cards, and the game soon begins.

I don't know anything about poker, but this is just a ruse. The real game isn't cards. It's a gamble of Alek's life.

"So," Borya says, his accent rolling freely, "business has been well?"

"What do you think? You get paid at the end of each month. You know it has been," Alek snaps, arranging his cards in his hands.

"Yes, we have all been most fortunate, but Aleksei, we are very disappointed in you not sharing with us. We are your closest friends, after all. We all have a role to play in this business to see it succeed. Astra and I cover our tracks while Oscar has the global connections we need. We are so good at what we do because we have worked together for so long. We all play a part in this well-oiled machine, but it seems you think you're suddenly better than us."

So it appears the four of them "work" together to make sure their bank accounts are never dry. But being the right-hand men won't cut it for them anymore.

The already tense air turns thicker, making it harder to breathe.

"You have known Astra and me since we were what...?" Borya asks, but he knows.

"I'm not here for a trip down memory lane," he replies, placing a card onto the table.

"Don't be like that, Aleksei. Your dear, sweet mother would be most disappointed in your manners."

Alek's shoulders rise, and if he had hackles, they'd be standing on end.

Astra's comment has me wondering just how long they have known one another. Because for her to mention his mother, it's evident they've met before. And what happened to Alek's mom?

"This change is unlike you," she continues, playing a hand. "Is it because you're trying to impress the American?"

"She has a name," Alek snaps, peering at her over his cards.

"Oh, yes, how could I forget. It's all I've been hearing about as of late."

This has both Alek and me sitting to attention.

"Your little speech was so...touching. Anyone would think you meant it."

"I did," Alek replies while Saint clenches his fists behind his back.

Astra laughs bitterly. "I've seen it all before. You'll grow bored with her like you always do. But until then, how about we all have some fun with her?"

Saint looks over his shoulder, nodding that it's time.

"I-I have to use the bathroom." I stand quickly, my legs trembling.

Alek places his cards face down on the table and removes his mask slowly. His face is one of pure fury. "How dare you come into my home and disrespect me."

Astra doesn't flinch.

Oscar, however, takes the bait. "That's rich, coming from you, as you have no qualms coming into other people's homes and disrespecting them."

"What are you talking about?"

Oscar throws his cards on the table, pushing back his chair with force as he stands. "It's okay for you to take as you please. But when someone else does, it's punishable."

"You have all gone mad!" Alek cries, shaking his head in disbelief.

"You came into my home, shaming me, and now, it's time we do the same."

And there it is. The real reason we're here.

"Go!" Saint whispers, his eyes urgent. But when I take a step toward the door, Borya stands coolly, reaching into his pocket and producing a gun.

"We're not done yet." He trains the gun on me.

I stop dead in my tracks, raising my trembling hands in surrender.

Alek comes to a quick stand, his body vibrating in absolute wrath. "How did you get that in here? Past security?"

My gaze swings to Saint for answers. Is this part of his plan? But when he interlocks his hands behind his nape, looking at this shitstorm unfold, I know he's just as surprised as I am.

Astra tsks him as she leans back in her seat, enjoying the show. "Your newfound...emotional tie to that girl makes you weak. Your men can see it. We all can. You're losing power. Your loyalty is slipping. Your guards betrayed you because they can see you've gone soft. They need a new leader, one who isn't afraid of getting their hands dirty."

"And who might that be, Astra?" he snarls, curling his lip in disgust.

Finally, she rises, graceful and composed. She runs a hand through her hair, smiling. "Why me, of course."

When Borya stands by her, his gun still aimed at me, she adds, "And my king."

"Over my dead body."

"That can be arranged," Borya says, watching closely as Astra lifts the hem of her dress and retrieves a gun from the leather holster attached to her thigh. She points it at Alek.

"So this game of poker was just a ploy to get me alone? Is that it?"

"Yes and no," she replies as I watch on in horror. "You were always going to lose this game, Aleksei. But the rules have changed. We want the name of your supplier. You give that to us, and we will let you and your little pet live."

"And if I don't?"

Borya's grin is malevolent as he peers at me. "Then we get creative."

"We don't want to kill you, Aleksei. We have been friends since we were ten years old. But watching you...pine after that girl is an embarrassment to us all. You show weakness, and we can't have that." There is no question Astra is the ring leader. I wonder if she was always this way.

"And what do you get out of all of this?" Alek focuses on Oscar, who is standing back and watching the show.

"A say in how we run things, of course. Oh," he adds casually, "and your ангел."

Saint advances forward, gripping Oscar by the arm and spinning him around fiercely. "That wasn't part of the deal. She was to go, unharmed."

Oscar smirks, running his fingers over Saint's grip. "I lied. Besides, I like her. I like watching what she does to you."

If it weren't for me watching this unfold, then I wouldn't believe it. But here I stand, witness to such atrocities, and there isn't a damn thing I can do about it.

Alek narrows his eyes, staring at the man he believed to be Dominic. "Saint?" he gasps, a wave of surprise passing over him.

With his ruse up, Saint rips off his mask and drops it by his feet. He meets Alek's eyes, unbending. "Hello, Alek."

Alek stumbles backward, running a hand over his gaping mouth. "It seems I have been played a fool by all." When he focuses his attention my way, I instantly avert my gaze, revealing my guilt. "You knew?"

Deep-seated guilt washes over me. "Yes," I whisper, unable

to lie a second longer.

"No." His gasp kicks me low, and I swallow back my shame. How could I have done this? I'm no better than the vile human beings surrounding me.

"Sorry, Saint, but he has to leave here alive. Whatever happens to the girl is none of my concern." Borya waves his gun my way, but I don't flinch.

"Is this what you wanted?" Alek cries, gesturing toward me. "For them to kill her?"

"Of course not!" Saint snaps, shaking his head angrily.

"Then what? What could they give you that means more to you than your freedom? And Zoey's?" Alek isn't trying to play the game. He appears stunned that his number one trusted confidant could betray him this way.

"Willow." When he finally speaks, the room falls quiet. "She means more to me than you'll ever know. And I would do anything, side with anyone, to set her free...from you."

Oscar watches on, aroused by Saint's dominance.

"What did they promise you?" Alek wants to know it all. And so do I because there is a catch. There is always a catch.

Saint squares his shoulders as he shifts slightly to use his body as a shield to shelter me from Borya's gun. "Your death," he replies with nothing but pure spite. "I was supposed to kill you, share your secrets with them, and protect them how I did you. I do all this...and Willow is free. They would ensure she leaves this country safe."

And there it is. The truth.

I can understand why he didn't want to share it with me because I would have told him no. But now, it's too late. He was never coming with me. There is no out for Saint, and there never will be. As long as he's alive, he's enslaved to them all.

"Change of plans," Astra says, untouched by Saint's admission. "I will let you live, Aleksei, because Saint is your dirty little secret, isn't he? He knows everything. Shame on you for showing weakness yet again. I was going to kill you, maybe torture you a little, but it will be far more fun knowing you're alive to see us destroy your legacy. You're done."

"That wasn't part of the deal. He has to die!" Saint shouts, anger vibrating from him.

I can't wrap my head around this because it seems so… implausible. But hasn't it always?

Saint sided with these monsters, promising to protect them and reveal Alek's secrets, on the proviso that I was to leave unharmed and that Alek died by his hand. He did all of this for…me.

But you can't trust a snake. They have played us all.

"He was never supposed to leave here alive! You promised me she would have your protection. You were to grant her safe passage back to America."

Oscar walks toward Saint, appearing to want to console him, but Saint punches him in the face, his nose squishing under the impact. "If the deal is off, then don't you fucking touch me, you sick asshole."

Oscar howls in pain as he cups his nose, blood pouring through his fingers. The fact Saint hasn't pulled a weapon means he's unarmed. But his hands are just as fatal.

His violence seems to have stirred something in Astra who looks over at Borya in concern. They are afraid of him.

They know he can end them just as easily as they can end him. But the catch is, they need him.

Alek won't spill the details on what they need. They want to take over his empire, but they don't want to do the dirty work. They want to expand on his loot but not start from scratch. "Okay, let's come to a compromise."

Borya waits for Astra to continue.

"We give you Aleksei, but she has to go too. She is a liability."

"Absolutely not," Saint snarls, removing the buttons on his jacket, one by one. When he sheds himself of such gentlemanly attire, shit gets real. "She leaves here. Safe. And beyond these walls."

"And what happens then? Who will look after her? We were the ones who were supposed to do that. But I'm sorry, that isn't going to happen now."

"I can look after myself," I spit in a not so convincing tone as Saint curses under his breath.

They only seem to realize I am standing here.

"You have caused so much trouble, little girl." Astra arches an eyebrow, examining me closely. "Do you really think the wolves won't tear you apart? Everyone wants to know what is so special about you. How someone so…insignificant could bring a powerful leader to his knees."

Alek breathes steadily while I look at him, ashamed of what I've done.

"Your need for vengeance has blinded you, brother. Now, what will you do?" Alek says to Saint.

"Shut up," Saint growls, barely holding back.

"Time is ticking, Saint. Best you make a choice now, or we will make it for you," Borya warns. No guessing what that will be.

"It's okay. I deserve this," I affirm, my fear subsiding. "I won't allow them to use you this way."

Saint spins to look at me, and the haunted look in his eyes has my resolve crumbling. "You don't deserve this!" he cries, passionately. "You never did."

Tears begin to well, and Saint shakes his head, saddened by the sight. However, when he begins to unbutton his shirt, that sadness turns to something else. Oscar's howls are muted as we all watch Saint disrobe with utter fascination.

What I see strapped to his body soon has that fascination transforming to dread. "No." I gasp, hand over mouth, shaking my head fiercely.

Alek's eyes widen, as do Borya and Astra's. "You didn't really think I trusted you, did you?" Saint condescendingly asks both Borya and Astra as they back away, terrified. "I wanted to give you the benefit of the doubt, but I've learned from the best."

Alek is the only one who stands his ground, not at all intimidated by the bomb strapped to Saint's body. "There was always a plan B," he mocks. "And that plan was you never leaving this house alive. Once I knew Willow was safe, you'd all get what you deserved."

"Saint, no!" I rush forward, heart in my throat as I desperately look for a way to dismantle the wires. But I'm no bomb expert. And this is foolproof. *This* was his plan all along.

He would never sacrifice Sara or allow these monsters to

live. He is ending it here, now. Putting an end to this reign for good.

"Why didn't you tell me?" I chastise, feeling foolish for not seeing this sooner.

"Forgive me, but I had to do it this way," he replies forlornly. "Ангел, go. Now."

"What?" I blink back my tears. "No, I'm not leaving you! I'm staying here with you."

With frantic fingers, I try to unfasten the straps around his body, but he pushes me away. "Go, now! Do what I tell you."

"I-I won't!" I yell, on the verge of hysteria. "No! It c-can't end this wa-way."

"It must, and it will," he exclaims, reaching out to brush the tears from my cheek. "Do you think I want to do this? But what choice do I have?"

"You can leave here now, with me," I reason with force, refusing to backdown, but it's useless.

"I wish it was different, and I tried. I really did. I made a pact with the devil, but it still wasn't enough," he says, and he did. He tried to put a different plan into motion to ensure my safety and end in Alek's death. His freedom would be stripped from him, but that was a sacrifice he was willing to make.

But they've double crossed him, which, judging by the bomb strapped to his body, he suspected would happen all along.

"I knew it wouldn't be enough," he continues, begging I understand why he's doing this. "Which is why I had to come prepared for every possible scenario. I thought for once, luck would be on our side. I thought wrong."

A sob leaves me.

"I wish there was a way for both of us to leave here, but as long as I'm alive, they will hunt me and the people I…love. If I'm not with them, they assume I'm against them. They will never let me go."

Astra only confirms what I know to be true. "He's right. There isn't an out for him. He knows too much. He will never be free from us, but more importantly, he will never be free of the sins of the past."

Saint lowers his eyes, ashamed for all he's done.

"He can kill us all, but our allies will ensure he pays. The reason we agreed to his terms is because we need him. That's why he's still alive. But we don't need you. And the moment you step out of here, alone, you'll be hunted. Without our protection, you'll never leave this country alive."

Saint clenches his jaw because Astra's tale is my reality, and there isn't a damn thing we can do. Or, maybe there is.

"Shoot them!" I cry. Saint is fast. He could disarm Borya and steal his gun without breaking a sweat. "Shoot them all." And by all, I mean Alek also. No matter what he's done, and the small glimmers of goodness he has shown me, he will always be the man who kidnapped me. And it's time he paid his dues.

Saint's sigh is heavy, alerting me to the fact that if he could have done so, he would have already. But it's not that easy. "And then what?" he questions softly. "Someone will always be ready to take over. By blowing up this place, I'll take out as many of those motherfuckers as I can. And…I can try and make amends for the damage I've done."

Saint's guilt for his sins has driven him this way.

"I won't allow you to do this," I challenge, frantically peering around the room for an out.

"The choice is made." He cups my cheek with a trembling hand. "All I can offer you is a life on the run where you'll forever be looking over your shoulder. I won't have that for you because you deserve so much more. I will only bring pain into your world. And I've already brought so much. I wanted a happy ending with you, I truly did. But I don't deserve one. I deserve *this* for all that I've done. It's time I atone for my sins."

"There's another way!" I bellow, refusing to accept this. But Saint has thought this through. This was never his first choice, but it's the *only* choice that sets me free. His first priority was getting me out of here safely, and then he'd deal with the consequences later.

"I can't fight them all, which is why I have to do this. If I... die, it'll end all of this for you. And that's all I ever wanted. For you to be happy."

The guns Astra and Borya hold are useless. One shot, and they ignite their deaths prematurely. "Let's come to a compromise." For the first time ever, I see fear, but it's too late.

"You were always one step ahead." It's Alek who speaks, his voice filled with nothing but admiration. "At least I die at the hand of someone I respect."

Saint inhales, tipping his chin to the heavens to ask for strength. I find out why that is. "You're not dying today."

"*What?*" It's me who expresses more surprise than Alek at Saint sparing his life.

"Astra is right. Now that the terms have changed, and you don't have her protection, someone needs to get you the hell out of here and keep you safe."

"Saint, please, you can't intend to blow us up," Astra says, paling.

"Watch me," he counters while Astra yelps, searching for a way out.

"No," I whimper, wrapping my arms around my middle, unbelieving he would leave me in Alek's hands.

But what he says next is what I knew to be true all along. It's the reason I couldn't allow Alek to be killed. "Even if we were to escape here, I can't look after you like he can. You need someone to protect you, and he is my best option." He takes a deep, painful breath. "I need someone who…loves you…as much as I do. That's the only way I know you'll be safe." Saint looks at Alek, who nods.

They've finally found common ground—their love for me.

"Saint, no." Uncaring, I rush forward, placing my hands to his cheeks, begging he doesn't do this. "Please, don't. We were supposed to leave here together. Where you go, I go. I don't want to do this without you. We should have fled when we had the chance."

Tears cloud my vision as I search every corner of his face, hoping to see reason. But I don't.

"We could have, but where would we go? We had no solid plan. With no ID, the fact I'm a criminal, and the issue with you being technically dead, thanks to your *husband*, we can't do this aboveboard. We can't go to the consulate. Too many questions will be asked. And besides, most of the consulate are on *their* payroll. Aren't they?"

Alek nods slowly.

"We wouldn't stand a chance on our own. I don't have the connections to guarantee your safety, which is why I agreed to do this in the first place. The odds are and were always stacked against us. I'd only put you in more danger, and I've already done enough."

"You'll allow him to go free? You'd sacrifice your revenge for me?" Because that's what he's doing. I know handing me over to Alek for safe keeping is as asinine as it sounds, but this is the lesser of two evils.

"Yes," Saint replies without pause. "You mean more to me than anything in this world."

And a small part of me dies at his bittersweet confession.

"We will always be hunted. And we are each other's weaknesses. They will exploit that in any way they can. But I won't allow it."

"No," I sob, throwing my arms around his neck. "I won't leave you."

"I wish it was different, ангел, but it's not. You are a liability to them. So this is my last resort. I've tried everything, but there is only one way to ensure your safety and your freedom. And that's my death."

"Don't be a martyr!" I shriek, refusing to let him go. He rubs my back and holds me tight.

"Forgive me for doing this. This was never the ideal plan. I don't want to leave you with him, but how can I kill him when he can do something I can't?"

I wait for his reply with bated breath.

"He can protect you."

"So can you! That's all you've ever done!" My pleas are broken, but I will never give up.

For a moment, when he presses his lips to my head, I believe he's changed his mind. When he holds me tightly one last time, I am certain this is just a bad dream, and I will wake up. But I never do. "Take her."

"Saint!" My grip on him tightens, but I'm no match for the strong hands that seize my waist, prying me off him.

"Get off me!" I kick and scream, but Alek lifts me, clutching me tight to his chest. "You bastard! I hate you! Let me go!"

Alek simply ignores me. "Thank you." His gratitude has me fighting harder.

"I'm not doing this for you," Saint spits. "Look after her."

"Your death will not be in vain. I will honor you."

"NO!" I thrash about wildly, about to use every self-defense move I know, but Alek won't let me go as he tosses me over his shoulder. He tears through the room, taking one last look at the three friends who betrayed him.

"Your greed killed us all," he says, his voice filled with regret.

"You're bluffing," Borya declares, raising his gun and aiming at Alek. "I will end them."

"Maybe I am? But if you shoot them, then you'll never know." I see him retrieve a remote from his pants pocket, one which has a switch to make all of this go *BOOM*.

"Alek, please. I will never forgive you if you do this!" I

squirm, desperate to break free. My heart threatens to burst from my chest as I look for an out, for anything to save Saint.

"In another lifetime, I will get my vengeance," Saint promises Alek, not wanting him to mistake his leniency for weakness.

"And I will accept it because I am deserving of everything you give. Goodbye, dear friend."

"Goodbye, Aleksei."

The blood whooshes through my ears as adrenaline courses through me. This can't be it. It doesn't end this way. But it does...and I will always remember the parting words my love said to me before he saved my life.

"I...love you, ангел. I always have. Thank you for bringing light into the darkness. I will be with you. Always."

The room explodes into pandemonium as Alek kicks open the door with me flailing around wildly, desperate to save the man who loves me, who is about to sacrifice everything to set me free. But it's too late. Astra is frenzied as she fires the first shot which goes straight through Saint's chest.

"No!" A scream strips my throat raw as I watch him stagger back a few feet before blood begins to trickle from his wound. "Please, God, NO!"

I am possessed as I fight with all my might, breaking free from Alek's hold. I scamper toward Saint, but Alek quickly grips my wrist, tugging me back toward him. When I fight him, kicking and biting, he slaps me—hard. Stunned, I stagger backward, which allows him to pick me up once again.

"Go!" Saint shouts, before stumbling, and I watch through eyes which aren't mine as he plummets to the floor. He meets my gaze with a smile, a smile finally swathed in freedom. And suddenly, in the blink of an eye, this hell on earth is crumbling to the ground with a BOOM!

All the king's horses and all the king's men…

The noise is thunderous, and the force of the blast propels Alek forward. But his feet never waver as he continues running, intent on staying true to his word.

The hallway fills with smoke as the walls collapse around us. The unknowing guests run from the house, bloodied and dumbfounded by what is happening. Some have limbs missing, others are lying dead in twisted heaps. So much carnage, so much death just to save me.

By the time we get to the trapdoor in the kitchen, and Alek unlocks it, I am hysterical, unsure if this is a dream. He descends the stairs, ducking and weaving so he doesn't hit my head. The echoing screams are the only sound I hear as we make our way through the damp hidden passage.

After a while, there is a hushed silence, and I know that's because I've passed out. Pieces float in and out of consciousness. I focus on Alek's harsh breath as he carries me through the tunnel. I don't want to close my eyes. I want to remember everything. All of it. I need to remember him.

"Come, quickly." I recognize the voice, but shock has taken over, and I barely know my own name.

"How can I trust you?"

"Saint has given me instructions."

His name tears me in two, and a guttural howl rips from my chest. I am sobbing, but I'm robbed of air. Nothing but a winded cough splutters from me.

Alek gently places me onto something soft—leather, I think—and coaxes me to lie down. I go willingly as my will to fight is dead.

Saint is…dead. He is dead because of me.

"Drive," Alek orders, suggesting that I'm lying in the back seat of a car.

The tires squeal as we take off into the night, our backdrop the burning castle, which once stood tall and proud. The silence is deafening.

"красная долина," Alek mumbles under his breath. "Irony at its best, for what I see before me, is a red valley indeed."

I have finally uncovered the meaning behind the name, but it doesn't matter. Everything is lost.

Gone.

Alek brushes his fingers through my hair, and I allow it. I'm too exhausted to fight. What do I have left to fight for? The only reason is gone, and I never got the chance to say goodbye. In my naïve mind, I actually believed we would be okay.

But he always knew to save me, he would have to sacrifice himself.

Closing my eyes, I allow the tears to fall as I express my biggest regret. "I didn't even say it," I whisper in a broken voice.

"Say what, ангел?"

The name only has me weeping harder. I don't want him to use it because it was his; it was ours. But to hear it means he will live on forever. In my mind. And in my heart.

"I didn't even say I…love you back, and now…he will never know."

"He knew," Alek says softly, commanding I sleep. And for once, I do what I'm told.

Saint would be so proud.

CHAPTER FOURTEEN

Day 92

"Does it hurt?"

I shake my head because it doesn't. My skin is numb. So is my mind.

Weeks have passed, but it still feels like yesterday when my world changed forever. I can still hear his voice and see those chartreuse eyes. But as dusk sets upon me, night after night, a small piece of his memory is lost to the wind.

"We're almost done."

I wish I could make conversation, but I can't. It hurts to speak because with words comes questions, questions I don't want to face. I just want to live in the darkness because I once felt safe here. But I have lost that feeling as I will never be safe again.

"It looks awesome. Take a look." The man passes me a mirror, but I wave him off. I don't need to see it. That's not the reason I got it.

I jump up from the table, paying in cash because I have to be careful not to leave a trail. That's my life now. Always looking over my shoulder and waiting for the other shoe to drop.

A black truck idles by the curb. A foe is now a friend. "All done?" asks Max as I get into the passenger seat. Max was the one who drove us away from the burning mess. He was the one Saint trusted.

I nod, buckling up.

We take the backroads as we can't be too vigilant now that the hunter has become the prey. A soft song plays over the radio in Russian, and thanks to me studying day and night, I can now recognize some words.

"Alek has been trying to find someone to help. So far, no luck." No surprise as we're fugitives now.

The orphanage, which has been my sanctuary, comes into view, and when I look at the high walls, I don't see them as my prison anymore. I see them as keeping out the noise. Max parks the car around back, using the garage to keep the vehicle out of sight.

We exit in silence, the sun making way for the gray clouds as summer has long passed us by. Sister Albina opens the side gate, peering from left to right before gesturing us in. I hate that my presence endangers them, but I have no other place to go.

I don't have a passport anymore as it's back at the villa and god knows what Drew has done with it, so I can't go to the American consulate. Not that it matters, however, because the moment I stepped within three feet, hoping that maybe the consulate could help, black vans swarmed me, warning me that I'm a wanted woman. I must pay for what I did to The Circle.

Oscar, Astra, and Borya may have been the main players, but there are others who seek revenge for what I, for what *we* did to their kin. Alek is seen as a traitor, and he too is now hunted.

The night of the explosion destroyed Alek's home, but it strengthened the need for someone to rule. At first, it was believed Alek perished in the fire, but when his body wasn't found, rumors spread, and his fate was doomed.

He was believed to have instigated it all as he wanted to flee to America with his American whore to start a new life. He had gone soft and wasn't cut out for his life of crime. The fact he paraded me around and showed weakness by being kind confirmed the rumors.

No doubt, Astra and Borya's men were the ones who started the witch hunt. No one knows the truth but us. The rest, we can only hope, are dead.

We have a target on our backs and, it goes without saying, a large bounty on our heads. The most feared man in all of Russia is now the most wanted, so we are on our own. No one will dare help us because it's their life if they do.

But Mother Superior has proven not to be just anyone. She opened her doors without question when Alek called, begging for sanctuary. No one would think to look for us here because no one knows Alek has close ties to this place.

We walk down the long corridor, and when we enter the orphanage, the happy shrills of children welcome me home. They run forward to hug me tightly, warming what remains of my broken heart. Sister Albina can read my fatigue and tells them we can play later.

I amble down the hallway, wishing I could appreciate the new finger painting taped to the walls. But all I want to do is go to my small room and lock myself away from the world. The moment I open the door, I sigh because a small part of me believes I will see him.

He'll tell me it was all a bad joke. That he is alive. And he is mine.

But it never happens because he is dead.

Saying his name is too painful, so I merely think it from time to time. But what I did today is a forever reminder that no matter what happens, he will never leave my body or mind. I may not be able to say his name, but I will look upon it and remember how it felt to be his.

Closing the door, I take off my baggy sweater and toss it onto the single bed. Mother Superior insisted I take a nicer room, but this is all I need. Simple lodgings while I wait…but wait for what? Divine intervention hasn't shown me the way, not that I would expect He would. I've been locked out of the pearly gates for good.

Slipping off my tank, I stand in front of the mirror that hangs off the back of the door. Gently unraveling the bandage, I gasp at what stares back at me. Although red and inflamed, its beauty still shines through because how can a name that denotes nothing but holiness be anything but beautiful.

Rubbing my fingers over the raised letters, I smile, allowing the tears to fall. It seems fitting that my first tattoo is for him because I owe everything to him…to *Saint*.

A single word in a cursive font tattooed on my flank. Saint was a sinner, and now, thanks to his name, I'm a saint. His tattoo read sinner. Mine reads saint. He is forever inked on my skin, just as he's embedded on my soul.

Peering out the window, I quash down the voice screaming at me that he isn't dead. He wouldn't give up that easily. That voice gives me hope, but my hope died the day Saint did.

I take care to put ointment on each letter, remembering the way his fingers caressed my skin just the same. Is this why Saint covered his body in tattoos? Did the pain help him feel?

Capping the tube, I toss it onto the bed and hunt for a fresh T-shirt. Needing to keep busy, I sit cross-legged on the floor and reach for my Russian textbook. It helps to keep my mind busy and the demons at bay.

Lost in words which are still so foreign, I don't hear someone pounding down the hallway until my door bursts open. I reach for the knife under my bed, ready for battle, but when I see it's Alek, I place it back.

His refined looks are no more. He's grown a full beard, his hair is scruffy, and his clothes are non-designer. He no longer looks like the billionaire I first met. Saint left me in Alek's care because he believed Alek would be able to help me leave this country for good. But how wrong he was.

The lingering guilt, my only friend, bubbles to the surface because when I muse over our situation, I can't help but feel responsible for his death because it was in vain.

"I'm sorry to burst in, but I have to tell you something."

"What?"

He attempts to catch his breath, which alerts me that

someone was following in hot pursuit. I don't have a chance to speak because who I see robs me of any words.

I blink once. Twice. But she's still here. They both are.

"Sara?" I squeak after seconds of staring at her, mouth opening and closing in shock.

I thought she perished because Alek tried everything to find her. Thanks to our limited resources, though, we had presumed the worst when he came up empty. But here she stands. She's free.

"Hi, Willow."

"You're a-alive?"

She nods, biting her lip. "It's thanks to him. He was always going to save me."

I close my eyes, unable to face this without crumpling into yet another mess. It seems she can't say his name either. But the woman beside her doesn't share the sentiment. What is she doing here? I thought she'd be long gone by now.

"His name was Saint…my brother, who saved all of you."

Opening my eyes, I take in Zoey Hennessy. She barely looks like the person I once remember her to be. She looks healthy and strong. Not the lapdog she once was.

Alek opens his mouth, but she silences him with a wave of her hand. How the tables have turned. "Get up," she spits, curling her lip in disgust when she looks at my feeble frame.

"Fuck you," I curse, not interested in being judged. She may not need to grieve Saint, but I do.

"Really? My brother saves you, and this is how you choose to live?" She flicks her hand with distaste around my small, dank room. "I thought you were a fighter."

"I have nothing left to fight for," I miserably confess, hating how weak and pathetic I sound.

"Bullshit! Get up," she commands once again.

I am done with her self-righteous shit. I'm happy she got her life back on track, but that doesn't give her the right to come in here and bark orders at me.

Sara shuffles her feet, and I notice she has on a pretty pair of sandals. I'm glad she's no longer in rags.

"Get out, Zoey. I don't want to talk to you."

She turns her arrogant nose in the air and folds her arms across her chest. She isn't going anywhere. "You owe him this."

Zoey's stubbornness must be a Hennessy trait because I can hear Saint's tenacity in her tone, and if she's anything like her brother, she won't leave until she has the last word.

Standing angrily, I stalk forward, leveling her with a gaze filled with nothing but hatred. "You don't think I know that? I owe him everything!" I cry, allowing the angry tears to burn my cheeks. "He sacrificed his life to save mine, but how can I ever repay him? He's dead!"

My wrath was supposed to scald Zoey, but it seems to have the opposite effect. "There she is. The fighter I need."

"What are you talking about?"

She smirks, and my god, I stagger back because she looks so much like her brother. "I need you. I need all of you."

Sara stands tall for the first time ever while Alek rubs the back of his neck.

"What's going on?"

Time stands still as I measure my breathing...

In...

Out...

"I need all of you to help me."

"With what?"

Zoey reaches into her back pocket, producing her cell. Her fingers hover over the screen, swiping with a poised confidence. When she passes it to me, I look at it like it's a live grenade.

"With this?"

With trembling fingers, I accept the offering, but nothing can prepare me for what I see. "No," I whisper, blinking rapidly, but the image is still there. "That's not p-possible." Everything closes in around me, and I suddenly can't breathe.

"It's very possible. Look at the poster on the wall. Look at the date."

I do as she says, still unsure what I'm seeing because surely, this is a cruel trick.

"No," I state more firmly this time because I don't want to believe this. Because if it's true, it means...

"He's alive."

Running a quivering finger over the blurred image of his face, I can't deny that it looks like him. Like my Saint. And the poster behind him, advertising a night market in the main street of Moscow, reveals he was alive as of two days ago. But the picture depicts a startling scene.

He isn't there by choice as he is being shoved by an unknown assailant into the back seat of a car.

"I-I saw him d-die." My eyes are fixed to the screen, waiting for Zoey to yell surprise! This is her way of getting back at me for everything I've done to her.

But she doesn't. "Did you? No one found his body, and

that picture proves he's still alive."

My mind flicks over the last moments I saw him. He was shot, and then the room exploded around him because he detonated the bomb strapped to his chest. But she's right. From what Alek and I could find, he wasn't listed as one of the dead.

But I can't accept this. It's too painful if she's wrong.

"Get out of h-here! All o-of you!" I drop the phone, unable to look at the man who looks like Saint a second longer. Turning my back, I thread my fingers through my snarled hair, unable to accept this as truth.

But Zoey won't give up. "I know it's hard to believe, but I'm telling you the truth."

"How do you know?" I spin around, unable to keep my feelings under control.

I'm expecting her to break into laughter, ridiculing me for being such a naïve fool. But she does neither. She takes a long breath, leveling me with nothing but sincerity. "Because...*I* was the one who blew that hellhole to the ground."

Nothing I can say will express what I'm feeling right now. But it doesn't matter because Zoey speaks for us all.

"He's alive...I know where he is...and I need your help to get him out."

They say one's life flashes before their eyes before they die, which is why I am certain I'm seconds away from embracing death. I surrender to the darkness, unsure what the light will bring.

FOREVER MY SAINT
Volume Three
coming September 2019!

ACKNOWLEDGEMENTS

My wonderful husband, Daniel. I love you. Thank you for always believing in me. You're my favorite.

My ever-supporting parents. You guys are the best. I am who I am because of you. I love you.

My agent, Kimberly Brower from Brower Literary & Management. Thank you for your patience and thank you for being an amazing human being.

My editor, Jenny Sims. What can I say other than I LOVE YOU! Thank you for everything. You go above and beyond for me.

My proofreader—Lisa Edward—More Than Words, Copyediting & Proofreading. You are amazing. I owe you dinner.

Lana Kart—best Russian translator ever. PS. I'm expecting voice messages every day!

Sommer Stein, you NAILED this cover! Thank you for being so patient and making the process so fun. I'm sorry for annoying you constantly.

My publicist—Danielle Sanchez from Wildfire Marketing Solutions. Thank you for all your help. Your messages brighten my day.

A special shout-out to: Christina and Lauren, Elle Kennedy (I LOVE YOUR FACE), Lisa Edward, SC Stephens, Vi Keeland (I LOVE YOUR FACE TOO), Penelope Ward, Adriane Leigh, Geneva Lee, Pam Godwin, Natasha Preston,

Staci Hart, Natasha Madison, Len Webster, Rachel Brookes, J.L. Drake, Audrey Carlan, BJ Harvey, K.A. Tucker, Kylie Scott, Mia Sheridan, Tijan, Tina Gephart, Kimberly Whalen, Gemma, Louise, Heyne, Random House, Kinneret Zmora, Hugo & Cie, Planeta, MxM Bookmark, Art Eternal, Carbaccio, Fischer, Harper Brazil, Bookouture, Egmont Bulgaria, Brilliance Publishing, Audible, Hope Editions, USA TODAY/ Happy Ever After, Buzzfeed, BookBub, PopSugar, Love Letters Convention—Berlin, Aestas Book Blog, Natasha is a Book Junkie, Hugues De Saint Vincent, Romance Writers of Australia, Paris, New York, Sarah Sentz, Ria Alexander, Rosa Sharon, Virginia Tesi Carey, Amy Jennings, Gel Ytayz, Jennifer Spinninger, Vanessa Silva Martins, Denise Reyes—Dreamy Reads, Amalie—Amalie Reads, Megan—Steamy Reads Blog, Sofia—Beddable Reads (Your videos are amazing), Cheri Grand Anderman, Lauren Rosa, Kristin Dwyer, and Nina Bocci.

To the endless blogs that have supported me since day one—You guys rock my world.

My bookstagrammers—This book has allowed me to meet SO many of you. Your creativity astounds me. The effort you go to is just amazing. Thank you for the posts, the teasers, the support, the messages, the love, the EVERYTHING! I see what you do, and I am so, so thankful.

My reader group and review team—sending you all a big kiss.

My beautiful family—Mum, Papa, my sister—Fran, Matt, Samantha, Amelia, Gayle, Peter, Luke, Leah, Jimmy, Jack, Shirley, Michael, Rob, Elisa, Evan, Alex, Francesca, and my aunties, uncles, and cousins—I am the luckiest person alive to know each and every one of you. You brighten up my world in ways I honestly cannot express.

Samantha and Amelia— I love you both so very much.

To my family in Holland and Italy, and abroad. Sending you guys much love and kisses.

Zio Nello, Zio Frank, Zia Rosetta, and Zia Giuseppina— you are in our hearts. Always.

My fur babies— mamma loves you so much! Buckwheat, you are my best buddy. Dacca, I will always protect you from the big bad Bellie. Mitch, refer to Dacca's comment. Jag, you're a wombat in disguise. Bellie, you're a devil in disguise. And Ninja, thanks for watching over me.

To anyone I have missed, I'm sorry! It wasn't intentional!

Last but certainly not least, I want to thank YOU! Thank you for welcoming me into your hearts and homes. My readers are the BEST readers in this entire universe! Love you all!

ABOUT THE AUTHOR

Monica James spent her youth devouring the works of Anne Rice, William Shakespeare, and Emily Dickinson.

When she is not writing, Monica is busy running her own business, but she always finds a balance between the two. She enjoys writing honest, heartfelt, and turbulent stories, hoping to leave an imprint on her readers. She draws her inspiration from life.

She is a bestselling author in the U.S.A., Australia, Canada, France, Germany, Israel, and The U.K.

Monica James resides in Melbourne, Australia, with her wonderful family, and menagerie of animals. She is slightly obsessed with cats, chucks, and lip gloss, and secretly wishes she was a ninja on the weekends.

CONNECT WITH MONICA JAMES

Facebook: www.facebook.com/authormonicajames
Twitter: twitter.com/monicajames81
Goodreads: www.goodreads.com/MonicaJames
Instagram: www.instagram.com/authormonicajames/
Website: monicajamesbooks.blogspot.com.au/
Pinterest: www.pinterest.com/monicajames81/
BookBub: bit.ly/2E3eCIw
Amazon: amzn.to/2EWZSyS
Join my Reader Group: bit.ly/2nUaRyi